He

Readers are sure to enjoy this playful tale...this book is bound to please anyone that is looking for an easy, satisfying read on the beach.
—*InD'tale Magazine*

"If you like your cozy mysteries complete with a cast of zany characters this is one for you. And guess what? Recipes are included which makes me really wish I could bake."
—*Night Owl Reviews*

"TASTES LIKE MURDER is an intriguing start to the *Cookies and Chance Mystery* series. I want to visit more with all of the quirky characters just to see what crazy and outrageous things they will do next!"
—*Fresh Fiction*

"Twistier than expected cozy read--great for beach or by the fire"
—*The Kindle Book Review*

BOOKS BY CATHERINE BRUNS

Cookies & Chance Mysteries:
Tastes Like Murder
Baked to Death
Burned to a Crisp
Frosted with Revenge
A Spot of Murder (short story in the Killer Beach Reads collection)

Cindy York Mysteries:
Killer Transaction
Priced to Kill

Aloha Lagoon Mysteries:
Death of the Big Kahuna
Death of the Kona Man

FROSTED WITH REVENGE

---

a Cookies & Chance mystery

Catherine Bruns

Frosted with Revenge

Cover design by Yocla Designs

Published by Gemma Halliday Publishing

Acknowledgements:

Special accolades to retired Troy Police Captain Terrance Buchanan, who is always available with the answers I need. Thank you to Judy Melinek M.D., Forensic Pathologist, for her assistance in the medical field. I am grateful to my wonderful beta readers Constance Atwater and Kathy Kennedy who never fail to come through for me and my husband, Frank, for his infinite patience. As always, thank you to publisher Gemma Halliday and her fabulous editorial staff, especially Danielle Kuhns and Wendi Baker, who always take such good care of Sally and her family.

Profound thanks to Frank and Patti Ricupero and Amy Reger for sharing their delicious family recipes. Special love goes out to my cousin Betty Ann Stavola for providing me with Aunt Selma's treasured recipe for maamoul cookies, an ancestral family favorite that I am excited to share with my readers.

CHAPTER ONE

"Hi, sweetheart," my mother purred into the phone. "Have you seen today's paper yet?"

I stared at the phone in disbelief. It was a midafternoon in July, and the air conditioning in my cookie shop, Sally's Samples, had suddenly stopped working. There was a line of people out the front door, and my mother wanted to know if I'd had time to read the paper yet.

The only reason I'd even bothered to answer my cell was because it was the third time she'd called in the last ten minutes, and I thought someone must have died. If there hadn't been customers watching me, I might have been tempted to bang my head against the wall.

"Mom, we're swamped here," I protested. "Can we talk about this later?"

It was Saturday, our busiest day of the week, and we had only reopened yesterday. There had been a devastating fire at my former location last month. For the past several days my best friend, Josie Sullivan, and I had been forced to temporarily relocate the bakery to my parents' home. Talk about your crazy carnival rides. Between my mother parading around the house in bikinis for an upcoming beauty contest and my father keeping a coffin in the living room to help with the "studying" process for his new career, I was afraid that when we did finally move into our new location the bakery would suffer. Or perhaps even go belly up and out of business completely. Given the crowd today though, it seemed that our hungry customers had forgiven us for our brief lack of judgment.

"Sal," Josie yelled from behind the display case, where she was busy scooping raspberry cheesecake cookies into one of our little pink boxes. "Get those fortune cookies out of the oven now, or they'll burn."

I wiped away the sweat gathering on my forehead with my arm and ran into the back room where the ovens were. "Mom, I have to go."

"All right, dear. But I wanted to tell you that your engagement photo is in the paper today. It came out beautiful! And don't forget about the cake testing in an hour."

I removed the fortune cookies from the oven and placed the tray on the wooden block table. "Mom! I thought you canceled that. There's no way that I can go. Plus, Mike's working too."

"Nonsense," my mother scoffed. "Your sister is on her way over to relieve you. Since she has today off, she said she'd be glad to help out in the shop for a while."

My wedding was exactly one week from today. The specialty bakery shop that my mother had hired months ago to make the cake had gone bankrupt and closed its doors suddenly last week. Talk about bad timing. Panicked, my mother had quickly found another bakery that agreed to take on the cake at the very last minute. In fact, DeAngelo's Bakery was a very elite shop that specialized in creating the perfect wedding cake. I had seen the invoice that Pepe, the owner, sent my mother and had cringed at the price. Since I was in the business myself, I knew she was getting ripped off, but she had accepted the price without argument or comment.

"Mike won't be able to make it," I argued. "He's doing a basement job. Can't we do this some other time?"

"Sally Isabella Muccio," my mother hissed into the phone.

That was all she said, but it was enough. Using my full given name—which my mother hadn't done since I was a child—meant that she was rapidly growing annoyed with me. This was unusual behavior for Maria Muccio who always looked at life through rose-colored glasses.

"Your father and I paid a lot of money for that cake," she said crisply, further riddling me with guilt. "We need to make sure it's perfect and exactly what you want."

At this particular moment I didn't care if we ended up

eating trail mix. I hadn't wanted a big wedding in the first place, having traveled that road before. But as usual, my mother had won out.

I reached for the bucket of fortune cookie messages on the shelf in front of me and strategically folded them into the center of each piece of cooked dough. This had to be done immediately after taking the cookies out of the oven or else the dough would harden, and the message could not be placed inside properly.

"I'm sure it will taste delicious." In truth, the cake bothered me but not for the reason my mother thought. Josie had offered to make me one, but my mother had gone ahead with her plans without bothering to consult me or her. Mom had laid down a hefty deposit with each bakery before I even knew what she'd been planning, and now I was stuck trying to put all the pieces back together. I knew it had hurt my best friend, and that was the last thing I ever wanted to do. Josie was my head baker—okay, my only baker—but she had a knack with desserts unlike many others. Without her talent, I would not have a bakery. She had gone to culinary school right after high school but decided to leave when she had unintentionally gotten pregnant with her first child.

Deep down, I knew Josie was upset by my mother's refusal, but she was too proud to say anything. We hadn't discussed the matter yet, but I sensed it might come to a head soon, for Josie had been acting a bit strange the last few days.

"Why don't you go sample it instead, Mom? You have impeccable taste."

"Sal," my mother huffed. "This is the most important day of your life. Don't you want to make sure that everything will be perfect?"

"It will be, Mom." I folded the cookies while balancing the phone between my ear and shoulder as we chatted. "I'm marrying the man that I love, which is the only thing that matters."

Mike Donovan had been my high school boyfriend and first love. Through a huge misunderstanding that occurred on senior prom night after I found him in a car with a girl dubbed Backseat Brenda, we'd broken up. I'd never given Mike a chance to explain back then about what had really happened. On the rebound I'd gone on to date and marry my first husband, Colin Brown. That marriage came to a quick end when I walked in on Colin and my high school nemesis having sex. By a bizarre chain of events unrelated to the affair, both Colin and his mistress were dead now.

"Sal!" Josie yelled. "Are those chocolate chips done?"

I was starting to resemble the oven, baking from the inside out. I stopped for a moment to plug another table fan in. "I really have to go, Mom."

"All right, dear. Are you and Mike coming for dinner tonight?"

I blew out a long sigh and pulled the trays out of the oven. "Um, probably. I'm not sure how late he's working, so I have to check with him."

"Good. We need to go over the seating arrangements one last time," my mother insisted. "I have to get the numbers to the country club by Wednesday. You aren't taking this seriously enough. And remember the baby shower for Betsy Taylor is tomorrow."

The air grew tight around me, more from suffocation than actual heat. This was all getting to be too much. I needed to get away—now. Saturday couldn't get here fast enough. Immediately after the wedding, Mike and I would be leaving for a week in Hawaii—tropical paradise. No construction jobs, baking cookies, or crazy parents—only me and my husband for one entire week. At this point it still seemed like a dream.

When we became engaged last January, we'd talked about flying off to Vegas and eloping. Somehow we'd been roped into this three-ring circus instead. I would have been happy with a simple ceremony at city hall and had hinted at that numerous times. But these were my parents, and nothing was ever simple with them. They were loud and proud and marched to the beat of their own drum.

I mumbled a hasty good-bye to my mother and ran back to the fortune cookies. I pulled a message from the jar and placed it in the center of the cookie, but the dough had already hardened. Shoot. There were six other cookies that hadn't made the cut either. I scooped more dough onto the cookies sheets, spread them into thin circles with the spatula, and then hurriedly thrust the trays into the oven. The ones that were ready, I rushed out front to the waiting display case.

Josie was counting change out to one customer while balancing an empty bakery box in the other hand, waiting for the next person to decide what they wanted. There wasn't a day I didn't wonder what I would do without her. When I glanced through the crowd waiting and saw a familiar face, I did a huge mental eye roll. My parents' next-door neighbor, Mrs. Gavelli.

She thrust a stubby finger in my direction. "It too hot in here. What you do, turn off air to save some money?"

Josie's face turned as red as her hair. "Listen, old lady. The air conditioner is broken. We didn't plan on it happening."

"Who you call old lady? And as for you." She turned to address me. "You get that boyfriend of yours over to fix. Right now. And you give me fortune cookie in the case. No, not that one. The one in front of it." She rapped on the glass and pointed at her cookie of choice.

The two young women behind Mrs. Gavelli exchanged a glance between them, but Josie and I were used to Nicoletta Gavelli's antics. She'd lived next to my parents since I was a baby and enjoyed making my life difficult whenever possible. Nicoletta had recently finished chemotherapy treatment for bone cancer, and despite her aggravating mannerisms, my heart went out to her. She'd been diagnosed last winter, but I had only found out a few weeks ago. Except for the green polka-dotted head wrap she wore, the rest of Mrs. Gavelli was the same as always, from her lined, leathery-looking face with a perpetual scowl to her outfit of a drab gray housecoat and black Birkenstocks, complete with knee-highs rolling down around her calves.

I handed her the fortune cookie, and she cracked it open while the young woman behind her tried to step around her to place an order.

Mrs. Gavelli grunted at the woman. "You wait. I not finished yet."

Josie wrinkled her nose. "You're holding up the line."

Mrs. Gavelli ignored her and read the message aloud. "*It's nice to be important, but it's more important to be nice.*" Angrily, she threw the paper on the blue and white checkered vinyl floor. "Is no good. I tell you, no more silly fortunes. Now I tell your grandmamma on you." With that she turned and flounced out of the shop, the bells on the door jingling merrily with her departure.

A little girl standing with her mother turned to watch Nicoletta leave. "Was that the Wicked Witch of the West?" she asked.

Josie laughed out loud. "Pretty darn close."

I smiled politely at the next woman in line. "Sorry for the holdup. What can I get you?"

She pointed at the tray of fudgy delight cookies. "I'll take six of those yummy-looking cookies with the chocolate in the center."

The bells on the door were set in motion again as my baby sister, Gianna, walked in and went immediately into the back room after a quick wave to us. She was getting ready to move into the apartment over my shop in the next couple of days and had just returned from a luncheon date with her boyfriend, Johnny, who also happened to be Mrs. Gavelli's grandson.

Personally, if I'd ever thought that there was a chance of my ending up being related to Mrs. Gavelli, I might have been tempted to stab myself in the eye with a frosting knife. Lucky for Gianna, Nicoletta seemed to like her.

Gianna was brilliant and beautiful with chestnut-colored hair that fell around her shoulders in perfect waves and large, soft-brown eyes. She'd recently been appointed as a public defender and after a bit of a rocky start, was enjoying her new career. People said we looked like twins, but I didn't see it myself. Her features were more delicate than mine. Plus my hair was darker and curlier and on days like this, perpetually frizzy.

She came out of the back room with an apron on and shooed me away with her hand. "Go on. You'd better get out of here."

"Where are you going?" Josie wanted to know.

"Cake testing," I said. "But I have to call Mike first and have him pick me up since my car is in the shop today. While I'm waiting I'll go make up some more fortune cookies." Usually we were better prepared, but the demand for them had been great lately, with people even requesting orders for parties. *Ugh.*

"You can take my car," Gianna volunteered.

I shook my head. "It's easier this way. Plus I want him to look at the air conditioner while he's here." I longed to see my fiancé. We'd both been so buried with work the past few weeks that by the time we were together at night, it was all we could do to stay awake and have a normal conversation for five minutes. Last night we'd fallen asleep together in front of the television.

I retrieved my iPhone from my pocket and pressed Mike's number, which I had on speed dial, hoping he'd pick up. Mike owned a one-person construction company, and during the nice weather, work was plentiful for him. He could barely keep up these days. I managed to scoop more batter onto the tray and pop it into the oven while waiting for him to answer. We could only bake a tray or two of the fortune cookies at a time because they hardened so fast.

Mike's sexy voice came on the line, but he sounded harried. "Yeah, baby, what is it?"

"Can you pick me up in twenty minutes?"

There was a brief silence before he spoke again. "Is something wrong?"

I knew Mike would have forgotten. "We have the wedding cake testing today, remember?"

There was a mumble of frustration on the other end. "I thought your mother canceled that thing. I can't leave now. I'm in the middle of digging out a basement. Can't you go without me?"

"It's your wedding too," I reminded him.

He sighed. "I know. But this isn't a good time."

"It's only for an hour," I pleaded. "It would be nice to see you for a little while."

"Princess, you don't want to see me right now. I'm a walking disaster covered in dirt, mud, and sweat. Trust me. You're better off going by yourself."

I hated to pull out the begging card, especially when I knew he was so busy, but went ahead anyway. Plus I knew he'd give in. "You could take a shower in Gianna's apartment. *Please,* sweetheart?"

Mike exhaled deeply. "Why can't I ever say no to you?"

I grinned. "Because you love me."

"Guilty as charged." He laughed. "All right. But that

means I'll be even later getting home tonight, so no complaints. I promised Greg I'd have this job done before the wedding."

Which can't come soon enough. "Do you think you can look at the air conditioner when you get here? It stopped working an hour ago, and it's hotter than an inferno in here. We had to stick all the cookies with icing in the fridge so they wouldn't melt."

"I'll check it out. See you soon, baby."

I clicked off and took the next tray of fortune cookies out of the oven.

Josie came back to check on my progress. "We're caught up out front. How long will you be gone?"

"It shouldn't be for more than an hour. The whole thing is a complete waste of time if you ask me." I began to fold the fortunes inside the cookies.

Josie was at my side and started to assemble cookies as well. She bent her head down low and seemed to be concentrating unusually hard. "See, this all could have been avoided if *I'd* made the cake."

Oh jeez. Here it comes. "Jos, I was fine with you making the cake. You know that. Please don't be angry. My mother made all the plans without even consulting me. When I confronted her she said she thought you had enough on your plate already."

"You're my best friend," she said, her voice suddenly choked up. "It wasn't an inconvenience. I wanted to do this for you."

Guilt overwhelmed me. "I'm sorry. I just can't seem to please anyone these days."

She squeezed my arm. "No, I'm the one who's sorry. I'm acting like a baby. But I did want to do something special for you on your big day."

"You're my matron of honor. I think that's pretty special."

"And Gianna's your maid of honor," she added stubbornly. "She's the one who gets to help you with your train and hold your bouquet."

I sighed. "Jeez, it's not like I could ever choose between the two of you, okay? Maybe you could help with the dress, and she could hold my bouquet. Why can't I have both of you filling a special role that day? My mother is already driving me crazy with the preparations, Mike's upset he has to go to the bakery, and now you're annoyed with me too." *Stick a fork in me. I'm done.*

"That's not true," Josie said. "I'm so happy for both you and Mike. You guys were always meant to be together. Maybe I'm a bit nervous about handling things at the shop alone while you're on your honeymoon."

We'd had hired help in the shop up until a couple of weeks ago and were really in need of more assistance, or at the very least a part-time driver to make deliveries. A teenager had come in yesterday who would probably be suitable for the driver position and perhaps could wait on customers as well. My grandmother had offered to assist Josie while I was away, but she was almost 76 years old, and I didn't like placing such a burden on her shoulders. As a matter of fact, my Grandma Rosa would turn 76 next Saturday—the same day as my wedding. Not a coincidence on my part.

"There's still a few days left." I spoke with optimism. "Maybe we can find someone before I leave."

I was holding a fortune in my hand, but the cookie had already hardened and couldn't be moved an inch. "Shoot. I'm never quick enough with these."

Josie waved a hand dismissively. "We got the rest of them. It's only one cookie, so no big deal. At least we should have enough to last the rest of the day. If things slow down, I'll make more."

Every patron got a free fortune cookie with their purchase. Even though customers appreciated the gesture, I had grown wary of the messages. They seemed to carry predictions of doom that came true for the most part, or at least in my case. I started to put the message back in the jar, but the musical notes of my phone interrupted me. I looked down to grab my cell, and that's when I noticed the words printed on the message.

Revenge is sweeter than this cookie.

Josie stared at me. "Are you going to answer that or what?" Then she noticed me examining the strip of paper and leaned over my shoulder. "Uh-oh. What's it say this time?"

Reluctantly I showed her the message, and she gave a

bark of laughter. "Sally Muccio, soon to be Donovan, you're way too sweet to be the vengeful type. That was written for someone like me. So who do you have it in for anyway?"

"Oh, cut it out." Josie knew how I felt about the cookies. The thought to discontinue them had crossed my mind several times in the past few months, but since one message had actually led to saving my life a few weeks back, I'd been relenting a bit. Okay, I couldn't be positive that it had saved my life, but the circumstances seemed a bit too unusual for me to consider it a mere coincidence.

Josie grinned. "I knew if we hung around together long enough, some of me would rub off on you eventually. You're too nice for your own good."

"And you're crazy," I laughed.

"Forget about that message," Josie said. "You don't have an enemy in the world. Well, at least no one who isn't already behind bars, that is."

A cheerful thought indeed.

CHAPTER TWO

Twenty minutes later, the bells on the front door of the bakery were set in motion again. Without even turning around, I sensed it was my handsome fiancé. Full of anticipation, I turned around eagerly to acknowledge his presence—those midnight blue eyes that always captured my heart, the dark hair that curled at the nape of his neck, his tanned, handsome face, and—

My jaw almost hit the floor.

Mike's face was blackened with dirt, and his T-shirt and jeans were covered with dark stains. He was standing by the front door and wasn't smelling that great, even from a distance. Two women customers who were in front of the display case stared at him openmouthed then cautiously avoided him on their way out of the shop.

Mike grinned and flashed his gleaming white teeth at me. "I warned you."

Josie burst into laughter. "This is the only time I've ever actually seen women run *away* from you."

I wanted to pull my hair out of my head but instead pointed to the wooden stairs behind the counter. "Upstairs to the shower. *Now*."

"Sal, we should forget about this," he protested. "We've got about five minutes to spare, and that's if I hit all green lights on the way."

"The air conditioner first," Josie whined and pushed him into the back room. "*Please*. I'm dying in here."

I sighed heavily and watched Mike disappear into the back room, dropping dirt behind him every few steps. Well, maybe being late was better than not showing up at all. Perhaps DeAngelo's was running behind schedule today. I could only hope. I took a minute to look up their number on my phone. I dialed it, and the call immediately went to voicemail.

"Where are your filters for this thing?" Mike hollered.

"There's one under the sink somewhere," Josie yelled as she ran back to show him. I took the moment to leave a hasty message that stated we would be about ten minutes late and apologized for the inconvenience.

Unlike my shop, DeAngelo's Bakery specialized in wedding cakes. Besides the cakes, they sold a very small variety of pastries as well. I hadn't been in there personally, but Josie had since she always enjoyed scoping out the competition. She said it was a snooty, high-end place, so perhaps they couldn't be bothered with something as trivial as answering phones in the middle of the day. I couldn't imagine doing that myself, but hey, to each his own.

Mike came out of the back room. "All set. I just had to replace the filter. Josie's standing in front of it cooling herself off."

Gianna sat down at one of the tables. "Do you have clothes with you?"

"I've got shorts and a tank somewhere in the truck that I use for the gym, but that's all. Looks like I'm going extra casual." He winked at me. "Is that okay, boss?"

I remembered Josie's description of the elite bakery and winced inwardly. "It'll have to be. Hurry. I'll go grab your clothes."

He leaned down to kiss me, and I started to gag while also giggling in the process.

"My bride doesn't want to kiss me? How come?" he teased.

"Get upstairs!" I laughed and then went outside to Mike's truck. After rummaging around inside it for a minute, I found the clothes in a gym bag under the seat. I ran upstairs with the bag and placed it on the bathroom sink. The water was already running in the shower.

"Your stuff is on the counter," I called out.

Mike stuck his wet head out from around the shower curtain, and his blue eyes darkened as they fixed on my face. "You could join me, you know."

He did make it difficult to refuse. "Tempting, but I don't think this is a good time. And *not* in my sister's bathroom, either."

He stuck his head back inside the curtain and laughed. "It's always a good time, princess."

All we had to do was get through one more week, and then we would be joined together for the rest of our lives. Why did things take forever to happen when you longed for them so? I ran back down the stairs and found Josie and Gianna studying the newspaper, deep in conversation.

"Did you know that you and Mike were in the bridal section today?" Josie asked, holding it out for me to see.

"Oh! My mother mentioned it. I don't understand why she even bothered to put the announcement in. No one even pays attention to those little blurbs."

"Little blurbs?" Josie echoed incredulously. "Your mother paid for the elite package, girlfriend. There's half a page devoted to you and Mike, your wedding, honeymoon destination, blah-blah. There's even a line about your cake testing today. I'm surprised she didn't insert an extra paragraph about baby making for the honeymoon."

I grabbed the paper from Josie's hands and stifled a groan. "Why does she do these things to me?"

"Okay, I don't think I ever want to get married," Gianna announced. "If I do, maybe I'll keep it a secret for ten years or so before I actually tell Mom."

I glanced at the picture of myself and Mike. He looked his usual handsome self, in a striped, blue and white dress shirt, staring at the camera with his arm around my shoulders. I was wearing a white linen blouse and also grinning at the camera—while I held a fork to my mouth with a piece of cake on it. *Ugh.* I was mortified. "Really? She had to take a shot while I was eating?"

Josie's grin widened as she stared at the picture again. "Aw. You guys look cute. And happy. That's from your birthday party a couple of weeks ago."

Mike came jogging down the stairs. He was dressed in blue Nike shorts, a white tank top, and a ratty looking pair of Nike sneakers. Okay, not my outfit of choice for him, but at least he was clean.

"Your boots are on the front porch," Josie said. "Gianna cleaned them off while you guys were busy fooling around upstairs."

I rolled my eyes at her. "Like we had time for that."

"Thank you, ladies." He grinned. "I'm sure Sal's also grateful for your efforts to make me look like a gentleman."

He sat down on a chair to tie his shoes, but I grabbed his arm and tried to push him toward the door. "We're already late. See you guys in a bit."

Gianna shook her head as she continued to stare at the newspaper article. "Our mother. She does take the cake—literally."

* * *

As we stepped through the entranceway of DeAngelo's, I glanced at my watch for about the fifth time in as many minutes. The time read 2:12, and I sighed. Well, it was the best we could do. I glanced around with uncertainty, wondering if my mother might be lurking in the shadows somewhere, ready to lecture us for being late. Thankfully she was nowhere to be seen.

There were a few people waiting at the counter, placing orders for items such as cannoli and croissants. A young girl in a spotless white jacket was behind the marble veneer countertop that supported the gleaming multitier glass display case. The case ran almost the entire length of the room and was at least twice the size of my own. The walls were a white marble, and crystal light fixtures hung from the high-raised ceilings. Glass-topped tables had been strategically placed by the large front window. A carousel sat in the center of the window seat, spinning around merrily. Wow. As much as I loved my little bakery, it paled in comparison to this sophisticated one.

Pepe DeAngelo came scurrying from the back room. He bowed and smiled at us and then made a not so subtle practice of checking his watch. *Great.*

"I'm terribly sorry we're late," I said. "I did leave a message. My fiancé got held up at work."

Pepe was short, about my five-foot-three-inch height,

with a handlebar moustache and thinning black hair that surrounded a wide bald spot on the top of his head. He wore a white dress shirt and black pants that were immaculate. I'd met him once before when he had come into my shop to purchase cookies. Perhaps that had been Pepe's own attempt to size up the competition. At least I hoped so. I surmised that Pepe didn't do much baking himself and probably stood at the pastry chef's side all day hollering orders in Italian.

"This is my fiancé, Mike Donovan." The pride in my voice was apparent.

Pepe's eyes settled on Mike, and I saw the expression in them change. It looked like disbelief, or even panic, as his gaze traveled over Mike's impressive biceps in the tank top, then to the shorts, and finally the worn-out sneakers minus socks. I thought I heard him suck in some air.

Mike held out his hand. "Nice to meet you."

Pepe's nose wiggled slightly, but he accepted Mike's hand. His manners, like his shop, were impeccable, and he bowed before Mike then held out chairs for the both of us. We settled at a table directly in front of the glass window.

"Your mama," Pepe crooned to me in a heavily accented voice. "She come to see me last week and explained the problem with the other bakery. They close, no?"

I nodded. "They went bankrupt."

"Such a shame." He made a *tsk-tsk* sound. "Your mama—a wonderful woman. We have coffee and talk for long time. She magnificent—one in a million."

"That she is." Mike grinned wickedly.

I shot him a warning look. "We decided to go with the traditional cake, and she said you had some suggestions for the filling."

He nodded eagerly. "I recommend the white chocolate ganache frosting. Is good? You like?"

I glanced at Mike, who merely shrugged in response. "Sounds doable to me."

Pepe shot Mike an incredulous look. From the horrified expression on his face, he acted as if Mike had passed gas in his bakery. He didn't understand that this was just my fiancé's way. Mike was more than happy to leave all the wedding details to me and my mother. Perhaps part of the problem was that he had never had much of a family. He'd grown up in a hurry, with a drunken mother and abusive stepfather. He was no frills all the way and couldn't have cared less if the cake had come in a Hostess Twinkie wrapper. It was one more thing that I loved about him.

"Your mama was unsure which filling you would prefer, so my chef has personally designed two mini cakes. One is with raspberry filling and another with chocolate mousse." Pepe's eyes gleamed as he said the words. "You will try both."

Mike rocked the chair on its back legs and grinned. "Great. I didn't have lunch today, and I'm starved."

Pepe narrowed his eyes then turned on his heel and disappeared into the swinging doors behind the display case.

I nudged Mike in the ribs. "You're going to be the death of him, you know."

He shook his head. "That guy is way too pretentious. He needs to loosen up a bit."

The front door of the bakery opened, and a woman about my age strolled in. She was tall and slender, dressed expensively in a designer blue suit and shoes that bore the distinct mark of Versace. Her hair was dark like mine and almost as curly. Icy blue eyes rested on me briefly for a minute before they turned and did a full body scan of Mike. Instantly I was on my guard.

"Is Pepe here?" she asked with an authoritative air.

"He'll be back out in a minute," I said.

She wrinkled her nose at me and then continued to stand there with arms folded, her right foot tapping a steady beat on the linoleum floor. Her eyes traveled back to Mike, and I bristled inwardly. She looked as if she was undressing him with her eyes. He didn't appear to notice as he took my hand and brought it to his lips while checking his phone with his other hand.

I didn't know who this woman was, but her actions weren't exactly scoring any points with me.

Pepe came back into the bakery with two china plates. He placed one in front of me and the other in front of Mike then clasped his hands together in delight. "*Buon appetito*."

The woman cleared her throat loudly and tapped Pepe on the shoulder. "Don't you remember who I am?"

"Miss Alexandra Walston," he replied smoothly and bowed. He ran over to the adjoining table and held a chair out for her. "You are early. Please sit down, and I will be with you shortly."

Her nostrils flared. "I don't have time to wait. I have a final dress fitting in an hour and need you to assist me. *Now.*"

Pepe examined his watch. "I am so sorry, *signora.* Your appointment is not until three. I will finish with this couple and then attend you. Would you like a pastry while you wait? Chef Georgio is putting the finishing touches on your cake. It will not take long."

Alexandra's face turned crimson. "Perhaps you aren't aware of who I am or who my parents are? My father owns several businesses in the state, as well as a restaurant and hotel."

I hated when people pulled out the "do you know who I am" card. In my opinion, no one was better than anyone else. Alexandra suddenly turned and narrowed her eyes at me, almost as if she'd heard my inner thoughts. I boldly stared back at her with unabashed defiance.

Pepe looked distressed. "Please, Miss Walston. I will take excellent care of you and promise that the wait will not be long."

Alexandra's thin lips formed into a sneer. "If my cake is not out here in five minutes, my mother will find another bakery to make it."

"But your wedding is this Saturday," Pepe protested. "How would you find another one in such short time?"

"Leave that to me. There are plenty of establishments that would welcome my business. Do you want the order or not?"

Mike and I exchanged a glance. He was most likely thinking the same thing as me. A spoiled little…

Pepe nodded and bowed before her royal highness. "I will talk to the chef. Please do not leave. I will have something for you right away."

I wasn't hungry, so I decided to wait a few minutes before sampling the cakes. The intense heat from the bakery earlier had killed my appetite. Mike had already polished off his piece of cake with the chocolate mousse filling and had started right in on the raspberry torte. He was oblivious to Alexandra who continued to eye him like he was a piece of cake himself.

Mike fed me a bite of the raspberry torte off his fork. "Try this one, baby. Pretty good stuff."

I couldn't help thinking that Pepe might have a cow if he knew patrons were referring to his masterpiece as "pretty good stuff." I accepted the bite and watched as Alexandra turned her head away in disgust. The raspberry filling burst with the fruit's natural flavors and ignited my taste buds. It mixed wonderfully with the chocolate, and I fought an urge to moan as I savored it in my mouth for as long as possible. "Oh, I think this is the one. It's absolutely delicious."

Mike's phone buzzed. He looked down at the screen and frowned. "I'm going to run outside and take this call. It's Greg, the customer whose basement I'm working on. He's probably wondering where I ran off to." He gave me a light kiss on the lips and then strode out of the bakery with the phone pressed to his ear. I watched as he walked around to the side of the building and then turned back to walk in the other direction. I'd discovered that when discussing anything work related, Mike was quite the pacer.

I turned my head and noticed that Alexandra was watching him too. His outfit looked a bit out of the ordinary for the shop, but there was no denying how good looking he was with the shorts and tank top enhancing his lean, muscular body. Mike could have been dressed in a paper bag, and it wouldn't have made any difference.

This woman was really starting to annoy me. If she was going to check out my fiancé, did she have to be so blatantly obvious about it?

Pepe came hurrying in from the back room with another china plate that held a piece of red velvet cake with white frosting. He placed it in front of Alexandra and bowed again. She stared down at the cake and then at Pepe with a look of annoyance.

"I don't want this kind."

Pepe bit into his lower lip. He must have wanted to smack her across the face—how could he not? Instead, he smiled politely. "But *signora*, this is the cake that you ordered."

She thrust a finger at the untouched raspberry torte on my plate. "I want to sample *that* kind."

Pepe looked pained. "Please, *signora*, I do not have any more of the raspberry torte ready for you right now."

The poor man. If this had happened in my shop, Josie would have thrown Alexandra out on her butt by now. I picked up my plate and offered it to Alexandra. "I didn't touch this piece. I don't have much of an appetite today, so please feel free."

She looked at me like I had offered her arsenic. Then to my surprise she grabbed the plate out of my hands. "I hope you didn't breathe on it."

My patience had worn thin with this woman. "What exactly is your problem? I was only trying to be nice."

Alexandra took a bite from the cake and glowered at me. "I don't do nice, so suck it up, cupcake." She closed her eyes and made a moaning sound. "Oh, yes. *This* is the one I want."

There must have been steam coming out of my ears. People like her with their arrogant and condescending attitude sickened me to no end. Alexandra gave new meaning to the term bridezilla, and I pitied her fiancé.

A man in a white jacket who I assumed was the pastry chef stuck his head out of the double doors. "Pepe, I need to have a word with you."

Pepe looked from me to Alexandra nervously. "Ladies, please excuse me." He bowed and hurried away, leaving me alone with her royal bitchiness.

Alexandra devoured the rest of the piece within seconds. She brought her napkin to her face and dabbed at her lips daintily. When she stared out the window at Mike again, I could have sworn I saw a bit of drool trickle out the side of her mouth.

"My word," she said in a low, breathless tone. "How did someone like *you* wind up with someone like *him*?"

Heat rose in my face. "Excuse me?"

"Sorry, honey," Alexandra purred. "You're okay, but that man is so hot that I'm melting just watching him." As if to illustrate the point, she rose from her seat and walked in front of my table, blocking my view of Mike as she stared unabashedly out the window at him, hands on her hips.

Alexandra waved a hand in front of her face. "If I wasn't engaged myself, I'd go outside and wrap my—"

She never finished the sentence. A loud popping noise filled the air, and the front window shattered into a thousand tiny pieces. The shock caused me to jerk back in my chair which then toppled to the floor, forcing me to smack my head painfully against the tiles. I uttered a groan and had a brief glimpse of Alexandra crashing into a nearby table.

Terrified screams filled the air as I lay there too stunned to move. I tried to make sense of what had occurred, but my brain was a mass of jumbled confusion. When I attempted to scream, no sound came out. What had just happened? Had someone thrown an object at the window?

The sound of the bakery bells jingled merrily as the door slammed open into the wall with a deafening sound. In seconds Mike was by my side, his face white as powdered sugar as he stared down at me. He sank to the floor and pulled me into his arms. I tried to sit up, but he threw his body over mine.

"Don't move. Stay down, Sal!"

Pepe was screaming in Italian, and a woman was crying—probably the young lady who had been working behind the display case. I couldn't see her from where I lay, so there was no way to tell for sure.

"Call 9-1-1!" a man's deep voice yelled—maybe the pastry chef?

Mike ran his hands over the sides of my face. "Are you all right, baby?"

"Wh-what was it?" I asked, my entire body trembling.

"Someone shot at the shop. Stay down," he ordered.

I turned my head toward the wall, still in shock, and that was when I saw her. Alexandra was lying on her side underneath an upended table, the lower part of her body hidden from my view. Her dark hair had chards of glass embedded in it. The effect was alluring and mesmerizing as the sun settled on the pieces, making it seem as if she was wearing a veil of sorts. *A bridal veil.* Her icy blue eyes were wide open and stared vacantly into space.

Then I spotted it—the perfect round hole in the middle of her forehead. Blood was seeping down the side of Alexandra's face. She was pale—lifeless, in fact.

I glanced down at my arms and saw blood. There was no pain, so I was unsure where it was coming from. I whimpered aloud and clung tightly to Mike who whispered reassurances in my ear. Despite the blackness that was closing in around me, I forced myself to turn and stare at her one last time—the silent face of a bride who would never see her wedding day.

CHAPTER THREE

DeAngelo's Bakery resided on a multiiuse street in a quiet neighborhood on the outskirts of Colwestern. An upscale apartment building was situated across the street and a private school located on the next with some charming homes surrounding it. I'd always enjoyed passing through this area to view the elegant homes and glorious changes in scenery during the four seasons of the year.

Mike and I leaned against the brick side of the building and watched the bedlam in front of us play out. The street was lined with police vehicles, EMT trucks, and even a television van parked next to the medical examiner's vehicle. Curious neighbors and onlookers were being held back from the crime scene tape by a policeman who told them "there's nothing here to see." Spectators gathered across the street in front of the apartment building, and a few even hung out of the windows, pointing and gawking at the scene below.

Alexandra's body was still inside the bakery. The medical examiner and police were with her, including one cop in particular that Mike and I knew fairly well.

"Unbelievable," Mike said in a low voice as he watched the perky blonde television reporter chatting amiably with Pepe, almost as if she were hosting a game show. Pepe was talking half in Italian and part in broken English, visibly upset. His hands whirled around in the air frantically as he stopped every few seconds to wipe tears from his face with a handkerchief while gesturing at the shop.

"How do they find out about this stuff so fast?" Mike wanted to know.

I didn't have a reply. An EMT had cleaned my arm,

which had a cut from the flying broken glass. I'd been examined but refused additional aid when they suggested going to the hospital to get checked out. I hated hospitals, and fortunately Mike hadn't insisted I go. He held me closely around the waist, and neither of us said much, still startled by what had happened. I'd had brushes with death before but never in this manner.

The technician said it was a miracle that I had not sustained any serious injuries and gave me a blanket to wrap myself in. Despite the warm day, I was chilled and suspected it might be from some degree of shock. Police had already taken our statements, but we had not been told we could leave yet.

Mike crushed me tightly against him. "You don't look well, baby. I'm going to get you out of here as soon as I can."

Up until that moment, I had been proud that I'd managed to maintain a calm demeanor, shock or no shock. However, when I looked into those beautiful midnight blue eyes of his that gazed at me with such concern and love, the tears started to gather in my own. That was when the realization hit me.

"You were outside walking past the window when the shot came," I whispered into his shoulder. "What if they'd—I mean, what if you had gotten—oh God…"

Mike said nothing as he kissed the top of my head. When I looked up at his face again, I noticed that his eyes had clouded over as well. He gave me a small smile, blinked, and then I officially lost it. So much for my cool exterior. Tears rolled down my cheeks, and I started to shake from head to toe.

"We're okay, baby," he spoke softly into my hair. "I'm not going to let anything happen to you, okay? Not ever."

"Sally and Mike, can I speak to you for a minute?"

At the sound of the familiar voice, Mike tensed against me. Officer Brian Jenkins stood there, nodding cordially at the both of us. He was a cop in Colwestern that I'd first met when I'd returned home from Florida after my divorce about a year ago. We'd become fast friends, and he'd made it perfectly clear that he had wanted to be something else as well. It hadn't taken me long to realize that I would never stop loving Mike, so Brian had never really stood a chance. He'd recently started dating an old high school acquaintance of mine which made me both relieved and happy for them.

Like Mike, Brian was easy on the eyes but a complete opposite of my fiancé as far as looks went. While Mike was dark haired and possessed a rugged, tanned face, Brian was fair, with thick, dirty-blond hair, an aristocratic-looking nose, and a Greek godlike profile.

Mike was aware of Brian's former interest in me, and I knew how difficult it was for him to maintain civility. When we'd first dated in high school, Mike had been very insecure and insanely jealous of any man I'd talked to back then. This had helped contribute to our breakup. He'd come a long way since then, and while Mike and Brian would never be friends, they at least treated each other with courtesy and a certain amount of respect these days.

"Jenkins," Mike greeted him. "Have you guys found out anything yet?"

"We're working on it." Brian was wearing his cop expression—similar to that of a poker face—totally unreadable. His eyes were serious as he glanced at me. "Are you okay, Sally?"

I nodded, and Mike's arm tightened around me. "Was this a random shooting, Brian? Do you think someone was targeting her?"

Brian gave a palms-up. "No way to know yet. The Walston family is very prominent in the area and all of New York State. The victim's father, Arthur Walston, owns some major commercial businesses. We did manage to notify her parents, who were in New York City for the day. They're on their way back of course. They in turn were going to reach her fiancé."

I was at a loss for words. I couldn't imagine how horrible it must have felt to receive a call that your child had been murdered.

Brian ran a hand over the stubble on his chin. "Did you talk to her at all? Was she acting nervous, like maybe someone was following her?"

I shook my head. "Not that I noticed. I don't want to speak ill of the dead, but she didn't strike me as a very nice person."

"She basically told the owner that if he didn't wait on her

within the next couple of minutes, she was canceling her order," Mike put in. "It seemed like she enjoyed watching him grovel at her feet. If she treated everyone like that then she must have made at least a few enemies during her lifetime."

"We'll be questioning her parents and her fiancé," Brian said. "Right now we're trying to determine where the rifle shot came from."

"How do you know it was a rifle?" I asked, trying to erase the vision of Alexandra's lifeless face from my mind.

"The coroner's office confirmed it as soon as they saw her," Brian explained. "The bullet exited her head on impact. There were also pieces of bone and brain spattered on the wall."

I put a hand to my mouth, afraid I might be sick. I had noticed blood and other substances on the wall but didn't realize what they were—up until now.

Mike glared at Brian. "You don't need to get into all the gory details. I think Sal's been through enough today."

Brian's face flushed. "I'm sorry. I know this isn't pleasant, and it had to be terrifying for you. Was she sitting next to you when it happened?"

Mike took a step forward. "We've already been questioned by one of your fellow officers."

I laid a hand on Mike's arm. "It's all right. She crossed in front of me at the very last second and was looking out the window." My voice quivered. "If she hadn't—it would have been me that got—"

Mike blew out a long ragged breath. "I don't want to think about that anymore. Jenkins, are we done here?"

Brian's bright green eyes with gold flecks continued to search my face for a moment, but he said nothing. I knew him well enough to surmise that he was forming his own theory about the shooting. What it was though, I had no idea.

"Jenkins?" Mike repeated, more impatient this time. "I want to take Sal home."

Brian blinked. "Uh, sure. Yeah, go home and try to forget about this mess."

Like that was even possible.

"I need to go back to the bakery and relieve Gianna," I told Mike.

He shook his head. "You're in no shape to go back to work. I want you to rest, and if you're feeling up to it, we'll still go to your parents for dinner tonight. Your mother wants to talk to you about last-minute wedding plans, and I think it would be a good distraction from all of this."

Brian nodded his approval. "I forgot your wedding is next week. Mike's right. You need to think about more pleasant things. If we have further questions, we know where to find you."

Mike snorted. "Yeah, you're good at that."

Brian ignored the remark and gave me a reassuring smile. "I'm glad you're okay, Sally. You've had an uncanny amount of brushes with death lately. You must have an angel watching over you."

As he said the well-meaning words, there was something in his face that made me nervous. He hadn't spoken in a lovelorn manner—it felt more as if he was keeping something from me instead. A small chill ran down my spine, and I tried to shake it off, telling myself I was letting my imagination run away with me again.

* * *

"It must be karma," my father announced. "Out of all days for this to happen. It's a sign of things to come."

I glanced at my father, who was seated at the head of the cherrywood dining room table. The entire family was gathered around it for one of Grandma Rosa's sumptuous dinners—my mother, father, Grandma Rosa, Gianna and Johnny, Mike and me. We all waited expectantly—or perhaps with dread—for my father to continue.

"Here it comes," Gianna mumbled as she refilled her wine glass.

Domenic Muccio was unique in many respects. He was an old-school Italian and thirteen years my mother's senior. Since his retirement a couple of years back, he'd kept himself busy with a variety of different projects. He was obsessed with death in any shape or form. He'd gone from planning his own funeral to driving a hearse and currently was planning to become a mortician. He even had a casket set up in the living room, claiming that it helped with his studying process.

My mother, sitting to his left, giggled as she placed a hand on his shoulder. "Have you ever met a smarter man in your life?"

Gianna rolled her eyes while Johnny put his head down and grinned. He'd been raised by Mrs. Gavelli ever since his mother, Sophia, Mrs. G's only daughter, had died from a drug overdose when he was five. Growing up next door to my family, Johnny was used to our original brand of wackiness.

Gianna and Johnny were still in the early stages of dating, but it was obvious how crazy he was about her. I adored Johnny, even though he had been a wicked little boy who once upon a time had enjoyed luring me into his darkened garage to play doctor. I'd always suspected he had a crush on my sister and was thrilled to see them so happy together.

Mike continued eating as if he hadn't even heard my father. I sighed and spoke up since I knew my father was waiting for someone to answer him. "What do you mean, Dad?"

My father sprinkled Parmesan cheese on his rigatoni. "Don't get me wrong, *bella donna.* What happened today was a horrible tragedy for that young woman and her family."

My mother made the sign of the cross on her chest. "Rest her soul." She was a devout Catholic who at the age of fifty-three, had recently landed a modeling contract for a magazine. Much to my and Gianna's chagrin, she was going to be an underwear model. She had a perfect size-four figure, long lithe legs, shoulder-length dark hair, a tiny nose, and teeth she whitened religiously.

It was a sad state of affairs when your mother looked better than you did most days. Despite her giggling school-girlish attitude and the embarrassing way she and my father carried on in public, I loved her dearly but wished fervently that she'd be wearing more clothes in front of the world.

"It's so tragic that she was going to be married the same day as you and Mike," my mother put in.

My father shoveled pasta into his mouth and then chewed thoughtfully as he stared at me. "I hope you don't mind if I use this as a new topic for my blog."

Gianna groaned, and Johnny held a napkin in front of his mouth, but I could still see him laughing behind it.

I stared at my father in disbelief. "You have a blog?"

He puffed out his chest. "Doesn't everybody? Yep. I set it up yesterday, and the first post goes online tonight. The blog is called *Slow Down—You're Killing Me*. It's my original take on life and death."

Mike snorted back a laugh while Johnny doubled over at the table and let out a howl, as if he was in pain.

Gianna nudged her boyfriend in the side. "I don't think this is funny."

"Sorry, sweetheart," he managed to say with a straight face. "I really do enjoy mealtimes with your family."

I looked across the table at my sister. "I think you're worrying for nothing. What's the harm? It's not like anyone's actually going to read it."

My mother gasped. "Sal, that's kind of harsh."

I finished off my glass of water. "Sorry, I didn't mean to offend you, Dad. But there are a million blogs out there." Plus my father typed with one finger, so it would take him a year to write a post. The thought that people would take the time to read his odd ramblings on life and death was almost comical. "What makes you think they'd read yours?"

"You're breaking my heart here," my father moaned. "It's going to be a huge success. I'd bet my life on it!"

"*Stupido*," Grandma Rosa grunted as she pointed at the china tureen which held my favorite dish, braciole. Braciole was tender, thin slices of beef pan fried with a filling of herbs and cheese then dipped into her rich tomato sauce. She stared at me with disapproval. "*Cara mia*, you have not eaten anything."

"I'm sorry, Grandma. I don't have an appetite."

Mike reached into the china tureen for another braciole. "It's really good, baby. You don't know what you're missing."

I raised an eyebrow at him. "After what happened today, how can you possibly eat?"

He grinned and kissed my cheek. "I can't help it. Digging out basements makes me hungry."

Grandma Rosa continued to watch me with her large, somber brown eyes. "I am so sorry you had to witness that horrible tragedy today."

Gianna sipped at her wine. "There are already articles online about Alexandra and the shooting. Her wedding planner was quoted as saying she was the biggest bridezilla that he ever had the misfortune of working with. Maybe *he* took her out."

"Jeez," I grumbled. "The poor woman isn't even cold yet. How can people be so cruel?"

Grandma Rosa scratched her white head thoughtfully. "Did they say that someone had been trying to kill her?"

"No one knows for certain." Mike piled more pasta onto his plate. "But they must have been."

Grandma Rosa locked eyes with me. "I am not so sure."

I adored my grandmother, but the look she gave me made me shiver inwardly. I turned to address my mother. "I think I'll skip Betsy Taylor's shower tomorrow."

A look of sheer alarm crossed my mother's face. "You can't skip the shower! I mean—I've already told them that you, Gianna, Grandma, and I will be coming. It would be terribly rude to decline at the last minute."

Good grief. "Mom, I don't even know her that well. She's your friend's daughter from church. I have a gift for her that you can take along. I'm sure they'll understand."

My mother exchanged a glance with Grandma Rosa, and I saw her lower lip tremble. She rose to her feet and quickly ran up the stairs on her tiny stiletto heels. Baffled, I stared at my grandmother. "What did I do?"

Grandma Rosa waved impatiently. "All these wedding plans are starting to make your mama a little cuckoo."

Gianna drained her glass. "Yeah, like she wasn't there already."

"Does anyone know when the funeral is for the Walston woman yet?" my father asked. "We should go pay our respects."

"We don't even know them," my sister protested.

My father pointed at me. "Sal knew the deceased. It would be tacky if we didn't show up."

My father loved going to wakes. "Dad, I talked with her for about two minutes before she died. I wouldn't exactly say that I knew her."

"She did save your life though," my father put in. "Why,

if she hadn't stepped in front of you—"

He didn't finish the sentence, and we were all silent for a few moments thinking about his words. My stomach muscles constricted at the thought.

Mike's hand tightened around mine, and I spoke in a shaky voice. "I think I want to go home."

"Sure thing, princess."

We rose to our feet. I kissed my father and stopped to talk to Gianna for a minute while Mike kissed my grandmother on the cheek, and she whispered something in his ear.

"Tell mom I'll call her tomorrow, and we can go over the seating arrangements then," I said to Grandma Rosa.

"No cheesecake?" Mike looked mournful.

It was terribly unfair how my fiancé managed to stay so lean despite the amount of food he could consume in one sitting, while I had to worry that my wedding dress would be too snug at my final fitting. "Maybe Grandma will let you take some home."

Grandma Rosa nodded in approval. "Of course. I will get some for both of you." She patted me on the shoulder. "Come with me while I get it ready."

I followed her into the large, sunny yellow kitchen where she spent most of her day. Up until last week, Josie and I had been running the bakery out of this room. It had been full of complications to say the least, thanks mostly to my parents and their whackadoodle ways, but had served its purpose until the new location was ready.

My grandmother cut two thick slices of her famous ricotta cheesecake and wrapped them in aluminum foil. She placed them in a paper bag and handed it to me. "It is not like you to not want cheesecake, *cara mia*," she said. "I hope you will be feeling better tomorrow."

I pinched the bridge of my nose between my thumb and forefinger. "Thank you. I think I might still be in shock on some level. I want to put the shooting out of my head and think about more pleasant things—like my wedding."

She said nothing, but the concern in her eyes unnerved me. Next to Mike, my grandmother was the other love of my life. Her words were always filled with wisdom, and on some level she was like my own personal fortune cookie, but a more pleasant variety than the ones I encountered at my shop.

"What are you thinking?" I asked.

She looked startled at the words and then smiled. "It is nothing. I am so grateful that you and Mike were not harmed in the shooting today."

"Me too." Still, I suspected that there was something else. "Are you sure nothing is bothering you?"

She patted my cheek gently. "Go home, *cara mia*. Get some rest. You are about to marry the man you love. Nothing else matters right now."

On the ride home I realized that she'd never answered my question.

CHAPTER FOUR

"There's something I should tell you," Mike whispered seductively in my ear.

I was lying in his arms, tired but sated, basking in the intimate moment we had just shared together. It was early Sunday morning, and he had successfully managed to stop me from thinking about the horrible events of the day before. There was a life lesson in this somewhere—I was sure of it. Never again would I take anything for granted. Especially him.

"What, you're ready for more?" I joked.

He chuckled. "For the record, you never have to ask that question. But that's not what I'm talking about. Okay, two more guesses."

"Hmm." I grimaced. "You know I hate guessing games."

Mike's mouth was at my ear. "Indulge me, okay?"

I buried my head into his smooth muscular chest. "You're in love with another woman?"

He played with my hair. "That's not even worth an answer. You're on your last guess, princess."

I sighed. "Well, that only leaves one thing. You're going to marry me on Saturday and make all my dreams come true."

"That is my plan," Mike admitted as he stroked my shoulders, "but not what I was referring to. I've got to tell you something that isn't going to make you very happy."

He had my full attention now. I propped myself up on one elbow to look him directly in the eyes. "Do I want to hear this?"

"Probably not," he admitted. "But since I'm about to be your husband, I think it's only fair to warn you."

Uh-oh. "Spill it. You're making me nervous."

"It's not that bad," Mike said. "Your mother is planning a surprise bridal shower for you today."

A groan escaped from my lips. I sat up in bed and pulled the sheet around me. "Please tell me you're joking. I told Mom I didn't want one."

Mike raised himself into a sitting position as well and kissed me. "Princess, you know that your mother never listens to you or anyone else for that matter."

He had a point. I wanted to scream, but that would have scared Spike, our black and white Shih-Tzu who was curled up in a ball at the bottom of our bed. Months ago I had explained to my mother that I didn't feel right about having a shower. I'd had one before—an expensive and elaborate affair when I married Colin. Sure, I knew people had multiple ones, and that was fine, but I didn't want people spending extra money on me. Plus, Mike and I had been living together since January. We were far from rich, but there wasn't anything we needed.

"Okay, but we've been engaged for several months," I said. "Why is she springing this on me six days before the wedding?"

He wrapped his arms around me. "In your mother's defense, she didn't decide until a couple of weeks ago to go through with it. Maria said she had so much fun at your surprise birthday party that she wanted to have another party. I guess she figured you might not mind so much. She told me she got an advance from her modeling shoot and wanted to put it toward the party. With the fire and everything else that happened, the plan suffered a setback, and she had to wait until things were back to normal. She only made the final arrangements last week."

I sighed. "Things will never be normal in my family. You know that. And why didn't my grandmother warn me?" Grandma Rosa was the only one I could count on in times like this.

"She was going to," Mike explained. "But I told her last night I'd take the rap for this one since your mother is bound to find out. I don't want her to be angry at your grandmother. Hell, no one has a right to ever be mad at that woman. You don't exactly have a poker face, Sal, so your mother is going to know you're not surprised the minute you walk into the restaurant. Last night when you said you weren't in the mood to go to the shower, you missed the panic in her expression."

"I knew something was up. Mom never worries about anything. Everything is always beautiful in her little world."

He traced a finger down the side of my face. "Your mother loves you very much. But for some reason she's weirdly obsessed about this wedding. Was she like this when you married Colin?"

I shook my head. "A little, but not to this extreme. Then again, she didn't like Colin." Actually, no one had. It was as if everyone had been able to see the writing on the wall back then, except for me. "She always liked you though."

"Score one for me then," Mike grinned. "Your grandmother thought you should be warned. I mean let's face it, the party would kind of be ruined if you weren't there."

"So this shower for Betsy Taylor is really mine?" I asked.

"The jig is up," he teased.

Great. I sighed and snuggled closer to him. "This is our only day together all week. I'd rather spend it with you."

He kissed me tenderly. "One week from today it will just be you and me. In paradise."

"Which can't get here soon enough."

"Try to enjoy the wedding preparations until then, okay?" A sly smile formed at the corners of his mouth. "We still have some time left today. Let's get in more practice for the honeymoon."

* * *

"You knew all about this, didn't you?" Josie demanded.

I was sitting at a table in Mama Lena's private dining room, flanked by Gianna on one side and Josie on the other. My mother was busy prancing around the room, chatting with people and looking sensational in a print, jeweled, light blue halter minidress. Grandma Rosa was standing next to her, watching the goings on, and I could have sworn she rolled her eyes at her daughter.

There weren't many occasions when I dressed up, but for

the occasion I had worn a pink sundress with spaghetti straps. It was a pretty dress and very comfortable, but I didn't look half as good as my mother. Actually, no one in the room did.

Gianna noticed me watching her. "That dress is from Forever 21. She showed it to me the other day when she bought it. Seriously, when is she going to act her age?"

"Your mother?" Josie asked. "She'll be wearing animal prints and bikinis until she's ninety." She elbowed me in the side. "Don't try to avoid my question. You knew about the shower. I could tell the minute you walked in."

I blew out a breath. "All right, but don't tell my mother, okay?"

Gianna paused, a forkful of salad in hand. "She already knows. I could tell from the expression on her face. Who told you, anyway? Grandma?"

I shook my head and stirred some sweetener into my iced tea. "Mike did. I wasn't exactly in the mood for a party today."

"Well, after what you went through yesterday, that's understandable." Josie squeezed my hand. "How are you holding up?"

I wiggled my hand back and forth. "I keep thinking about the fact that a woman who was getting married the same day as me is now dead. What if I had been the one who got shot instead of her?"

Gianna shuddered visibly. "Sal, you have to stop thinking like that. Alexandra probably had tons of enemies. I read about the way she treated other people. Apparently she had a job working at her father's hotel and did nothing all day but order everyone around. Someone just got fed up and decided to take her out. I've seen these cases before. Too bad it had to happen in front of you, though. I can't begin to imagine how terrible the ordeal was for you and Mike."

Josie cleared her throat. "I saw Officer Hottie on the news last night talking about the shooting. How are he and Ally doing?"

I shrugged. "Good, I guess. It's not like Mike and I spend a lot—or should I say any—time with them, you know."

Gianna cut into her chicken. My mother had ordered an

Italian dinner for everyone, complete with antipasti, a choice of chicken parmigiana or lasagna, salad, and rolls. Sure, their house was paid off, and my father had a good pension from the railroad, but I hated that they were spending all this money on me.

"Funny that you should mention Ally. I just saw her on my way to the restroom," Gianna commented.

Josie's blue eyes went wide with surprise. "Did you invite her to the wedding, Sal?"

I shook my head. To be honest I had briefly toyed with the idea of asking Brian to the ceremony but ultimately decided against it. I didn't think Mike would be thrilled, and it almost felt like I would be rubbing our love in Brian's face. "No. She must be here for another reason."

"Ally was on her way out. She had a catering menu in her hand and mentioned something about holding an anniversary party here for her parents next month," Gianna said. "She was asking me questions about the service, and could you enter the room directly from the parking lot—blah-blah, you know, for the whole surprise factor. Things like that. Oh, and she did tell me to congratulate you."

"That was nice of her." I took a long sip of iced tea and stared down at my plate. The food looked delicious, but I wasn't hungry. Shootings were a great motivation for my diet.

Gianna grinned. "I have to confess that I got a little nosy and asked her how things were going with Brian."

Josie leaned closer to my sister. "And?"

Gianna wiped her mouth with a napkin. "She said things were good but that he had been distracted the last couple of days. She thinks it's because of the shooting."

"Well, he is a cop," I said defensively. "I'm sure there are many days when he takes his job home with him. It must be hard not to."

My sister raised an eyebrow at me. "For some reason I don't think that's what she meant. When your name was mentioned, she looked uncomfortable. Is she aware that Brian had feelings for you?"

"What a nice way to put it," Josie smiled wickedly. "I would have said, 'Was Ally aware that Brian lusted after your body?'"

Ugh. "Cripes, do you have to be so crude? In answer to the question, I have no idea. It's all ancient history anyway."

Josie leaned back in her seat, laughing. "If Brian was a moron, he would have told Ally about his feelings for you. Chances are she guessed. He still gets that dewy-eyed expression when he's around you. Any woman would catch on to that."

I groaned. "Would you quit it? They seem happy together, and I'm glad for them. I hope he marries her and they have a dozen kids."

"Oh, Sal," Josie sighed. "You take the fun out of everything."

A man in a white serving jacket appeared at my left side. "Done with your plate, miss?" He was cute, with short, curly brown hair and a boyish face that was emphasized by his clean-shaven look. Then I stared into his eyes and was momentarily taken back. They were dark and cold, gazing into mine without expression.

My mouth went dry. "Yes, thank you."

"Are you the bride?" His eyes remained focused on me, and a chill formed between my shoulder blades.

"Of course she's the bride," Josie chortled. "Can't you tell how she's lighting up the entire room?"

He laughed good-naturedly then. As he reached across me for my plate, his sleeve rode up a bit on his arm to reveal a rose tattoo on the back of his wrist with the letter *M* next to it.

He bent his head so that his lips were near my ear. "May you always have good fortune, miss. Lots of *luck*."

My napkin fell to the floor, and I bent down to retrieve it. When I straightened up, the waiter had disappeared. The chill between my shoulders traveled down my spine at an alarming rate. The man's eyes had been the most notable factor about him—blank and cold, with a lack of any type of emotion. I had seen eyes like that before during some very dark moments of my life. Why did his words bother me? *Oh, for goodness sake, Sal. He was just trying to be nice. Stop thinking the worst about everyone you meet.*

My mother clapped her hands together. "Attention, everyone! Sally is going to open her gifts now."

She motioned to the three of us, and we all stood, with a bit of reluctance. My mother guided us to the platform where three velvet chairs were lined up behind a table covered with a white lace cloth. The chair in the middle had a banner over it that said *Bride-to-Be*. On either side of my chair were banners that read *Maid of Honor* and *Matron of Honor.*

"Jeez Louise," Gianna murmured. "She's getting a little carried away with this, don't you think?"

Josie and Gianna were my only attendants for the wedding. My mother had wanted to include a few distant cousins, but for once I had put my foot down and refused. I wanted those closest to me in the wedding party this time and no one else. I had also insisted that Grandma Rosa play a special role in the day as well. At her suggestion, she would be reciting a poem.

The three of us sat down, and my mother handed Gianna a pad of paper to write down who the gifts were from. Josie was given the tedious job of transferring gifts from the nearby table for me to open. Josie went to the table laden with presents that were wrapped in silver and gold paper. She brought over three packages for me to start with.

I absolutely hated to be the center of attention. Several of these women didn't even know me and vice versa. They were friends of my mother's from her real estate office and church or relatives that I only saw at weddings and funerals. Well, I had to make the best of it, so I smiled gaily at everyone and tried to act gracious.

My mother's gifts to me consisted of several pieces of barely there lingerie and an assortment of baby onesies in both pink and blue. When I held up the gifts, everyone roared with laughter.

"Someone really wants to be a grandmother!" A plump woman with a round, pleasant face and short blonde hair sat at a table directly in front of us and elbowed my mother in the side. Mom, being half the woman's size, nearly fell off the chair from the impact.

Josie whispered in my ear. "Do you know who that is?"

I glanced at the woman, who gave me a little finger wave when she noticed my staring. I looked down at the next package so that she wouldn't know we were talking about her. "No idea."

Josie pretended that she was showing me a name on the inside of the card she held out. "That's Marla Channing's mother. You know. The one who has the apartment across the street from the bakery."

At her words, I almost fell off *my* chair. "The stripper who dated Mike?"

"Who's a stripper?" Gianna leaned toward us with interest.

"*Shh.*" Josie pointed at the card again and gave a fake giggle. My sister and I both laughed on cue as well. "I told you before they only went out a couple of times. She was obsessed with him, not the other way around."

I glanced around the room in a panic. "Marla isn't here, is she?"

"No." Josie pretended to help me untie the bow. "I think your mother knows her mother from church. I'm not sure that Marla even goes to church. From what I hear, she'd keep the confessional pretty busy."

Cripes. I hoped this woman would not bring her daughter to my wedding. I'd have to talk to Mom about it. I knew Mike hadn't exactly been a monk in the ten years we'd been apart, but I had no intention of making friends with a woman my fiancé may or may have not been intimate with.

Josie brought over a square package wrapped in vintage blue paper with red roses on it. She turned it upside down. "Maybe the card's inside."

I unwrapped the package and opened the box to reveal a giant silver fortune cookie. I held it between my hands then lifted it up for everyone in the room to see.

"What is it?" someone yelled.

"It's a fortune cookie jewelry box," Mrs. Channing cackled. "They sell them online." She winked at me. "What a perfect gift for you, honey."

There was a groove in the center of the box that could be moved apart with your fingers in order to lift the lid. The entire object was about four by six inches in size. It wouldn't hold much jewelry, but the overall effect was cute.

"How adorable is this," Gianna squealed as she touched it. "And so fitting."

"Open it up. I want to see the inside." Josie peered over my shoulder.

I lifted the lid. There was a tiny mirror, and the box was lined in white satin. A piece of paper was folded up in the middle. My stomach muscles constricted as I reached for it.

"Oh my God! It even has a fortune. This is so original. Read what it says," Gianna urged.

I opened the piece of paper and stared down at the message that had been printed in large block letters with a black felt marker. A message that had clearly been meant for my eyes only.

Bang, bang. Next time I won't miss.

CHAPTER FIVE

A clanging of bells commenced inside my head. They continued to toil away ominously, growing louder and louder until I thought I might pass out from the noise alone. I struggled against the overwhelming panic that spread through my body. A little voice in my brain reminded me to stay calm. There was no way I could let the guests know what had happened.

Gianna gasped, and the expression on Josie's face was grim. Sixty women were sitting in front of us, watching with curiosity and waiting expectantly for us to share the message with them.

Josie found her voice first. "You guys will have to forgive Sal," she said in a tone that sounded both hoarse and shaky. "She's a little shell-shocked."

"What's it say?" Gladys Shelby, a woman who had worked in real estate with my mother, asked.

Gianna removed the message from my trembling hands, folded it up, and placed it back inside the jewelry box. "Uh, it says that Sal is going to have ten kids. She and Mike have always wanted a large family, but even she's a bit overwhelmed by this. Sal's going to have to bake a lot of cookies to feed that brood."

Everyone laughed and clapped.

Josie handed me another package. She noticed my hands were shaking and in an attempt to steady me, covered them with her warm ones for a minute. Without asking she then began to rip the paper off the box herself. "Sal pinched a nerve in her hand yesterday while baking, and she's a bit tired from opening all these presents, so I'll do the rest."

Fortunately there were only a couple of gifts left. I held

them up for the crowd to *ooh* and *aah* over but couldn't even remember what they were. I kept thinking about the jewelry box and the message of death inside.

The shooting at Pepe's bakery. That had to be what this was about. All along I had been thinking that someone had deliberately tried to kill Alexandra Walston. It made sense at the time. During the two minutes I'd known the woman, it was obvious that she was mean, insulting, and pretentious. Of course someone wanted *her* dead.

I placed a hand over my heart in an attempt to steady myself. The truth stung like an angry wasp. Alexandra hadn't been the intended victim. Someone wanted *me* dead. But why? The realization was both terrifying and mind numbing. I had to call Brian. I needed help—police help—right away.

My mother was at my side. "Sal, it's time for you to cut the cake."

Several women had started to gather with their phones and cameras for pictures. The cake had been provided by the restaurant, a beautiful red velvet masterpiece with vanilla filling. Plates of Grandma Rosa's sumptuous Italian wedding cookies surrounded the cake. Josie had confided to me earlier with pride in her voice that my grandmother had asked her specifically to come over and help with the preparation of the cookies earlier in the week. I didn't say anything but knew Grandma Rosa didn't need any help. It was her way of attempting to include Josie, and I loved her all the more for it.

I swallowed nervously. "Mom, I need to go make a phone call. Can't you cut it?"

She frowned. "Who do you have to call?"

The women were chatting amongst themselves and not paying us any mind, but I did notice that a couple of them, Mrs. Channing in particular, had their ears tuned in to our conversation.

Josie placed a hand on my arm. "I'll go with you to call him, Sal."

"Call who? Mike?" My mother's expression was puzzled.

"I'll help with the cake," Gianna said quietly.

My mother shook her head. "The staff will serve the

cake. But Sally has to be the one to cut it. *She's* the bride." She bent close to me, and despite the numbness in my body, I couldn't help noticing that the strapless halter dress was riding a bit low on her chest and threatening to expose the girls.

"Mom, you need to make a slight clothing adjustment," I whispered.

My mother giggled and turned her back to the crowd while she fixed her dress. "There, all better." She reached for my hand. "Come on. I want to get some pictures."

"Mom, please," I implored. "Just let me make the call first. It can't wait."

She narrowed her eyes at me. "Sally Isabella Muccio, you are ruining this shower with your stubbornness."

Gianna's face reddened. "Stop it. No one cares about the stupid cake, Mom!"

Silence filled the room. Everyone stared open-mouthed at beautiful, elegant Gianna who looked as though she couldn't believe what had happened herself. I could almost hear the whispers between the women. "That public defender job has gone right to her head," and, "How disrespectful to talk to your mother like that."

Gianna put a hand to her mouth. "I'm sorry," she whispered. "I didn't mean for it to come out like that."

My mother bit into her lower lip, stared at Gianna with tears in her eyes, and then turned on her heel and hurried out of the room.

I shut my eyes and wished that I could disappear. What a mess.

Gianna gave me a slight push. "Go call Brian. I'll take care of everything in here."

As Josie started to follow me out, she squeezed Gianna's hand. "Good luck. They might try to lynch you before we get back."

I started toward the dual metal fire doors that led to the parking lot. Josie grabbed my arm and shoved me in the opposite direction, toward the carpeted main hall in front of the dining room.

Bewildered, I stared at her. "What are you doing?"

"You'd be like a sitting duck out there," she said. "You

can't afford to take any chances. We'll call Brian from the ladies' room."

The scant chicken that I had eaten earlier wasn't settling well in the bottom of my stomach, and I prayed I wouldn't be sick. Josie half dragged me to the bathroom. Fortunately no one else was in there as I pressed the button on my phone for Brian's contact information.

To my surprise, a female voice answered. "Hello?"

"Ally?" I asked. "Is that you?"

There was a long pause. "Who's this?"

"It's Sally—Sally Muccio," I stammered. "Could I speak to Brian for a minute?"

Another long pause. "He's in the shower. Can I ask what this is regarding?"

Her voice sounded snippy, and I blinked. This wasn't the Ally I knew. Sure, we hadn't kept in touch since high school, but she'd always been pleasant to me, and even though we'd hung out with different crowds back then, I'd always considered her a friend.

The last time I had seen Ally was a couple of weeks ago at Colwestern Hospital where she worked as a nurse. Someone had tried to attack both Josie and me with a knife. I'd needed stitches in my hand and had run into Ally afterward. Brian had been present as well, and they'd left the building together. At the time Ally couldn't have been sweeter to me.

"Please, Ally, it's very important," I pleaded.

I heard her talking to someone in the background, and then Brian came on the line. "Hi, Sally. Can I help you with something?" He was using his cop voice again—maybe for Ally's benefit this time. I wondered briefly about what Josie said earlier—did Ally know that he had been interested in me before?

"Brian, I'm sorry to interrupt your time with Ally, but I have a serious problem."

His tone changed from aloof to concern. "What's wrong?"

"The shooting yesterday at the bakery," I whispered. "I think that bullet might have been meant for me."

There was no gasp on the other end, no muttering of expletives. Brian's voice was calm, cool, and very businesslike.

Policelike. "I was afraid it might have been."

What the heck? "Brian, if you thought so, why didn't you tell me this yesterday?"

"Sally, I wasn't positive," he admitted. "When it comes to your track record, it was something I had to take into consideration. I didn't want to alarm you since I didn't know for certain. What happened to make you think the shooting was intentional?"

A woman opened the door to the restroom, and Josie waved her hands in the air and jumped up and down.

"Nervous bride-to-be in here," Josie said. "Come back later."

The woman gave us a funny look but hastily backed out of the room.

My mouth was dry as unbuttered toast. "I received a message in one of the gifts at my bridal shower today. A fortune cookie message that read *Bang, bang. Next time I won't miss.*"

"Where are you?" Brian wanted to know.

I blew out a breath and tried to steady myself. I had never been much of a drinker, but a shot glass of Amaretto sounded pretty darned good right about now. Brian would make sure nothing happened to me, right? "I'm at Mama Lena's Restaurant. What if this person has booby-trapped my house? Maybe they're lying in wait for me or Mike."

Silence ensued on the other end. "We can do a search. How much longer will you be at the restaurant?"

"Everyone's having cake, so probably about a half hour or so. Mike's bringing his truck over to help me with the gifts, but I need to stop at my parents' house first." I'd have to tell my mother and Grandma Rosa what was going on but didn't want to do it here.

I heard Ally talking in the background again. Brian must have put his hand over the receiver because his voice became muffled. Still, I could hear the angry tone of her voice resonating through the phone. *Great.* Now I was causing problems between the two of them. "Brian, I'm sorry. Let me call the station and get someone else to help me. You're obviously not working today."

He cleared his throat. "I'll meet you at your parents' house." Then the line went dead.

I disconnected and looked up at Josie. "He's going to meet us at my parents' house in half an hour." I dashed off a quick text to Mike, telling him I was ready to leave. I'd wait until he got here to let him know about the death note. He'd go nuts for sure.

"Maybe it's not as bad as we think," Josie said. "Maybe someone knows about what happened yesterday and is playing a crappy joke on you."

God, I wanted to believe that so much. "I hope you're right."

Gianna rushed into the bathroom, followed by my grandmother. "Everyone's out there inhaling cake and cookies. Some of the women are already packing up and leaving. Are you okay?"

I nodded. "It may have been a practical joke."

Gianna looked relieved. "Do you really think so?"

Grandma Rosa examined my face closely. "*Cara mia*, do not take any chances. You should call your officer friend and pluck his brain."

Josie let out a bark of laughter. "Is he a chicken now?"

"You mean pick his brain, Grandma," I said.

She shrugged. "That is good too."

"Where's Mom?" I asked.

Gianna closed her eyes for a minute and exhaled. "She left."

"Left?" Josie and I both said simultaneously.

My sister looked embarrassed. "I'm sorry. I know I was too hard on her, but she was being ridiculous. She's acting like this is her wedding and not yours. And all those nosy biddies out there, gossiping together and whispering!"

"I'm sorry they were cold to you," I said.

She waved a hand impatiently. "Don't worry about that. The best part was when Mrs. Gavelli gave me the finger. She said I must have inherited disrespect from you. Then she said she was going to force Johnny to break up with me."

A smile formed at the corners of my sister's mouth. Gianna knew that was never going to happen. As much as he adored his grandmother, Johnny was putty in Gianna's hands.

Even though I felt bad for Gianna, I couldn't help but

giggle at the image of Mrs. Gavelli making an obscene gesture. Soon everyone else joined in as well. It felt good to laugh with the people that I loved and for a brief moment, forget that some lunatic might be out to get me.

CHAPTER SIX

We were gathered in the living room of my parents' house—Mike, Brian, Gianna, Josie, and me. My father was perched at his workstation, typing away merrily on his laptop. I assumed he was hard at work on his death blog—the nickname Gianna had given it. At this rate, I might have some material for him to use soon.

Grandma Rosa descended the stairs slowly and sat down next to me on the brown couch with its green floral pattern. "Your mama—she says that she has a headache and is going to bed."

"Oh, for cripes sake," Gianna grumbled. "How long is Mom planning to carry on like this for? She's such a drama queen."

Grandma Rosa shot my sister a warning look. "That is enough. Sometimes things are not always as they appear."

Grandma Rosa was never afraid to voice her opinion when her daughter acted like a teenager, so I found it interesting that she was now coming to my mother's defense. Something was up, but I'd have to find out what it was later.

Mike placed a protective arm around my shoulders. "Jenkins, I want to know what you and the rest of your precinct are doing to protect Sal from this whack job."

Brian looked pained. "We don't have any concrete proof yet that someone's trying to harm her."

From the way my fiancé looked at Brian, I worried that Mike might be thinking about harming *him.*

"She needs police protection or else she's not leaving our house until the wedding," Mike insisted. "After our honeymoon, if this nut hasn't been caught yet, we'll have to move elsewhere."

Bewildered, I stared at him. "I can't live that way, Mike. I'll just take some extra precautions until this person is found."

His blue eyes were dark as they stared into mine. "I'm not taking any chances with your safety."

"What about the past murder investigations Sal's has been involved with?" Josie asked Brian. "Can you find out if anyone has gotten out of jail? Maybe someone is pissed off at her for helping to put them away and is looking for revenge."

Brian nodded. "I'm already looking into this and should have some answers shortly." His gaze met mine again. "Was anyone acting suspicious at the shower?"

I shook my head. "Not that I can think of." A vision of the well-wishing waiter then came to mind. "Well, there was this—no, I'm sure it doesn't mean anything."

Brian leaned forward. "At this point, please don't disregard anything, Sally."

"The waiter." I turned to Gianna and Josie. "Did you guys see him?"

"He was talking to you when he removed your plate," Josie said. "I didn't really see his face though. That was the only time I saw him all afternoon."

"He asked me if I was the bride," I explained to Brian. "Then he said something like, 'Best of luck. May you always have good fortune.' He sounded like a fortune cookie."

"Maybe he was Chinese?" my father asked and continued to type away, in his own little zone like always. He didn't notice the incredulous looks we all shot his way.

"I'll call the owner of the restaurant and check it out." Brian gestured to Mike. "You know, there's a chance that the note, if it was referring to the shooting, could have been meant for you and not Sally."

Mike frowned. "I'd rather it was but think that's doubtful. What, has a customer got it in for me because I screwed up their foundation, and now they want me dead? Forget it. I'm not buying that theory. It's someone who knows about the fortune cookies in Sal's bakery. They're out to get her, not me."

Brian clenched his teeth together as if aggravated. "You were at DeAngelo's Bakery with Sally when the shooting occurred. Perhaps someone was trying to get you, and they put the message in the jewelry box to torment her. They obviously know you're getting married. Do you have any enemies? Anyone who doesn't like you?"

Besides Brian, that is.

I saw a muscle tick in Mike's jaw. "Not that I'm aware of."

"No angry ex-girlfriends looking to even a score?" Brian prompted.

Mike's tanned face reddened in anger. "Where are you going with this, Jenkins?"

I glanced sideways at Josie who raised her eyebrows at me in return. I cleared my throat before speaking. "Um, I didn't want to say anything, but the mother of one of Mike's former girlfriends was at the shower today. A Mrs. Channing."

"Who?" Mike asked, baffled.

"You dated her daughter, Marla," I reminded him. "She has an apartment across the street from the new bakery."

"Too close for comfort," Gianna mumbled.

Mike looked at me as though I was speaking a foreign language. "What does she look like?"

Typical male. When I first came back to town a year ago, Josie had mentioned that Mike had dated a lot of women in the years we were apart so I probably should have been grateful that he didn't remember her. "Blonde. Petite, slim, very pretty."

He continued to stare at me with a puzzled expression. "When did I go out with her?"

Josie leaned forward in her chair. "A few months before Sal came home."

"She works as a stripper," I volunteered.

"Mama mia," Grandma Rosa shook her head.

Mike suddenly looked embarrassed. "Oh, *her.* We went out once, maybe twice. She was kind of clingy. It wasn't anything serious."

Maybe not for you, but…

Brian interrupted my thoughts. "I'll have a talk with her. You say that she lives across the street from the bakery?"

Uh oh. "Please don't talk to her," I implored him. "She's been in the bakery, and this would make things very awkward. She hasn't actually done anything to me."

Well, that wasn't the total truth. She'd patronized the bakery at its old location, and gave every indication she'd be a frequent customer at the new location as well, given the close distance to her home. When she had discovered—probably from her mother—that Mike and I were getting married, the nice, polite attitude had stopped towards me. She had been in the bakery on Friday, the day we had reopened. I'd heard her announce to Josie, loud enough so that I could overhear in the back room, that she'd bedded every guy she'd dated. What an accomplishment to be proud of. I'd come out of the back room in a hurry before Josie tried to shove one of the fudgy delight cookies down her throat.

"Her mother was a bit loud and annoying at the shower, but there's no proof they're involved," I said.

"Well, if it's not them," Brian said, "who else knew you were having a shower today at Mama Lena's restaurant?"

Gianna's nostrils flared. "*Everyone* knew, thanks to our mother. She put Sal and Mike's wedding announcement in the paper yesterday. The article was almost an entire page long. God knows how much money she shelled out for it. There were details about the church, the rehearsal dinner, the cake testing—"

Mike rubbed a hand across his eyes wearily. "There you have it. This psycho knows every move that Sal's going to make this week."

That wasn't a comforting thought. If I was the intended target, it certainly would explain how the shooting at DeAngelo's came to occur, especially since the killer would have known what time we were scheduled to be there. Also, Alexandra's facial features were similar to mine from a distance. The shooter could very likely have thought she was me. I tried hard to swallow the panic rising in my throat.

"Well, will you look at this," my father said suddenly.

We all turned to stare at him.

"What is it now, Dad?" Gianna asked in an irritated tone.

My father rubbed his hands together in delight. "Jimmy Talarico tweeted about my new blog."

"You tweet?" Gianna asked, surprised.

"Sure, I'm on Twitter," my father bragged. "I have five followers too."

"What is this thing for twits like your father?" Grandma Rosa wanted to know. "Can anyone join, like the Facebook helper?"

My father looked at me. "Speaking of Facebook, I posted on your Sally's Samples page this morning and told everyone about my new blog."

Josie swore under her breath while I groaned out loud. "Dad, I really wish you wouldn't have done that."

"Sorry, Domenic," Josie said. "I designed that page. It's all about our cookies and nothing else. Death doesn't really go well with dessert."

"Sure it does," my father insisted. "Too much of a good thing can kill you. Hey, Sal, that's a great line for a fortune cookie."

Jeez Louise.

Josie took her phone out of her purse and brought up Facebook. "We're up to over 2,000 likes on that page, and we're not going to lose them because of your morbid blog." She pushed a few buttons. "There. I just killed it. No pun intended, Domenic."

"Aw, come on," my father protested. "I need the social media exposure."

"Can we get back to the problem at hand?" Mike asked. "Jenkins, I really think this is about Sal and not me."

Brian made another note. "If we're considering past murder investigations Sally's been involved with, we know Colin's killer is dead, so that only leaves a couple of other people for me to run through the system, which I'll do tonight." He stared up at me. "Did your mother post about the shower as well? It seems that the waiter or Mrs. Channing could have easily planted the jewelry box in the restaurant."

Gianna clenched her fists at her side. "Mom put that tidbit in a different paper, one she knew Sal wasn't likely to see since the shower was supposed to be a surprise."

"I'm sorry." A small voice spoke softly from behind me.

We turned around to see my mother standing on the staircase, clutching the railing between her slim fingers.

My father looked up and blew her a kiss. "Hi, hot stuff." He then returned to typing with one finger, humming to himself.

Gianna glared at our mother. "You should be sorry. You put a target on your own daughter's back. Why couldn't you leave well enough alone? Did you tell people about her final fitting tomorrow too? Why does everything have to be about *you*?"

"Stop it," I whispered. "This isn't her fault."

Gianna rose to her feet and walked over to our mother. "But it *is* her fault. Your life is in danger now because our mother is so selfish."

"That is enough." Grandma Rosa spoke in a sharp voice that stopped all of us cold. "You will not speak to your mama like that. Yes, she was foolish. But she was acting out of kindness."

My mother stared at Gianna and attempted to blink back tears. It was the first time I had ever seen her when she wasn't looking like a million bucks. Her face was devoid of makeup, her dark hair frizzy and uncombed, and she had wrapped herself in a pink satin robe, with no body parts showing for once.

Mom stared at me and hiccupped back a sob. "I'm sorry, honey." She dashed back up the stairs, and we heard her bedroom door slam shut.

I put my head in my hands. It wasn't my intention to make my mother feel bad about this. I knew that she loved me and was truly excited about my upcoming nuptials. Yes, she'd been difficult at times to deal with during the wedding preparations for Colin as well, but it was much worse now. As I'd explained to Mike earlier, I think my mother had known that marriage wouldn't last. I hadn't admitted to anyone that I'd had doubts as well, so her support back then had meant the world to me.

Brian stared down at his phone and then rose to his feet. "Ally's texting me. I need to go."

"My, she's got you on a short leash already," Josie quipped.

I shot Josie a dirty look, and she stared down at the carpet. Mike and I both stood and walked Brian to the front door.

"Jenkins, you haven't answered my question," Mike said. "I want to know what the police are going to do to keep my fiancée safe."

Brian ran a hand through his dirty-blond hair. "We can send a car by your house a couple of times a day. Other than that, there's not much else we can do."

Mike stared at him in disbelief. "You're kidding, right?"

Brian shook his head. "I'm afraid not. This is a small town. We don't have provisions for this type of thing in our budget, and we can't provide 24-hour-a-day protection. I don't know of a precinct around here that can."

Mike reached for my hand. "Maybe we should leave tonight. We'll fly to Vegas to get married and then go on to Hawaii from there. I'll call the airline when we get home."

My head was spinning from all of this. What would we do with Spike? What about the bakery and the jobs Mike had contracted for? We had responsibilities to fulfill and couldn't just leave at the drop of a hat.

"I don't want to run away," I protested. "We don't even know for sure that the note was meant for me. Like Brian said, it could have been intended for you."

"I don't care about that," Mike said. "My only concern is keeping you safe."

A sob stuck in my throat. If something were to happen to Mike, I wasn't sure I'd survive. I loved him more than anything on this earth. Right now I was terrified enough for the both of us.

"I have a gun," Mike announced to Brian, "and I'm going to look into hiring a bodyguard for Sal."

Startled, I placed a hand on his arm. "I think this is going too far."

Mike gripped me by the shoulders. "It already has gone too far." He addressed Brian. "Have you found out anything about the shooting yet?"

"We've been concentrating our efforts on trying to locate where the rifle shot came from," Brian explained. "My partner and I went door to door at the apartment building last night, asking if tenants heard anything, saw something funny, had managed to take a video of the area, etc. We also spoke with the landlord. He indicated that there were a couple of units with suspicious tenants where the shots could have come from. We're running checks on them and may end up getting search warrants for their apartments if anything funny shows up."

"Gee, that makes me feel better," Mike said in a sarcastic tone.

Brian looked at me. "We may bring you in to identify a few people in a lineup. One of them could be the waiter from the shower. You never told me what he looked like."

"He was good-looking," I said. "Maybe about my age or a little older. Brown, curly hair and clean-shaven. His eyes were strange though."

"Strange? How do you mean?" Brian asked.

"I don't know how to describe them," I said honestly. "It was as if there was something wrong with him. When he stared at me, it felt creepy, like he was looking right through me. His eyes were emotionless, cold. He also had a tattoo on his wrist. It was a red rose with the letter *M* next to it."

"There were roses on the wrapping paper of the present too," Josie put in.

"Do you still have the wrapping paper?" Brian asked.

Gianna looked mournful. "I threw it away at the shower."

Brian reached for the doorknob. "For the record, we've talked with Alexandra Walston's parents. It seems that she had her share of enemies, with one possibly being her fiancé."

"Are you kidding?" I asked.

"Alexandra's mother mentioned that the couple had a huge fight earlier this week," Brian said. "He accused her of cheating on him."

The news didn't come as a surprise. I knew for a fact that Alexandra would have been more than happy to sweeten Mike's cake at Pepe's bakery the other day.

"I don't know why a note would have been left for you or Mike if her fiancé was the killer, though." Brian narrowed his eyes. "The guy doesn't have a prior record, but still, who knows? Maybe it would be a good idea to have Mike drive you to and from work. Neither one of you should be alone, to be on the safe side."

Mike snorted. "Nah, we don't have anything to worry about. We have police protection, right?"

Brian shot him a clear look of irritation and then quietly closed the door behind him.

"Hey!" my father called out. "I've got comments coming in on my blog! I knew it was a winner!"

I stood there, feeling like someone had just knocked the wind out of me. "So maybe this is a practical joke, right? Someone knows that we were at the bakery the other day when the shooting occurred and is messing with us. There's nothing to worry about, right?"

Mike drew me into his arms and spoke over the top of my head. "Nothing is going to happen to you, Sal. I won't let it."

CHAPTER SEVEN

"Sal," Josie yelled from the back room. "What time is your dress fitting?"

I was placing jelly cookies and genettis into one of our little pink boxes for Mrs. Josten, an elderly woman who lived down the street. "Two o'clock. Do you think you can manage without me for a while? I could ask my grandmother to stop by."

Josie came into the front room with a tray of fortune cookies for the display case. I was always happy for the additional business they provided but secretly wished they weren't so popular. Some days they did unnerve me a bit.

"No. Your grandmother's probably busy nursing your mother's hurt feelings today." Josie grabbed a piece of wax paper and placed the cookies inside the case. "I'll be fine. The new driver can help me out if necessary."

I raised my eyebrows. "You went ahead and hired Mickey Steiger without asking me?"

She set the empty tray on top of the case. "Look. We can give him a try this week, and if he doesn't work out, we'll let him go. He'll be here at one thirty." She squinted at the clock on the wall. "Ten minutes, I mean. I need him to deliver that order to the Belvedere Banquet House. They're having a retirement party for one of their employees tonight, remember? The restaurant is paying good money for that tray of cookies."

I was too tired to fight it. "Yeah, okay. I really don't know anything about him though, and that bothers me. We haven't exactly had good luck with hiring employees in the past."

That was an understatement. We'd hired helpers in the past, and neither occasion had worked out well. The two women who I'd employed at different times had not been ideal for us, with one actually stealing a recipe that we had planned to use in a baking competition. We'd also had a part-time driver who'd been murdered.

Josie broke into my thoughts. "Rob said he's a good kid." Josie's husband played in a softball league with Mickey and his older brother, James. They were supposed to play every Sunday since Josie didn't work, but because Josie had been at the shower with me yesterday, Rob had skipped the weekly game when they couldn't find a babysitter.

"Of course," Josie said wickedly, "I couldn't help noticing the other day when Mickey was here filling out his application that he kept gazing at you in all your loveliness."

I did a major eye roll in response. "I think you're imagining things. How old is this kid again?"

"Eighteen," she replied smoothly. "Legal age. He wouldn't be the first one to fantasize about an older woman, right?"

The entire thought was unsettling and ridiculous. "Okay, you need to stop this. It's—disturbing. We'll try him out for one week. When he gets back from the delivery, maybe you could show him how to work the register and some other simple things around here. Make sure he fills out his I-9 and W-4. At least I'll feel better knowing that you won't be alone here this afternoon."

The bells sounded on the front door, and one of the last people I wanted to see—Marla Channing—sauntered in. She was dressed skimpily as usual, with a white halter top made of a thin, silk-like material that showed the curve of her massive chest and made it blatantly obvious that she was not wearing a bra underneath. The white jean shorts she had paired with the top were tight fitting and barely covered her rear. Her canvas, high wedge platform heels showed off toes that were painted a hot pink. I couldn't help thinking the outfit would have looked great on my mother. Unfortunately, Marla was no slouch in it either.

I watched as she wiggled her body over to the counter and gave me a small prissy smile. I could understand why Mike—or any man for that matter—would have dated her. Despite the sleazy way she dressed, I had to admit she was beautiful with her long, tousled blonde hair, large amber-colored eyes, and a heart-shaped face with delicate features.

Her eyes scanned the T-shirt and jeans I had donned. The white bib apron that I wore over them was covered in chocolate stains from the cookies I'd just frosted.

"Hi, Sally," she giggled. "I think I'll take a black and white cookie today. Same colors as you're wearing. *Tee-hee.*"

I clenched my teeth together and reached down into the display case. I placed the cookie into one of the little white bags and handed it to her. "That's a dollar fifty."

Marla handed me two singles, and I rang up her order.

"How's Mike?" she asked, in a voice that was both breathless and seductive.

I froze, my back to her, and exchanged an eyebrow-raising glance with Josie who was standing nearby cleaning off the espresso machine. "He's fine, thanks."

"Oh, you forgot my fortune cookie," Marla said.

Josie narrowed her eyes at the woman and spoke in a tone so low that Marla couldn't hear. "I'll get her a cookie she won't forget."

Marla let out another high-pitched giggle. "It's funny. I never thought about Mike being the marrying type. Do you know what I mean?"

Stay calm, Sal. She's trying to get a rise out of you. "No, I don't know what you mean," I said quietly.

Marla took the fortune cookie from Josie's outstretched hand. "He always struck me as the love 'em and leave 'em type. At least that's the way he was with me."

She fluttered eyelashes that I was positive were fake and gave me a coy smile.

Suddenly I was thankful that I'd already given Marla her order because that cookie might have wound up smashed in her face. "You're entitled to your own opinion."

She gave me a wide-eyed, deer in the headlights look. "You don't seem his type."

I bristled inwardly and reminded myself that I had what she wanted, and there was no reason to get into a hair pulling fight with this woman. "I guess you'll have to ask Mike what his type is then."

Josie folded her arms across her chest. "You dated him—what? Once? Twice at most?"

"True," Marla admitted. "But it's what we actually did on those dates that counted."

My hand rose slowly into the air, aching to slap that smug smile off her face. Since I was behind the display case, I didn't think Marla had seen the movement. I had never hit anyone in my entire life, with the exception of my sister when we were children and having typical sibling arguments.

Josie moved closer to my side and covered my hand with hers. "Yes, I see that spot on the case, Sal. Don't worry. I'll clean it off now."

Marla gave a slow toss of her head and reached into the bag for her cookie. She took a tiny ladylike bite and continued to stare at us. "Well, if you hadn't thrown a leash around his neck, I bet we could have made an awesome couple." She took another bite and chewed thoughtfully as she mocked me with her smile. "That man is *hot*."

"Get the hell out of here," Josie growled.

I walked around the counter until there were only inches between myself and Marla. She looked surprised at my action and backed up a step as if afraid I might strike her.

"I'm delighted that you think my fiancé is hot, Marla." Although hopping mad on the inside, I made an extra effort to keep my voice on an even keel. "I think he's pretty hot myself but will be sure to pass the message along."

Josie let out a bark of laughter while Marla's mouth dropped open. She started to say something then turned on her heel and stormed out of the bakery, almost knocking down a teenaged boy who'd been just outside the entrance talking on his cell phone.

Josie slung an arm around my shoulders. "Sal, I have to hand it to you. If that chick had talked that way to me about Rob, I would have rearranged her face."

I blew out a long breath and stared down at my hands, which were shaking. I hated confrontation of any sort, and it had taken all my restraint to keep from smacking her. The woman was a lawsuit waiting to happen, and I wouldn't risk my business on her petty ways. I was furious that Marla also had the nerve to throw in my face that she had slept with Mike at a time when we weren't even together. What he had done back then was his business. I didn't plan to ask him about it because I had no desire to know what had happened, just as I was positive he didn't want intimate details about my marriage to Colin either.

When I came back home a year ago, Mike had confessed that even though he had dated several women during the ten years we'd been apart, he'd never gotten over me. Of course that was satisfying for my ego to hear, and the same had been true on my part. I'd gone on to date and marry another man on the rebound after our breakup. It had ended in disaster because of his infidelity to me, but perhaps deep down Colin had known that I still cared for Mike. The only thing that mattered now was that we loved and trusted each other. As long as we had both these elements in our marriage, nothing would come between us.

"Don't you think," I said, "that acting like that after only going out with someone for one or two dates might constitute unnatural behavior?"

"Oh, she's definitely stalker material," Josie said. "She was in here one day when the two of you were talking in the back room. I swear that there were daggers in that chick's eyes. Plus, he hasn't had anything to do with her in over a year. She isn't playing with a full deck."

We looked at each other and seemed to be thinking the same thing.

"Sal," Josie said softly. "We should see if Brian's spoken to her yet."

I wrapped my arms around myself for warmth. It was nerve wracking to think that someone might actually want to kill me. Sure, I'd had people try to hurt me before, but not in this manner. Usually I became involved when someone close to me was in trouble, like when Gianna was suspected of starting my bakery on fire when her client's body was found inside, or when Mike had been arrested for Colin's murder. I didn't go around asking for trouble, but it still seemed to find me anyway.

"Okay," I agreed. "I'll call him when I get back from my fitting."

The bells on the door jingled merrily, and the boy who'd been standing outside, Mickey Steiger, hesitated in the doorway. He nodded to Josie and when our gazes met, his face turned red, and he hung his head downward.

Actually, there wasn't much about Mickey that wasn't red. He was a true carrottop in the sense of the word, with freckles all over his arms and cheeks. Large brown eyes were set in a serious square face. He was about five foot nine inches tall and so skinny I thought I could quite easily pick him up.

"Hey, Mickey," Josie greeted him. "Let me go grab your forms." She walked into the back room and left me standing there alone with the chatterbox. Mickey kept his eyes glued on the floor.

I smiled, although I wasn't sure he could see it. "I hope you'll like working here."

Mickey glanced up, as if startled by the sound of my voice. When he saw me looking at him, he flushed and stared down at the floor again. "Uh, yeah. Thanks."

Gee, this was going well. Thankfully Josie appeared at that moment and guided him toward one of the little tables set up in front of the bay window. "After you fill these out, I'm going to send you out on your first delivery," she said. "When you get back, you can help me behind the counter for a little while until Sal gets back."

Mickey sat down in the chair Josie indicated, his long legs stretched out casually in a pair of faded jeans. He accepted the pen she gave him and then stole another furtive glance in my direction. *Eek.* Josie may have been right after all. From the way he was looking at me, I was either the object of his affection or had snakes in my hair like Medusa.

The bells on the door sounded again. Mrs. Gavelli walked in and pointed a stubby finger at me.

"Aha!" she said. "I know I find you here."

Josie leaned against the counter. "She works here. You're a regular brain surgeon, aren't you?"

Mrs. Gavelli glared at Josie. "You always troublemaker, ever since a little girl. You make this one a troublemaker too. She try to work her wiles on my grandson years ago, and now she make Gianna a hussy too."

Oh, brother. "How about a fortune cookie?" I asked in a cheery tone. "On the house."

Mrs. Gavelli snorted. "You try to bribe me. It no good, but I take anyway. Now I go get your wedding gift today. Is big surprise. Good gift."

Josie's eyes twinkled as she handed her a fortune cookie. "She doesn't want a chastity belt, Mrs. G."

I bit into my lower lip to keep from laughing.

Mrs. Gavelli's jaw dropped. She glared at me and then shook her finger menacingly at Josie. "You go to hell for that remark." She cracked the cookie open. "Aha! See. Finally you give me good fortune."

"What's it say?" Josie teased. "You will live long enough to torture many more souls?"

She let out a loud harrumph. "Just for that, I no tell you." She whirled around and pushed open the front door with a vengeance, setting the bells off in a frenzy.

"She shouldn't talk to you that way."

We both turned to look at Mickey. I was shocked that he had opened his mouth, let alone dared to voice his opinion of my personal tormenter. When Mickey saw us staring, he looked back down at his forms and continued writing without another word. His ears had turned as red as his hair.

* * *

Becky's Bridals was a small dress shop run out of a duplex in Colwestern. Becky Winchester, sole proprietor, owned the entire building. One side was devoted to the shop and the other her personal residence. The building was white with pink shutters, and a large sign in hot pink letters hung on the front door. *Be a Becky Bride and Put Some Romance in Your Life.*

Becky was my mother's age. In fact, they had gone to school together. She was loud, brash, and very good at her job. She'd been divorced three times and knew everyone's business in town. Her daughter Lydia was one of the seamstresses and stood at attention nearby, ready to assist if the dress didn't fit to perfection.

The salon was cute, with pale pink walls and a rose-colored carpet. Becky had tried to talk me into a pink wedding gown, but I had politely declined. The shop itself was split into two rooms. One side contained racks of wedding gowns in almost every color, from white to her favorite, a prominent pink, and I had even spotted one in an arctic blue shade. There must be someone who longed to be a Disney princess on their wedding day.

The other side of the room held bridesmaid gowns and mother-of-the-bride dresses. My mother had picked out a jeweled, strapless silver gown with a slit up the right side so high it threatened to reveal her underwear. Don't get me wrong—she looked sensational in it. My only hope is that she would actually be wearing underwear.

"Oh, honey," Becky crooned as I came out of the single dressing room. "This dress was made for you. Your young man is going to go wild when he sees you in it."

I stared at my reflection in the full-length mirror. I did love this dress. It was light and comfortable, an ivory satin with a lace overtone. Tiny sleeves were also covered in lace, and the V-neck design complimented my chest, where I was a little more endowed than I preferred to be. Josie, who was almost as flat as a board, had told me on several occasions over our lifelong friendship that she'd be more than happy to trade with me. I guess you always want what you can't have.

Becky bustled over and started plucking the material at my waste, pinching it between her fingers until she found me.

"Ouch." Her nails were long and painful, and I was grateful that the pin she held was in her other hand. "What are you doing?"

She frowned. "You've lost weight since last week. I can tell by the extra material at your waist."

"It feels fine," I protested. "The dress is very comfortable."

She wagged a finger at me. "Don't tell me you're on that freakish diet where you eat nothing but carrots for two weeks before the wedding. You don't want to pass out on your way down the aisle, do you?"

Another cheerful thought. Right now my primary goal was to reach the aisle—alive. *Okay, stop it, Sal. That gunshot wasn't meant for you. You don't have any enemies.* At least I hoped not. I needed to ask Brian about the results of his search as soon as possible.

The back door buzzed, and Lydia went to see who it

was. Becky pointed at two large garment bags that were hanging from a rack by the register. "Gianna and Josie's gowns. Gianna said she didn't have time to come by and try it on." She rolled her eyes. "That girl will never learn. Did you want to take it with you?"

Gianna and Josie were both wearing pastel gowns made of a chiffon material with rounded necks and slightly puffy sleeves. The dresses were tea length, and they looked gorgeous in them. "Sure. That's fine."

Lydia closed the back door and approached us, waving a small box in her hand. "I just found this outside the door. It has a note on top that says *For the bride-to-be*."

"Well, that helps," her mother said dryly. "We have three other brides coming for fittings today. Maybe there's a name on the inside."

A tiny prickle of fear shot through me as I watched Lydia remove the top from the box. She held up a gold chain and offered it to me. "Sal, it must be for you. It's a fortune cookie necklace."

I stared at the necklace but refused to touch it. The tiny gold fortune cookie on the chain didn't have a place to hold messages, but it appeared that my fan club had struck again. Lydia looked at a slip of paper in the box, and her face immediately paled.

I bit into my lower lip. "What does it say?"

She hesitated then read aloud in a puzzled voice. "*One person's wedding might become their funeral*."

CHAPTER EIGHT

Somehow, I managed to drive back to my shop. I'd pulled over once, afraid that I might be sick, and tried to blame it on the fact that I'd not eaten breakfast. Nauseated, I was forced to confront the truth. I was being targeted by a crazy person. Someone meant business, and the chances were excellent that I was the intended victim—not Mike.

For the first time ever, I found myself constantly checking the rearview mirror in a mind-numbing sense of panic. Was someone following me? I couldn't tell. Despite the car's air conditioner turned on full blast, sweat broke out in a river on my forehead. *No.* I was not going to live like this. I'd call Brian when I got back to the shop. The police must have some leads by now.

I found Josie alone in the shop. She was making up a batch of her famous whoopie pies that had been ordered specifically for a church gathering tonight.

I looked around. "Where's Mickey?"

"We got a delivery call for two dozen genettis," she said. "An office party. Thank goodness I had them on hand. He should be back shortly. How'd the fitting go?"

"Not very well. I got another surprise." I showed her the slip of paper. "I'm scared, Jos. I don't think this person is playing."

Josie's eyes went wide with alarm. She moved past me and looked out the front window. "Do you see that car parked across the street?"

I followed her out to the front room, careful to stop at a distance from the window. *This is what terror does to a person.* A dark blue Buick LaCrosse sedan was parked directly across the street from my shop. The windows were tinted, and I couldn't see the person inside. I tried to swallow the fear rising in my throat. "What about it?"

"I noticed it earlier," Josie said. "It disappeared right after you left, and now the car is back. Coincidence? Probably not. I think this guy is following you, and it may be the same person who's out to kill you. Should we call the cops?"

This wasn't a time to be taking chances, so I pulled my phone out of my purse. I hated to keep bothering Brian, but he was my prime contact at the police station. Plus, I knew he would do whatever he could to help. As I dialed his number, I prayed that Ally wouldn't answer the phone again.

"Officer Jenkins."

Thank goodness. "Brian, it's Sally. I have a problem."

There was a long pause. "What's wrong?"

"There's a guy parked out in front of my shop. I think he might be following me." Or else I was getting extremely paranoid. "He's in a dark blue Buick. If you're busy—" I thought of Ally again, "maybe you could ask one of your fellow coworkers to come by and check it out?"

"I'm on duty," Brian said. "As it happens, I'm only about five minutes away. I'll swing by and have a little chat with him."

Relief spread through my body. "Thank you so much, Brian. You don't know how much this means to me."

"I'll see you soon." He clicked off.

I went into the back room where Josie was spooning the creamed filling onto the cakes and then assembling them. "Brian's going to come over and check it out."

"By the way," Josie said, "his old ball and chain was in while you were at your fitting. I kind of got the impression that she wanted to talk to you."

Wonderful. "What did she say?"

Josie put the leftover filling aside. "Ally asked if you were around, and I told her no. Then she started making small talk. She was the only one in the shop at the time, so I was able to chat with her for a few minutes. You know, about the usual stuff. How the kids were, how long you and Mike had been engaged, if you and Brian had slept together, how good our jelly cookies were—"

What? "Whoa. Back up a second. She asked if I'd slept

with Brian?"

My best friend gave me a coy smile. "Well, she didn't come right out and say that. Ally has too much tact. She asked how long you'd known Brian, and I told her you'd met him when you first came back to Colwestern last summer. He was the cop on duty when skanky Amanda's body was found on our front porch."

Amanda Gregorio had been my high school nemesis. Blonde, rich, beautiful, and meaner than a snake. To top it all off, I'd walked in on her while she'd been in bed with my then husband, Colin.

Josie prattled on. "Of course, like everyone else, Ally hated Amanda. That witch was rotten to everyone, especially you. Anyway, Ally asked if you'd ever dated Brian and…well, I was honest."

Wasn't she always? "Not too brutally honest, I hope."

Josie snickered. "I told her he was interested but that you had always been in love with Mike, so Officer Hottie never stood a chance. I thought that would reassure her, but she seemed more ticked off than ever. She paid for the cookies and left without another word."

I twisted a strand of hair around my fingers. "Oh, this is just great. She thinks he's still carrying a torch for me. The last thing I want to do is come between them."

Josie moved past me into the front room and placed the tray of cookies on the counter. "It's not your problem. You have enough going on in your life without having to worry about those two. You're getting married in a few days, and someone might be trying to kill you or your fiancé. Let Ally deal with her own insecurities."

I looked up just in time to see the driver's side door of the Buick open. My stomach lurched as a man of Asian descent, possibly Korean, got out of the vehicle. He was over six feet tall and dressed in an expensive dark gray suit. He slammed the door and started striding toward my bakery with purpose.

"Oh my God," I whimpered. My feet were frozen to the floor, and I couldn't move.

"Duck!" Josie commanded as she pushed me down onto the floor behind the display case.

"No!" I hissed in a panic and clutched at her leg. "He'll shoot you!"

Josie shook me off. "Let him try. We've got a camera in here now. He won't get away with it."

"That won't make me feel any better if he pulls the trigger first," I whispered.

She reached for the tray on the counter. "Relax. I've got it covered."

The bells sounded over the door. From where I sat on the floor behind the case, the man couldn't see me, but I could view him from the waist down. Josie's hands remained on the tray as she addressed our so-called customer.

"Hi there," she said in an unusually cheery voice. "Can I help you?"

"I'm looking for Sally Muccio," he said in a deep velvety tone.

Josie was perfectly still. "She isn't here."

There was silence for a moment. "I followed her here a few minutes ago, miss. I *know* she's here. I need to speak with her right now."

Oh my God, oh my God. He's going to hurt my best friend. I clutched at Josie's leg, trying to force her down onto the floor, but she shook me off.

"You're following Sally?" Josie asked with a slight tremor again.

I watched him reach into his pants pocket. "As a matter of fact, I am. You see—"

Before the man could say anything further, I screamed and Josie started throwing the whoopie pies at him with the intensity of a Major League pitcher. With both of them being preoccupied, I rose to my feet. The man's face was covered with filling, and pieces of the chocolate were all over the front of his suit. He staggered backwards like he was intoxicated until his head connected with the glass of the front door, and then he crashed to the floor.

My jaw dropped. Josie was strangely calm, armed with a cookie in one hand and her phone in the other. She wore a triumphant smile. "All those hours playing baseball with the kids in the backyard have finally paid off."

Josie and I slowly moved around to the front of the case and stood there looking down at my possible assassin. All I could see was dark hair dotted with splotches of whipped cream. His entire face was covered. Seemingly dazed, he moaned and tried to wipe the cream from his eyes as he blinked up at us.

Josie whipped a frosting knife out of her pocket. I had to hand it to her—the girl was always prepared. "Don't try anything, loser. The cops will be here soon, so you'd better plan on spending the night in the slammer."

He continued to stare at us openmouthed, but no sound came out. At that moment Brian's squad car pulled up across the street behind the Buick. He got out, walked to the side of the vehicle, and then turned to look over at the shop. Since Mr. Assassin's body was blocking the door, I stood at the front window frantically waving my arms and jumping up and down in the air. Brian ran toward the shop as Josie prodded our would-be attacker with the toe of her shoe.

"The cops are here, and you're right in the way," she said sharply.

"Uh." The man grunted and pressed his hands against the floor as he tried to raise himself up.

Josie kicked him with her sneaker, and he collapsed on the floor again. "Never mind. You're not going anywhere."

Brian opened the door slowly and managed to squeeze his body inside. He stared down in shock at the man. Then his mouth twitched slightly as he turned to me and Josie. "This is the guy you were telling me about?"

My voice was trembling. "Yes. He was getting ready to pull a gun on Josie."

Our would-be attacker wiped at his face again with the sleeve of his jacket. "Officer, this is a huge mistake."

Instinctively, Brian's hand went to his gun on his belt. "Would you mind telling me why you're harassing these women?"

The man stood and brushed more cookies and whipped cream from his body. It was a useless effort since both he and his suit were a walking disaster. He reached a hand streaked with whipped cream into his pocket while Josie and I took a step backward.

"Careful, Brian. He's going to shoot you!" I screamed.

The man swore. "Ladies, I'm not going to shoot anyone. I'm a private investigator who was hired to protect Miss Muccio, not harm her." He flashed identification at Brian.

Brian examined the photo then glanced up at the man. He handed the card back to him. "Ralph Chang. Oh sure. I've heard of your company. R.C. Investigations, right?"

Ralph nodded and reached for napkins on the nearby table to wipe his face. "Yes." He glared at Josie. "Although after the encounter with Miss Muccio's employee, I think it's safe to say she doesn't need a bodyguard."

Josie's face was suddenly pale underneath the freckles. "He's a b-bodyguard?"

Brian bit into his lower lip to keep a straight face.

Ralph checked his suit coat, sighed then took it off, and loosened his tie. "I was hired by Mr. Michael Donovan to keep his fiancée safe."

I couldn't believe that Mike had actually gone through with the plan, and without telling me first. "He hired me a bodyguard? Are you serious?"

Josie clapped a hand over her mouth in horror. "I'm so sorry," she stammered. "I had no idea. Wait, let me help you clean this mess up." She ran into the back room and returned in record time with two hand towels, one damp and one dry. She started to help clean off Ralph's coat, but he waved her off.

"No offense, miss, but I'd rather you stayed as far away from me as possible."

Brian's mouth twitched. "Well, I see that one mystery has been solved."

I exhaled a long, steady breath. "This is all my fault. I just got back from my dress fitting, and someone left a present on the bridal shop's porch that was meant for me." I showed Ralph and Brian the fortune cookie and its message.

Brian's smile disappeared as he examined the slip of paper. "Let me take this for evidence. We can try to run it for fingerprints, but chances are we won't find anything."

Ralph put a hand to the back of his head where it had connected with the front door. "Sorry, Miss Muccio, but I need to go home and change. And take a couple of aspirin. I'll phone

Mike and tell him I'll be back later on. *Maybe*."

Josie shifted nervously from one foot to another. "I'm really sorry, sir."

He had one hand on the door but turned to look back at her. "You've got a mean right arm, Miss. Maybe the Yankees could use your help."

The bells were set in motion as Ralph opened the door and staggered across the street to his waiting car.

Brian watched him leave, hands on his hips. "The poor bastard. They say being a cop is a tough job because we put our lives on the line every day. Being hired to look after you has got to be worse though."

"Hmm." I frowned. "Thanks for the compliment."

He narrowed his eyes. "Sorry, Sally, but it's the truth. Your world is a bit scary these days."

Yeah, don't I know it.

Josie heaved a sigh. "I hope he doesn't quit. You obviously need someone watching your back."

"She should hire you," Brian grinned. "Problem solved."

Josie gave him a sharp look then snorted back a laugh as she went into the back room to get a broom and clean up the cookie mess.

"Thanks for coming." I smiled at Brian.

He watched as Josie started cleaning the floor. "Do you think we could talk privately for a moment, Sally?"

Josie looked up at the both of us. "Don't worry. I can take a hint. I need to make up some more whoopie pies for tonight anyway. My stock has somehow been depleted." She hummed a little tune low in her throat as she returned to the back room.

There were three small tables painted white with matching chairs in front of my large bay window. I sat down on one of the chairs, and Brian took a seat opposite me. "Can I get you some coffee?"

He shook his head. "No thanks. I'm trying to cut down. I have enough trouble sleeping lately as it is."

When he smiled, I couldn't help noticing how those green eyes of his shone in the sunlight that was reflecting through the window. A pang of recognition set in, and I winced.

Not again. I thought Brian had finally accepted that there was nothing romantic between us. Disappointment flooded my body. I really wanted him as a friend but nothing more. I was in love with someone else and always had been. This infatuation needed to end.

"What's up?" My tone sounded a bit reluctant.

He placed his elbows on the tablecloth Grandma Rosa had crocheted so lovingly for me and leaned forward. "This is really hard for me to say."

I couldn't deal with this any longer. "Brian, you're a really nice guy, but—"

"Sally, you need to stop calling me."

I prattled on, oblivious to his words. "I'm getting married on Saturday and thought you had accepted the fact that there would never be anything—"

Wait a second. What did he just say?

Brian looked apologetic. "I confess that I was really taken with you for a while. When you turned me down and decided to get back together with Mike, it hurt a great deal. For a while it affected me so much that every time I dated another girl, all I did was compare her to you. But I'm over that now."

"Oh." I didn't know what else to say. For some odd reason, it felt like I'd been rejected. "Well, I'm glad that you and Ally are happy."

At the mention of her name, his face lit up. "I'm crazy about Ally. We've gotten close in the last couple of weeks. *Very* close in fact."

Okay, way too much information for me.

He stared down at the table, refusing to meet my eyes. "When you called yesterday—well, Ally got kind of pissed. I know it sounds unreasonable of her, but somewhere she'd heard that I'd pursued you to go out with me and that we might have even *been together,* if you know what I mean."

I knew what he meant, and this didn't make me feel any happier about the entire situation. Now I understood the reason for Ally's visit today. Josie's earlier assumption had been correct. Even though I was getting married on Saturday, Ally thought I might still have designs on Brian. Or worse, that we were carrying on. "I see. I hope you set her straight."

He nodded. "I told her that, yes, I had asked you out before, but nothing ever happened between the two of us. I'm not sure if she believed it though. Then when you called yesterday—well, she kind of snapped."

I didn't like that word. I had seen people snap before, and it wasn't a pretty sight. Since I had an idea where Brian was going with this conversation, I decided to help him out. "So next time I should call 9-1-1 for assistance instead of bothering you?"

His answer was to reach out and cover my hand with his. I briefly thought about moving mine away, but the gesture wasn't construed by me as a romantic one.

"I still care about you and always will," Brian continued. "But I really want to make this work with Ally. So, yes, if you could please call someone else in the future, that would be great. I'm still involved in this case and promise to call or stop by whenever I have new information. If you could avoid contacting me directly in the future though, I would appreciate it."

I nodded mutely. Of course I understood where Brian was coming from and didn't mean to take advantage of him, but his request had hurt me. At the moment I really needed his help. My life might be in danger, and Brian knew better than anyone else about the past involvements I'd had with some shady individuals. It seemed only natural that I would call him for assistance. To learn that Ally was acting this way surprised me as well. I wondered if she might be getting too possessive of Brian already but didn't feel it was my place to ask.

He reached into his pocket and handed me a card. "If something happens, call my partner, Adam. You've met him before."

I stared down at the card for a minute before I responded. "Sure, no problem. I appreciate the thought."

Brian rose from the table. "I'm glad Mike's looking after you and hired Ralph. From what I hear, he's the best at what he does, and you should be safe. Well, if Ralph decides he still wants the job, that is."

My laugh sounded hollow to my own ears. I was saddened by his words for this felt like a good-bye of some sort. I didn't want to lose Brian's friendship but forced myself to look at things from his perspective. He was trying to make a future with Ally and didn't need me screwing things up for him.

If a woman who I thought might have been involved with Mike in the past—say, Marla—kept calling him to fix a leaky faucet, would it bother me? *Okay, bad example there.* Mike and I had been through so much since we first started dating at the age of sixteen. After five years of being with Colin then another five as his wife and then learning about his indiscretions, it had been difficult for me to learn to trust again. I had no doubts about my relationship with Mike or his love for me, but after all this time apart, it had come at a high price.

"I'll call you tomorrow if I have any updates," Brian continued. "I also wanted to let you know that I checked out all other assailants from past cases you were involved with and everyone is still behind bars. From the time Amanda was found dead on your doorstop to when we arrested the party responsible for killing Gianna's client and burning down your bakery a few weeks ago. But if you think I've forgotten someone, feel free to let Adam know."

For some reason, I felt like someone had been overlooked, but who that might be escaped me for the moment. "Of course. Thanks, Brian."

He paused at the door and then turned around to look at me one last time. "Best of luck, Sally." His tone was husky. "You deserve to be happy."

CHAPTER NINE

"You could have told me."

I tried very hard to keep the disapproval out of my tone. Mike had my best interest at heart, of that I had no doubt. Ever since we'd gotten back together, he'd gone to extreme lengths to prove his love for me, to show me he was over the jealousy issues and insecurities that had plagued him through his awful childhood and teenage years. The bodyguard hiring was his attempt to protect me, but the truth of the matter was it had almost ended in disaster.

Mike pulled his truck into my parents' driveway behind Gianna's Ford Fiesta. He had picked me up at the bakery and insisted that I wasn't going anywhere alone if Ralph was not available to babysit me. The bodyguard was mysteriously missing in action tonight. Go figure.

We had grabbed a quick bite to eat at a fast food restaurant and were now dropping off Gianna's maid of honor dress. She was moving into the apartment later this week but was at my parents' tonight. The day couldn't come soon enough, she had said.

Mike reached for my hand and brought it to his lips. "That was why Ralph came into the shop, to tell you, baby. He hadn't counted on your wacko partner going all mental on him."

Wacko partner? Real nice.

He went on. "Plus, I didn't think he was available to start until tomorrow, so I was all set to patrol the bakery myself. Ralph's been a good client of mine. I installed siding on his house a few months ago, did his roof last week, and he has more work for me. Most important, he's great at his profession."

The miracle of it all was that Ralph still wanted the job.

He couldn't be that desperate for business, could he?

"How much is this costing?" I asked through the open window as Mike went around the front of the truck.

He glanced up and down the street before he opened my door. "You let me worry about that."

"Mike—"

He wrapped his arms around me before I could even attempt to move from the seat. "I don't care. There's no price on your life, baby." He kissed me tenderly. "If it makes you feel any better, the cost's not as bad as you think. I've done a great deal of work on his house, so we're trading off a bit."

"How much?" I asked again.

He ignored my question. "I don't think we should go through with this wedding at the country club. We need to come up with a new plan."

I blew out a sigh. "Mom's going to freak."

His blue eyes shot angry sparks. "Well, that's too bad. No way am I taking any chances with your safety, and I would hope that she'd feel the same way."

Well, if my mother was normal, she'd feel that way. Of course I knew she loved me, but the woman went through life seeing only what she wanted to see. Ever since she had started planning this wedding, she had been acting stranger than usual, and that was hard to believe. Perhaps she thought this was the only wedding she'd ever get to arrange. Gianna had told me numerous times that she wanted a career before settling down, and she was uncertain about children. We couldn't be more different in that respect. Gianna saying the words to my mother would be similar to thrusting a knife in her back.

I reached for the garment bag next to me on the seat and handed it to him. "That's sure to go over well."

As we walked down the sidewalk and toward the front door, it was opened by my grandmother.

"I saw you pull in," Grandma Rosa said as I hugged her.

The best part about returning to my childhood home was—and always had been—spending time with my grandmother. She had come to live with my parents after my grandfather had passed away, when Gianna was a baby. Growing up, there were many times she had been the only one who'd ever really listened to what I was saying.

"Are you hungry?" she asked. "There are leftovers and a butterscotch parfait that Nicoletta sent over."

"I'm glad she's feeling well enough to make her famous dessert again." The dessert was four layers of delicious, rich butterscotch and whipped cream goodness, but I'd barely been able to choke down my cheeseburger.

Mike shook his head. "No thanks, Rosa. We already stopped for a burger."

Grandma Rosa frowned as she looked at me. "You have lost weight. Becky called your mother today. She is all worried about your gown not fitting right. And your mama is all upset about who is going to make the cake. Pepe has closed the shop down until next week."

I struggled not to roll my eyes. "The gown fits fine, and I know all about Pepe. He already phoned me." There was no way I could be angry with the man for canceling my order. Heck, if I were Pepe, I wouldn't want to be involved in cake preparations for me either. I'd managed to transform his elegant shop into a disaster zone.

"Josie's making the cake," I said as we walked inside. "That's the way it should have been from the beginning."

Grandma Rosa nodded in approval. "That is good, yes. But your mama is a bit touched in the head these days, more so than usual. She is in the kitchen waiting for you both. Do not say I did not warn you."

Gianna came out into the foyer, hugged me, and took the garment bag from my hands. "Thanks for picking it up."

"No problem." I watched as she hung it in the nearby closet. "You're not going out with Johnny tonight?"

Gianna shook her head. "He's spending time with Nicoletta tonight. His grandmother is feeling a bit jealous since I entered the picture." She glanced at Mike. "I hate to be a pest, but is the apartment ready to go?"

Mike nodded. "I'm going to put the final coat of paint on tomorrow, and you should be able to move in the following day."

She sighed in relief. "You're the best. Thanks."

My father shouted from the living room. "Yeah, baby! The blog is getting hits. I knew death would be popular!"

We all peered into the room. My father was sitting at his workstation, next to the mahogany coffin that stood open, and fortunately empty.

I walked into the living room hand in hand with Mike. "That's great, Dad."

"People are even commenting on it." He leaned closer to the screen to read a post and spoke in a dramatic halting tone. "*You make death sound so appealing*. I got a thousand hits today! I'm famous!" He pounded the desk with his fist and gave a loud whoop.

"This is just wrong on so many levels," Gianna said.

My mother was sitting at the kitchen table with a pile of index cards in her hands and a cup of coffee nearby. She looked up and smiled at us. "Hi, honey. Hello, Mike."

I leaned down to kiss her cheek. "How are you feeling, Mom?"

"Never better, darling." She was all dressed up in a sparkly, one-piece gold number that was cut low in the chest and ended about midway down her thighs. It appeared that everything was once again right in Maria Muccio's world. Until Mike sprang his news on her, that is.

Mom waved the cards at me. "I've got the seating charts here. We still have ten people that haven't responded. I'm going to call them in the morning then give the final count to the country club by—wait, what's tomorrow? Wednesday? I need to give it to them by Thursday."

Mike's face was stern as he sat down next to my mother. "Maria, I want you to know that I appreciate everything you've done for me and Sal. I'm looking forward to being a part of your family."

She reached over and patted his cheek and then giggled. "It's my pleasure, honey. I'm looking forward to it too."

He cleared his throat and looked uncomfortable. "I hate to do this to you after all the work that you've put in, but under the current circumstances, maybe it's best that we cancel the wedding, or at least the reception. I'm happy to pay back any money that you've lost as soon as I can. I'm worried about Sal and this potential maniac that's out there trying to kill her. She got another message today, and because of the information in the newspaper the other day, it's likely that this person knows exactly where she's going to be on Saturday. Maybe we could find another place for the reception, and they could perform the ceremony there as well?"

My mother's face paled under her carefully applied makeup. "We can't find another place now. The wedding is in five days! What on earth are you thinking?"

Mike's face colored slightly. "I'm thinking of my wife, and your daughter. I'm fine getting married at city hall or wherever Sal wants. The important thing is that she's safe. It's all that matters to me."

There was a lump in my throat as I reached for his hand. "Thank you for saying what I couldn't."

Gianna dabbed at her eyes with a tissue. "That was beautiful."

My mother's face went from pale to crimson in the blink of an eye. "I see. So after I spent all of these hours working on the preparations and put down a hefty deposit, you want to cancel it all of a sudden? Hey, no problem."

"I'm sorry for the trouble," Mike said. "But I love your daughter more than anything. We'll run off and elope if we have to, but I would like you to be part of our special day."

My mother rose quickly out of her chair, knocking it over in the process. Her eyes glazed over, and she was breathing heavy. For a brief moment I didn't recognize her. "Well, how thoughtful of you," she said.

"Mom," I broke in. "I think it's for the best. We didn't want a big wedding anyway."

She stared at me like I had two heads. "I never thought I had raised such a selfish daughter."

To say I was stunned would have been an understatement. The woman in front of me was no longer my mother. *What the heck is she thinking?*

"*You* didn't raise us," Gianna interrupted. "Grandma did. You were always busy flitting around with friends, shopping, or trying out some new career. You've always put yourself first."

My mother bit into her lower lip, and tears streamed down her cheeks. "I take that back. I have *two* selfish daughters."

Grandma Rosa grunted and clapped her hands loudly

together. "That is enough. Maria, stop acting like a child. This is Sally and Mike's day, not yours."

My mother slammed the cards down on the table. "Of course. Perhaps you don't want me there at all."

"*Pazza,*" Grandma Rosa muttered under her breath. "You must stop living in the past. It is unhealthy. Learn to accept things as they are."

"So now my own mother thinks I'm crazy too." She stared at my grandmother in disbelief then clamped a hand over her mouth before she ran out of the room sobbing.

Grandma Rosa sighed and reached into the cupboard for a bottle of anisette and shot glasses. She placed them on the table in front of us.

"Okay," Gianna said. "Let's have it. What's really wrong with her? And don't tell me it's the change. There's more to it than that."

My grandmother poured herself some liquor and looked questioningly at us. Mike accepted a shot which he downed within seconds, but I shook my head.

Gianna reached into the fridge and poured herself a glass of wine from the nearly empty bottle. "I may need to open another one at this rate."

I addressed my grandmother. "Mom is acting really weird, even for her, and I think you know what's bothering her. Did I do something? Is it the wedding?"

Grandma Rosa downed her shot in one gulp and immediately poured another. She gestured at Mike with the bottle, and he shook his head. "No, *cara mia*. She has always liked Mike and not that buffoon you were married to before." She made the sign of the cross on her chest. "Rest his soul."

Gianna crossed herself as well. "Sorry to say, Sal, but no one liked him."

Jeez Louise. This was going to haunt me forever. "Yes, I'm well aware."

Mike grinned as he put his arm around me. "You did so much better this time."

"Not full of ourselves, are we?" I teased.

Grandma Rosa stared down at her empty glass. "Your mama has become one of those people in that reality show on television. You know, the woman who gets married and acts like a crazy fool. Godzilla."

"It's bridezilla, Grandma," Gianna corrected her.

She waved a hand dismissively. "That is good too."

Mike suppressed a smile.

"So what's bothering her?" I asked again. "Grandma, you know what it is, don't you?"

A stupid question because my grandmother knew everything. Sometimes I even wondered if she was a bit psychic.

Grandma Rosa nodded. "Yes, she seems more *pazza* than usual, but there is a reason for her crazy tantrums. When the time is right, and if she is in agreement, I will tell you. Until then, try to be patient with her." She pointed a finger at Gianna. "Especially *you*."

Gianna's mouth fell open. "Come on, Grandma. You know what I said is the truth. She's always been self-absorbed. Does she love me and Sal? Yes. Do I love her and Dad? Absolutely. But she's always done exactly what she wants. It's like she has blinders on and can't see anyone else. Am I right, Sal?"

I hesitated before looking into my grandmother's kind and wise, large brown eyes. My emotions were getting the best of me, and my voice trembled. "Honestly, I don't know what we would have done without you all these years." Mike kissed the top of my head as I steadied myself. "I didn't want a big wedding, but since it seemed to mean a lot to her, we went along with it. I wanted the ceremony held on your birthday because of how much I love you. You've always done so much for me and Gianna."

Gianna nodded in approval.

Grandma Rosa frowned. "Bah. That is silly. My birthday is no big deal. We all have them. At my age, it is just another day on the calendar. Please do not worry about me, *cara mia*. This is *your* day. You two have been through so much, and it is your time to shine. What does it matter if your wedding is at the Tahoe Mahal or in your living room?"

Gianna laughed. "It's the *Taj Mahal*, Grandma, and it's located in India."

She shrugged. "I thought it was in California. What is it

you say—my bad? Bah. All I want is for my granddaughters—and my new grandson—to be happy."

Mike leaned over to give her a kiss on the cheek. "Thank you for that."

I twisted a napkin between my fingers. "I think Mike's right about canceling the reception at the country club. Hopefully Mom will come around and agree. And I hate seeing her and Dad lose money on this."

"I meant what I said." Mike's tone was quiet but firm. "I'll pay her back."

Grandma Rosa waved a hand impatiently. "There are more important things to worry about right now."

My father appeared in the doorway of the kitchen. "*Bella donna.*"

He wore an odd expression on his face, and for a moment I worried he might be having another stroke like he had back in January. "Dad, what's wrong?"

He crooked a finger at me. "I think there's something you should take a look at."

Mike and I both rose to our feet in a hurry. "Is there someone hanging around outside of the house?" I tried not to panic.

Dad shook his head and started back toward the living room, indicating we should follow. He sat down in his swivel chair and pointed at his computer screen. "I've been getting comments on my newest blog post. I called it 'You'll Know When It's Your Time to Go.'"

"For cripes sake," Gianna groaned. "This is embarrassing. Please tell me you're not using your real name."

My father shook his head. "I call myself Father Death. But I did post on Twitter using my own name."

Gianna snickered. "Yeah, we remember about the five followers."

Dad smiled up at her, obviously pleased with himself. "Make that over two thousand now. I'm starting to feel a bit like a rock star here."

"Holy cow. What is wrong with this world?" Gianna wanted to know.

My father's usual jovial looking face was grim as he

stared into my eyes. "I did post on your Sally's Samples page, remember, until Josie took it down. I had a link to my blog on it, which might explain how this person knew where to find my posts and write you this—note."

The tension in the room had become thick enough to slice through with a frosting knife. "What are you talking about?"

My father scrolled down the page of comments until he found the one he was looking for. "I think this one might have been left for you, my sweet girl."

We all leaned forward to read the post, Gianna at my right and Grandma Rosa to the other side of my father. The writer went by the name of Miscellaneous.

"That's odd," Gianna mused. "Most people use Anonymous. I don't think I've ever seen anyone sign their name like that before."

Then she gasped.

After Mike finished reading the screen, he was gripping my shoulders so tightly that the bones started to ache. As for me, normal breathing had become extremely difficult. The post read:

Hey, Father D, you've hit the nail right on the head. Marvelous post. I'm so glad I found your blog. We might not want to face these things, but we all know when it's our time to go and should make the best of it. - Miscellaneous

P.S. Tell Sally that her time has come.

CHAPTER TEN

"I just talked to Lena Coletti," Brian said over the phone to me the next morning.

"Who?" I asked, momentarily confused. My brain was in a state of disarray these days. I'd tossed and turned all night after reading the message intended for me on my father's blog. The first thing this morning, I phoned Brian's partner, Adam. Less than ten minutes later, Brian had called me himself.

Brian cleared his throat. "The owner of Mama Lena's Restaurant. Sally, she said there wasn't any male staff working at the restaurant the day of your shower. Even her two chefs are female. She has one full-time employee in his fifties and a couple of part-timers barely out of their teens. Neither one matched the description you gave. Plus they weren't scheduled to work that day."

A chill the size of New York spread through my body. "I saw him with my own eyes. Josie and Gianna saw him too. We're not making this up."

"I didn't say that you were," Brian said quietly. "There might be another explanation."

His intended meaning hit me like a brick wall, and I sucked in some air. "Oh my God. He was only there because of me, wasn't he?"

Brian paused. "It's very possible he knew you were going to be there. From what you've already told me, it sounds like your mother broadcasted every last detail to the world. He might have even called the restaurant himself to confirm the day and time of the event. The way the place is laid out, he could have slipped into the private dining room from the parking lot unnoticed. Lena said they unlock the doors about an hour before the place opens. He may have put the package on the table before anyone else got there and was hiding out or pretending to be a patron in the restaurant. Lena said that whenever there's an event, the kitchen turns into a madhouse, so he could have gone unnoticed. From the sound of things, he managed to blend right in. I talked with a few other employees who worked that day, and no one recalled seeing him."

I clutched the phone tightly between my hands. "Brian, this isn't exactly making me feel any better."

"Sally, I'm sorry this is happening to you, but I have to ask. Are you still planning to go through with your original plans and the reception at the country club? Because frankly, I don't think it's a good idea."

I placed more chocolate chip cookies in the display case. "Mike and I told my mother last night that we wanted her to cancel the reservation. My grandmother was going to remind her again this morning. We've made an appointment to get married at city hall instead."

Brian coughed into the phone. "There's no proof that this so-called waiter is involved, but we are circulating your description of him around. Who knows? He could have been planning to kill you at the shower, looking for a precise moment. This sounds awful and terrifying, but you have to face the facts here. It might be the only thing that keeps you alive until your wedding day. Afterward you and Mike will be thousands of miles away and hopefully out of this lunatic's path."

I'd never realized before how terrifying it was to live in constant fear. I was standing in the middle of the front room of my bakery, at a respectable distance from the window. I could see Ralph's sedan parked directly across the street. He had the windows down about halfway, and another man was sitting shotgun with him. Mike had called him last night when we got home and instructed that I was not to be left alone for a second. He'd wanted to stay with me himself today, but I'd urged him to finish his job. One babysitter was more than enough. Besides, Mike seemed to agree that Ralph was better qualified than he was to protect me in this particular instance. His pride wouldn't allow him to admit it, but I knew the way his mind operated.

The entire ordeal was similar to being under water.

Every time I tried to fight my way to the surface, someone pushed me back underneath, and I struggled to breathe again.

Josie was in the back room making a cake—my wedding cake, that is. She was humming away, but I knew she was anxious too. Everyone was. Perhaps what had really terrified me last night was the look in my father's eyes. Life—and death for that matter—had always been a carefree topic for him. When he had told me about the post, his expression had been frightened. That wasn't something I had enjoyed seeing.

Four days to go until our wedding. Mike had already decided that if this lunatic was not caught by the end of our honeymoon, we would not be returning to Colwestern. I didn't even want to think about that possibility.

It was as if Brian had read my mind. "Maybe you and Mike should take off early before the wedding and elope. Like, say, tonight."

I inserted a K-Cup into my Keurig to fix my third cup of coffee this morning and reached into my purse under the counter for an aspirin. My breakfast of choice lately. "We discussed it last night. He's got Ralph giving me 24-hour-a-day surveillance. This has to be costing a fortune, and he refuses to tell me how much."

Brian's voice was gruff. "Sally, he loves you. Cost isn't important when it comes to protecting someone you care about."

Raindrops had started to sprinkle onto the ground outside in the form of a delicate summer shower. As I stared out at the sight, my own floodgates opened as well. I hoped the pending storm that had been predicted might keep people from coming to the shop because I wasn't feeling very social today.

"Can you think of anyone else who might have it in for you?" Brian asked.

"You already confirmed that everyone I've been involved with before is still behind bars," I said. "There's really no one—"

I stopped in midsentence as my eyes fell upon the framed award certificate with a giant cookie emblem in the corner of it proudly displayed on the wall of my bakery. Last January, Josie and I had competed in the reality baking show *Cookie Crusades*. We'd claimed first prize along with a check for

$20,000. It had been a depressing and anxious time in my life as Mike had just been arrested for the murder of Colin. A woman we'd hired to help in the bakery had stolen one of our recipes for the contest. She had also blamed me for an accident that concerned my ex but had nothing to do with me.

"Mitzi." I knew there was someone I had forgotten about.

"Mitzi," Brian repeated. "Wait a second. Isn't that the woman who worked in the bakery? The one whose fiancé was killed by the drunk driver Colin let walk out of his bar?"

My heart started to hammer against the wall of my chest as the unpleasantness of that entire situation hit me with full force. Colin had been working as a bartender in Florida after I'd left him and failed to cut a patron off one night. The inebriated man had gotten into his car and then proceeded to plow it into the side of a car Mitzi and her fiancé were in. Mitzi's fiancé had been killed. The driver got off with a ridiculously light sentence, and through the fancy footwork of an attorney, Colin had never served any time.

"Yes," I said finally. "The same exact one."

"But the accident had nothing to do with you," Brian protested.

I shut my eyes for a moment. "Well, that didn't matter to her. She said that Colin had destroyed her life, and she wanted to ruin me because of it."

"What was her last name again?" Brian asked. "I'll run a check on her."

My mind was drawing a blank. "Jos," I called into the back room. "What was Mitzi's last name?"

Josie stared up at me in confusion. She was getting ready to place the cake pans in the oven. "The wacko who worked for us for one day and stole my recipe? Graber."

I managed to contain my smile. When it came to anything cooking related, Josie never forgot a single detail. "Graber."

"All right. I'll look into it. In the meantime don't go anywhere alone, and keep Ralph close by."

I glanced out the window again. "I don't think he's going anywhere. Mike's hoping to finish his job sometime tomorrow, so we might take off right after that. I might not need Ralph's services after today."

"He's trained to provide quality protection," Brian said. "Mike isn't. Please don't take any unnecessary risks, Sally."

I disconnected and walked into the back room where Josie was placing dirty mixing bowls and utensils in the sink. She looked up expectantly. "Does Brian think that fruitcake is involved?"

I shrugged. "We're trying to consider all options."

The bells on the door sounded, and I jumped about ten feet in the air. Josie reached out a hand to steady me. "Sal. Nothing's going to happen to you while I'm here."

I blew out a breath. "I don't like being afraid."

"There's nothing to be afraid of." She glanced past me, and I saw her body go rigid. "Okay, maybe I spoke too soon."

I turned around to see Ally Tetrault standing near the front window watching us and looking very uncomfortable. It was enough to make me want to face a firing squad instead. *Almost.* She smiled tentatively as we came through the doorway leading to the front room.

"Hi, Ally," I greeted her. "Can we get you something?"

She cut her eyes from me to Josie and swallowed nervously. "I was wondering if we could have a little talk, Sally. Just the two of us."

Great. "Of course. Why don't you sit down?" I turned to Josie. "You can go back to what you were doing."

Josie gave Ally a look that would freeze the sun. "Are you sure, Sal?"

I nodded. "Ralph's out front. I'm fine."

Ally sat down by the window and ran her hands nervously over the white tablecloth. She was tall and slender with short auburn hair the same shade as Josie's and striking gray eyes that now regarded me with suspicion. "Who's Ralph?"

"My bodyguard."

Ally's mouth opened in surprise. "Your *what*?"

I folded my hands on the table. "Didn't Brian tell you we think someone is trying to kill me?"

She gave a slight shrug. "He might have mentioned it. I guess I thought that you were all overreacting a bit."

I shook my head. "Afraid not. We think the bullet that killed the woman at the bakery the other day was meant for me. And now someone's sending me threatening messages through my father's blog and other means too."

She stared at me with a veiled look that I tried to make out and failed. Doubt? Dislike? Perhaps some warped sense of satisfaction to see me suffer? I didn't think the last one was possible, but then again, this wasn't the same Ally I had known in high school.

Ally was a nurse. Her lifetime was devoted to helping people, not putting them through pain. Perhaps I was an exception to the rule.

She gave me a tight smile. "I'd like to ask you something personal, if you don't mind."

I had a sense of what was coming and braced myself. "Go ahead."

"Were you and Brian ever involved at any point? You know…" She broke off. *"Involved."*

Oh brother. "You mean *together*?"

Her face flushed, and she nodded.

I shook my head. "Nothing ever happened between the two of us." Sure, I'd kissed him a couple of times, but jeez, did she really need to know every sordid detail?

She reached out and grabbed my hand in a tight grip. "I'm in love with him, Sal. Please don't screw this up for me."

What was with this woman? Ally had always seemed so self-confident and together, but now she was unraveling right before my eyes. I didn't want to say anything since it was none of my business but thought I knew Brian well enough to surmise he wouldn't like the idea of a woman clinging to him. Yes, he had indicated to me that he was crazy about her. But if she wasn't careful, she might drive him away.

I didn't want anything to do with this mess. For crying out loud, I had my own problems to deal with.

"Ally," I spoke gently. "I have only loved one man my entire life. After many years of being apart over a stupid misunderstanding and going through a horrible relationship with someone else, I'm finally marrying him on Saturday. No offense, but I have no interest in anyone else's love life, and that includes

Brian's. You have my word that I'm not trying to screw anything up. I'm actually very happy for the both of you."

She glanced at me doubtfully, and I had a sudden urge to shake her. Why did she still think I was lying?

Ally twisted a tissue between her hands. "I appreciate your honesty. I don't want you to think I'm some clingy type that can't live without a man because nothing could be further from the truth."

Although sorely tempted, I didn't comment because that's exactly what I *was* thinking. "My opinion doesn't matter here."

"My ex-boyfriend did quite a number on me," she continued. "He stole money, cheated on me, and was more than happy to let me support him for over a year. Do you have any idea what that's like?"

I had a strong urge to ask her if his name was Colin. "Yes, as a matter of fact, I do."

"I've finally met a great guy, and I want to make this last." Her face flushed. "I'd love it if we could get married someday."

I reached out to pat her hand. "I hope everything works out."

She stood, hoisted her purse over her shoulder, and gave me a limp smile. "It will. Oh, and I'd appreciate it if you didn't mention our conversation to Brian either."

I nodded in understanding. "It's already forgotten."

"Thanks, Sal," Ally smiled. "It feels good to finally take control of my life. Brian and I will work everything out. I'm sure of it."

She gleefully pushed open the front door to the bakery, and I watched as she floated across the street to her vehicle. I went into the back room where Josie was standing hands on hips, shaking her head in disbelief.

"I heard every word. Oh yeah, and I'm sure Brian's all set to get married after only dating her for two weeks. Another woman I'd nominate for Desperate Chick of the Year award." Josie snickered. "She never seemed that needy in high school."

I groped around in my purse for an aspirin then remembered I'd just taken one. "I feel kind of sorry for her.

When a man uses you like that, it can change you forever. It's been tough to get over Colin's treatment of me, so my heart goes out to her. I only hope she doesn't let it end up ruining things between them."

Josie raised an eyebrow at me. "Oh, please. She's nuts. You *should* tell Brian about this. He'll start running for Canada."

"No!" I said sharply. "I promised I wouldn't. Don't go stirring up any trouble, Jos. Maybe they will end up getting married someday. Brian's going to make some lucky girl a wonderful husband."

"You're too nice for your own good," Josie remarked. "A woman who's that desperate for a man will do anything to keep him. Trust me, I've seen her type before. Watch out for Ally."

The front door opened, and Josie peered around the corner. "Please tell me that's not her again."

We were both surprised to see Mickey standing in the center of the room. He didn't approach us but waited patiently for Josie and me to come to him instead. He was dressed in jeans and a windbreaker and carried a plastic bag in his right hand. Josie followed me into the front room, wiping her hands on a dishtowel as she walked along.

I smiled at the teenager. "Hi, Mickey. I don't think you were scheduled to work today."

Mickey's face flushed, and he stared down at the floor. "No, Miss Muccio. I was in the neighborhood and figured I'd stop to see if you had anything for me to do."

Poor kid. Maybe he really needed the money. "Well, we're kind of slow today, probably because of the rain and thunderstorms they're predicting for later. How about a dozen chocolate chip cookies to take home with you?"

He nodded without looking up. "Sure."

I went to the display case and scooped the cookies into one of our little pink boxes for him. Mickey accepted it with another nod and addressed the floor again. "Thanks. Do you mind if I eat some here?"

"Of course not," I said. "Josie and I will be in the back room if you need anything else. We've got some cleaning to do. See you tomorrow?"

Mickey lifted his head, glanced at me, and then nodded.

He quickly lowered his head again when he slid into a seat by the window. I turned my back on him as I left the room yet could still feel his eyes on me. I shook off the slightly creepy sensation and grabbed a broom from the corner to start sweeping the floor.

"Sally's got a boyfriend," Josie whispered in a singsong tone.

"Cut it out," I hissed back at her. "Don't you remember what it was like to be that age? Vulnerable and shy? Oh wait, *you* were never shy."

She chortled. "Sure, I remember. Let's see, you'd broken up with the love of your life over something really stupid, and I'd just gotten knocked up by Rob. My parents were ready to strangle me *and* him. So yeah, maybe I don't totally get what he's going through."

"You never quit." The bells jingled, and I peered out the doorway in time to see Mickey scuffling across the road toward his beat-up Ford Escort. I checked the table, but he'd left it clean, except for a long-stemmed red rose placed strategically in the center. I picked up the flower and waved it at Josie.

"Aw," she crooned. "Isn't that sweet. It's too late for the prom this year though. Maybe he'll ask you to homecoming in the fall."

"Cut it out." Seeing the rose made me remember the server from my shower the other day, and I gave an involuntary shiver. Okay, maybe Mickey was a little weird, but he wasn't killer material. "Since this place is dead, what do you think about a field trip?"

She glanced up at me suspiciously. "What sort of field trip?"

"I was thinking that maybe we could do a little investigating. What if we went over to the apartment complex across the street from DeAngelo's Bakery to see if anyone might know the so-called waiter? I can give them a pretty good description. What if he lives there?"

"Hasn't Brian already checked that angle out?" Josie asked.

"Maybe, but I can't just sit here and continue to do nothing."

Josie narrowed her eyes. "If Mike finds out his fiancée

has been running around town looking for a possible killer—her own killer, in fact—he's not going to be happy. Plus, what about Mr. Magnum, P.I. out front? He won't let you go anywhere without him."

"Jos, I'm aware of this, and it's fine. We'll tell him we're going to see a friend."

She let out a bark of laughter. "Oh right. He's going to rat you out to Mike for sure."

No doubt. I reached under the counter for our *Be Back Soon* sign to put in the front window. "That's something I'll worry about later. I'm tired of being afraid."

She stared at me for a long moment. "All right. But what if we happen to find the killer? Then what?"

That was something I hadn't thought about and in all honesty wasn't sure I wanted to.

CHAPTER ELEVEN

I was positive Ralph didn't believe my rather lame story about Josie and I wanting to go visit a sick friend at the Paradise Isles Apartments. Of course he knew what had happened at the bakery last Saturday. However, when we insisted that we were fine with Ralph accompanying us and also presented him with an assortment of fresh baked cookies at the side of his car, he wavered a bit. The selection included jelly, black and white cookies, genettis, and raspberry cheesecake bars. No whoopie pies in sight. He glared at me while he selected a jelly thumbprint cookie.

"Mr. Donovan left strict instructions that if you went anywhere outside the bakery, I was to go along. I'll be letting him know about this little trip. You will *not* go inside the building without me," he said pointedly. "Also, you make sure to let me get out of my car first so I can scope out the area."

Cripes. I'd watched *Unfaithful* on television last week and kept thinking about the private detective Richard Gere's character had hired to watch his wife's every move. These were different circumstances, of course, since I wasn't cheating on Mike, but the whole situation was so restrictive. I needed to find this person so I could stop living my life in fear. This experience in terror was starting to suffocate me, and I wasn't sure how much more I could stand.

I had been hoping Ralph might conveniently forget to mention the visit to Mike after we presented him with the cookie bribe, but it didn't look like that was going to happen. Instead, I tried to make light of it. "Oh, he won't mind my going out. Plus I do kind of have an in with Mr. Donovan myself, so I'm sure it won't be a problem."

Josie laughed out loud, while Ralph continued to frown at me, clearly not amused.

We took Josie's minivan, with Ralph following closely behind. Josie parked in the paved parking lot behind the building. Ralph exited his car first, surveyed the area, and then gestured for us to get out of the vehicle while he rapidly walked toward us.

The rain was pouring from the sky at a furious and almost blinding pace. Thunder rumbled in the distance, and lightning flashed across the sky in bright silver-colored sparks. The good part about this storm was that it most likely would cool down the temperatures for the next few days. I'd checked the paper this morning, and they'd predicted that Saturday would be a lovely day in the mid-80s with low humidity. Of course there was a chance that Mike and I would be getting married before then. While I was happy about hurrying up our wedding day, it also saddened me, wanting the event to be the same day as Grandma Rosa's birthday. Oh, well. I had learned during my lifetime that things rarely went as planned.

Ralph was holding out an umbrella which Josie gratefully accepted. I was wearing a beige raincoat and hood, so I let him and Josie share the umbrella while we made a mad dash for the back door. There was an electronic keypad on it, so we hurried around front to a steel door that was marked *Office*. Two small windows were located on either side of the door, and we could see a light on inside. We tried the knob, but it was locked. There was a button above it that said *Press for Service*. A buzzing noise sounded, and the door unlocked.

As we wiped our feet on the mat inside the door, I glanced around at the surroundings. The office was small and airless with walls that appeared to have been white at one time but were now a dingy yellow, probably from the cigarette smoke that lingered in the room. Thin commercial gray carpeting ran underneath our feet, and two oak desks filled the room, one right behind the other. An adjoining room in the back held cardboard boxes on steel shelving, and I could see a door marked *Restroom.*

A heavyset older woman with short white hair and chunky gold hoop earrings was using a computer at the first desk. She looked up and smiled at us. "Can I help you?"

Okay, time to lie. "Hi. I'm looking for someone who I believe lives in the complex. He's a friend of a friend."

I swear that Ralph snickered from behind me.

The woman stared at me, puzzled. "You *think* the person lives here?"

"Well, I thought if I described him you might be able to help us out," I said.

Ralph must have had enough of my fibbing. He stepped forward and flashed his badge at the woman. "We're looking for a person who might have been involved in the shooting across the street."

She nodded in full understanding. "The police have already been here talking to Tony. He's the landlord. "Hey, Tony!" she yelled into the back room. "More questions about the shooting."

"How many times are they gonna ask the same stuff? Can't you take care of them, Susan?" a male voice yelled back.

After a few seconds the man who I assumed was Tony waddled into the room. He was balding with thick sideburns a mixture of light brown and gray hairs. Like his female employee, he was heavyset, with black suspenders holding up a pair of dark blue Dickies pants. He wore a short-sleeved, blue plaid shirt paired with them. His face was an unhealthy color that reminded me of powdered sugar. He stared at Josie first, his eyes lingering on her, then at me, and finally Ralph.

"Well, look who's here," he joked. His accent had a bit of a Southern twang to it. "Charlie's Angels and their boss in the flesh. You're missing a girl, ain't ya?"

Ralph ignored his remark and stuck out his hand. "Ralph Chang from R.C. Investigations. We'd like to ask you a few questions related to the shooting Saturday."

Tony stuck his fingers underneath his suspenders. "Look, I told the cops everything I know. Sure, a couple of tenants have guns, but they already checked out. I wasn't even here the day of the shooting, so no idea if the bullet came from this building or not."

Ralph turned to me. "My associate has a couple of questions for you as well."

Associate? That was rich. "About how many tenants do you have in the building, Mr., uh…Tony?"

"Benson." His eyes rested on my chest.

"Her face is about a foot higher than where you're looking, mister," Josie snapped.

He jerked his head up, shot Josie a dirty look, and his pale face instantly colored. "This building has twenty-five units, five on each floor. I know everyone who lives here."

"We're looking for a young man," I volunteered. "He has curly brown hair and brown eyes. Nice looking and maybe about five feet ten? In his late twenties or so."

He snorted. "That's not much to go on, honey. Anything else?"

"He has a tattoo on his wrist. It's a red rose with the letter *M* next to it."

Tony shrugged. "I don't spend much time looking at people's wrists."

No, only their chests it seemed. "So you don't know of anyone like that?"

He shook his head. "Sorry I couldn't help you. If I think of anything, I'll be sure to notify you."

Ralph nodded at Tony. "Thanks for your time."

I knew it was a long shot, but at least it made me feel good to think I had done something to help. Tony lumbered into the back room, and the *Restroom* door closed behind him.

"Wait a second," Susan said.

We all looked over at her. Susan motioned with her finger for us to come closer. "There's an apartment on the third floor that's been empty for the last couple of months. Tony took a woman in to see it Friday morning. The police checked it out the day after the shooting, which was Sunday. Tony was here that day and said that they thought the shot might have come from there."

"And?" Josie prompted her.

"Tony said he assured the cops there was no way anyone could have gotten in there." Susan grinned. "What a liar. He confessed to me later on that he'd forgotten to lock the door after the showing. When he took the police up to the apartment, it was still unlocked. He didn't tell the cops because he was afraid that the owner of the building might find out and he'd get canned."

Ralph folded his arms across his chest. "But he told *you* instead?"

Susan stuck her chin out defiantly. "Of course he told me. We're sleeping together. He thinks he can trust me, the dumb bunny."

Ew. Way too much information for me.

Ralph shook his head in disbelief.

Disappointment flooded through my body. "You said it was a woman? About how old was she?"

Susan shrugged. "Not sure. Maybe around your age? She was wearing a big straw hat that covered part of her face. She had blonde hair, but come to think of it, that may have been a wig. It didn't look natural. Anyhow, she wasn't very chatty while she waited for Tony. Didn't even say good-bye or thank you when she hurried out the door to leave. I'm telling you, people have no manners anymore."

Of course this was a long shot. I had been looking for a man with a rose tattoo, not a woman. Still, the timing did seem a bit odd. "Did she talk about anyone else? A husband? Boyfriend? No one was with her?"

She shook her head. "Like I said, I didn't show her the place. She was alone and didn't say much to me at all. But when you asked about the rose tattoo, that was what made me think. She said her name was Rose Stanley."

A shiver ran down my spine as I exchanged glances with Josie. This was too coincidental for my taste.

"Was there a way for her to get inside the building on Saturday to shoot at the bakery?" Josie asked. "The doors were locked when we tried them."

"She could have gotten another tenant to let her in," Susan explained. "The police are checking the surveillance footage as we speak."

"Can you get a search warrant?" I asked Ralph hopefully.

He shook his head. "You'll have to go through the police for that." Ralph handed Susan his card. "Thanks for your time. Will you let me know if you see this woman again?"

Susan eagerly leaned forward. "Do you think she was

involved with the shooting?"

"Hard to say. We'd only like to talk to her," Ralph said calmly.

She placed the card inside her purse. "I'll keep you posted."

We stepped outside. It was raining harder now, so we dispensed with any niceties as Josie and I ran for her van. We could discuss everything with Ralph when we got back to the bakery.

"What do you think?" Josie asked. "Could there be a connection with this woman wanting to see the apartment the day before?"

"Maybe." I leaned my head back against the seat wearily and closed my eyes. "The whole rose thing is kind of weird too. First we have the tattoo and then a woman named Rose? I guess it could be a coincidence. Maybe."

"Roses are supposed to be a sign of love, especially red ones," Josie said thoughtfully. "Look at the one Mickey left you earlier." Then she gasped.

Josie's eyes veered from the road to lock with mine as we both thought the same thing. The van swerved slightly.

"Look out!" I yelled. Her vehicle had started to move into the opposite lane.

Josie's hands were shaking at the wheel. "Holy crap. This is making me sick."

I wasn't feeling that great myself. "Come on. Mickey doesn't want to kill me. It's impossible."

Josie stopped for a traffic light and looked at me with blue eyes that were large and serious. The freckles on her face stood out against her fair skin. "But *someone* wants to kill you, Sal. And Mickey has a major crush on you. What if he's angry you're getting married on Saturday? I've read about this kind of stuff before. He can't have you, so no one else can either."

"Okay, this talk is seriously creeping me out," I said. "Mickey won't even look at me, but you honestly think he might want to murder me?"

Josie pulled the van up behind the store. "We have to consider everything. Remember, no one is above suspicion."

We made a mad dash for the back door. Unlike our old

location, the back of the building didn't have anything overhead to protect our vehicles from the weather. This was going to be a major drawback in the winter when there was six feet of snow piled on the ground, but we'd deal with that issue when the time came. Hopefully Mike could put up a carport by then or an overhang of some sort.

"Ugh," Josie said as we entered the back room, and she fussed with her hair. "I feel like a wet dog."

I pulled my raincoat off and hung it on one of the brass hooks connected to the wall. "I didn't get wet at all." The coat was one of the best presents my mother had ever bought for me.

"Well good for you," Josie grumbled as she flicked on the light, and I laughed.

The crackle of thunder boomed in my ears, and lightning flashed across the front window.

"What a weird summer storm," Josie mused.

I stared across the street and was suddenly nervous. "Wasn't Ralph behind us?"

Josie looked up from the display case where she was straightening the tray of shortbread cookies. "I saw his car when we were at the traffic light on Green Street. He was two vehicles back."

"Maybe he's changing shifts with someone." Still, I thought it was strange that he hadn't said anything about it to us, but then again, we didn't have a chance to talk when we'd left the building. I stared at my watch. "It's after five, and I'm exhausted. No one's coming out in this. What say we close up and go home early?"

Josie untied the apron she'd just put on. "You've got my vote. As a thank you, I volunteer to put the garbage out."

My cell phone started ringing. "Sounds good to me. Take my coat so you don't get soaked." I drew my phone out of my jeans pocket and glanced at the screen. "Hi, sweetheart."

"Princess." Mike's voice sounded strained. "Ralph just phoned me. He said you guys decided to do a little investigating on your own today."

Gee whiz. I hadn't thought Ralph would rat me out quite so soon. "He was with us the whole time. We didn't—"

"I don't care," Mike said angrily. "I will *not* have you

taking any more chances like that. Understand? I reamed Ralph out good, and now you're going to hear it too."

The thunder rumbled from outside again, the noise so loud it frightened me. Or perhaps it was Mike's voice that scared me even more. He had never talked to me like this before. I hated the fact that I'd made him so upset, and my eyes quickly flooded with tears.

I hiccupped back a sob. "Mike, I don't want to live like this. I'm not going to sit around and wait for someone to take another shot at me."

He blew out a long ragged sigh. "Don't get upset, baby. I'm sorry. Ralph also wanted you to know that he got a flat tire on the way back from your escapade. He said to stay in the bakery until he gets there."

Uneasiness washed over me. It was silly, of course. I hadn't wanted a bodyguard in the first place, but now that Ralph was on the job, it felt good to know that someone had my back at all times. I went to the front door and checked the lock then drew the blinds down. "As soon as he gets here, Josie and I are heading home. The shop's been dead all afternoon anyway, and I have some packing to do for a certain trip I'm taking with my husband very soon."

I knew that he was smiling on the other end. "Some pretty little nighties are all that you're going to need."

"You're so bad," I grinned.

"We're getting out of town as soon as possible." Mike said. "I'll be finishing up here in about an hour or so and then only have a couple of things to take care of tomorrow. I'm spending this evening with my soon-to-be-wife and no one else. No bridezilla mothers-in-law, no death-loving blogging fathers-in-law. Just you and me, baby."

"And some lingerie, right?" I teased.

"*Especially* lingerie." The tone of his voice had changed to soft and sexy. "Be good. I love you, princess. More than anything in this world. Don't ever forget that."

My voice trembled with emotion. "Me too."

I disconnected and smiled to myself. The life I had dreamed of for so long was finally within reach. Was it too much to ask to be with the man I loved? Why was someone trying to ruin this for me? I thought about Alexandra. True, I hadn't known the woman, but I'd always have to live with the knowledge that her death was my fault. Maybe I should try to contact her parents, but what would I say? *I'm sorry your daughter died because of me*? How awful to have someone you love taken away like that. It was something I couldn't fathom and didn't want to.

I looked out the front window again. Still no Ralph. I wished he'd hurry up and get here. "Hey, Jos?" I walked into the empty back room.

Maybe she'd gone to get something out of her van. I stuck my head out the back door. Her van was there, but Josie wasn't in it. At least she didn't appear to be. The green dumpster we used was propped open against the rear side of the building, but Josie wasn't standing beside it.

Fear rose from the pit of my stomach and slowly enveloped the rest of me. The rain continued to pour down on my head as I walked hurriedly alongside the van. That's when I saw her.

Josie was lying facedown in a pool of muddy water in front of the vehicle. Her body had been blocked from my view at the back door due to the position of the van. Her arms were stretched out in front of her and lifeless, like the rest of her body which lay on the soaked gravel ground.

I screamed and ran toward my friend, my heart pounding so hard I thought it might leap out of my chest any minute.

"Josie!" Sobbing hysterically, I fell to my knees beside her.

There was a trail of blood along the back of my raincoat, which commenced near her right shoulder. With trembling hands, I turned her face gently. She let out a low moan, and I breathed a sigh of relief.

"Thank God. Don't try to move, honey." I had no control over my shaking fingers as I pulled out my phone and dialed 9-1-1. The rain was soaking both of us, and I reached my arms over her protectively, although, not wearing a coat myself, there wasn't much I could do for her. My entire body would not stop trembling, and the rain now mixed with the tears running down my face. My vision blurred as I punched in what I hoped were the correct three digits.

Josie's eyes were half-open slits as she gazed up at me, and then they closed again. The words that fell from her lips confirmed what I already knew.

"Sal," she whispered. "I think I've been shot."

CHAPTER TWELVE

"It's all my fault."

I buried my head into my hands and sobbed. This couldn't be happening. It was bad enough that someone wanted me dead, but now my family and friends were in danger as well. Who was doing this? Why did someone hate me so much?

Mike wrapped his strong arms around me and kissed my hair. The intent was to comfort me but only led to my next crying jag. We were sitting in the waiting room of Colwestern Hospital—Mike, Rob, Grandma Rosa, Gianna, and me. Rob had been home with the kids since he worked nights when I'd managed to call him—between bouts of hysterical crying, that is. He'd found a neighbor to come over while he rushed to meet us at the hospital. He'd been here when Josie and I had both arrived in the ambulance. There was no way I would have left her side for a second.

"Come on, sweetheart." Mike's voice was gentle and reassuring. "You can't blame yourself for this."

Grandma Rosa, who was sitting on the other side of me, patted my hand. "He is right, *cara mia*," she said. "Be strong. Josie is a tough girl. She will be fine."

Rob was sitting across from us with Gianna next to him. At Grandma Rosa's words he ran an agitated hand through his hair and rose to his feet. He was a good-looking guy—brown hair in a buzz cut, serious brown eyes, and a well-trimmed beard. He turned and gazed at the large glass window that stared out onto the emergency room parking lot. His voice registered the impatience we all felt. "What the hell is taking them so long?"

"The doctor said that the surgery could take a couple of hours," Gianna said. "It's always longer than they initially tell you."

The door to the waiting room opened, and Brian walked toward us dressed in full cop ensemble. He nodded to everyone. "Any word on Josie?"

"She's still in surgery," Mike said.

Brian sat down in Rob's vacated spot then turned his full attention on me. "Ralph's flat was no accident. Someone must have followed all of you back from the apartment building. There was a bullet hole in his tire."

My mouth went dry, and Mike's arms grew tighter around me. "So obviously someone has been watching closely. They're aware that Ralph's been hired to protect Sal. They—him, her—it. Whoever this lunatic might be."

Brian's gaze met mine. "Sally, I ran a check on Mitzi Graber. She's living in Vermont with her parents. Looks like she's been there a few months."

Gianna gasped and brought her hand to her mouth. "Isn't that the one who worked for you?"

I felt myself go cold. "Yes. For one day."

"Didn't she blame you because her fiancé died in a drunk-driving accident caused by an inebriated man Colin refused to stop serving?" Gianna asked as she gripped the arms of her chair.

I nodded in response and addressed Brian. "Her parents are from Vermont. They were contestants on *Cookie Crusades* with Josie and me. I forget which part they're from though."

"Bennington," Brian said. "An officer from their force is going to pay Mitzi and her parents a visit tomorrow. I'll keep you posted on all the details."

The door to the waiting room opened again, and a man in scrubs and surgical cap stared over at us. "Is there a Mr. Sullivan in here?"

Rob turned from the window where he was standing and moved quickly to the man's side. "That's me. How's my wife?"

The man nodded and held out his hand. "Dr. Wells. Mrs. Sullivan is in recovery. She came through the surgery fine and should make a complete recovery with no long-term issues."

Everyone seemed to breathe a collective sigh of relief. I hugged Mike, too choked up to say anything for a moment.

"Praise the Lord," Grandma Rosa said as I echoed the sentiment in my head.

Rob's face was tight and drawn. He compressed his lips together, and I knew he was struggling for composure. "Can I see her?"

Dr. Wells nodded. "I'll take you back in a minute. But I wanted to tell you that there must have been someone watching over your wife today. The bullet fragmented when it entered her body and just missed her subclavian artery and vein. Instead it hit her upper shoulder and went through muscle and soft tissue. If there are no further complications, she might even be able to go home by Friday. Of course, she shouldn't return to work for a while. She was very lucky."

"Can I stay with her tonight?" Rob asked quietly.

Dr. Wells nodded. "We can move a cot in for you."

They disappeared from the waiting room while I sank back into the chair and proceeded to burst into tears.

Grandma Rosa stroked my hair. "Dearheart, you must stop blaming yourself for this. Josie would not want you to carry on this way."

Of course I blamed myself. But more than that I was angry—furious in fact. It was bad enough someone was out to get me, but now they were hurting people I loved, and I wouldn't stand for that. This maniac was going to be stopped, even if I had to be the one to do it.

"Did you hear me, baby?" Mike asked suddenly.

I glanced up at him. "No, sorry."

"Ralph's associate, George, will be taking over tonight. He's going to be parked in front of our house. There's nothing for you to worry about."

Sure, not a thing. I squeezed his hand and tried to put on a brave face but figured I'd failed miserably when I saw him watching me with anxious blue eyes.

"We can arrange to leave an officer here at the hospital overnight," Brian said. "Since someone made an attempt on Josie's life, it can be authorized. I'll send a patrol car up and down your road as well if you like."

Mike nodded in approval. "It's not much, but we'll take it." He kissed the top of my head. "Want some coffee, princess? I could use a cup."

"Sounds good." Normally I would be worried about the caffeine keeping me up but already knew there was no way I'd be able to sleep tonight.

"I will go too," Grandma Rosa said. "I am tired of sitting."

As they left the room, Gianna's cell phone buzzed. "Johnny," she mouthed at me. "I'll be outside."

That left Brian and me. I gripped the arms of the chair tightly and counted to ten. I was fighting a war against the rage growing inside me, but it was pointless. I had already lost the battle.

My face must have been a dead giveaway. "Are you all right?" Brian asked worriedly.

"No," I said through clenched teeth. "I'm not all right. I'm angry at this person who is trying to destroy my life. It's bad enough that someone wants me dead, but now my family and friends are targets too? I won't live like this, and they will *not* suffer anymore because of me."

He stared at me, thunderstruck. "Sally, don't interfere. Let the police handle it."

I didn't answer.

"Sally," Brian leaned forward and gave my arm a small shake. "Promise me you'll stay out of this. Run off with Mike tomorrow and get married."

I folded my arms across my chest. "There's no way that I'm going to leave my family here at the mercy of some crazy person. My best friend was shot. Do you know how that makes me feel? I've never been so upset in my entire life." *Or terrified.*

He sighed. "If you're gone, I don't think whoever is doing this will come after your family."

"But you can't be positive."

Brian's expression was pained. "No, I can't be positive. Look. We'll find this wacko, okay?" He rose then sat down next to me and patted my hand reassuringly. "I'll do everything I can to help you. That's a promise."

The door of the waiting room opened, and Ally walked in. She was dressed in street clothes of jeans and a T-shirt and seemed to be heading in the direction of the reception desk. She stopped dead in her tracks when she saw the two of us—or more specifically—Brian's hand resting on top of mine. I glanced at my watch—nearly eight o'clock. I knew she worked three twelve-hour shifts, so I guessed that she was probably coming on duty now.

Ally's usually pleasant-looking face was pinched tight with anger, and her eyes shot daggers at me. Her gaze then shifted to Brian who in turn stared down at the floor. Her expression changed as she continued to look at her boyfriend, but she made no attempt to come near him. Ally remained frozen in place, watching him with a forlorn look that reminded me of a lovesick puppy. She then disappeared behind the receptionist's counter without a word to either one of us.

I stared at Brian questioningly. "Well, that was just a bit awkward."

His jaw hardened. "Let it go, Sally."

But of course I couldn't. "What happened between the two of you?"

He pinched the bridge of his nose between his thumb and forefinger. "We had a huge fight. I think it might be over between us."

My stomach clenched. I had promised Ally I wouldn't tell Brian about her visit and intended to keep my word. "Please say this didn't have anything to do with me."

Brian smiled. "Okay, I won't tell you then."

"Brian…"

He looked at me, and his adorable Greek godlike face was stern. "Somehow your name got mentioned, and she let it slip that she went to see you. I was furious at her. Angry for her not trusting me and putting you in the middle of all this."

What a mess. "It's okay, really. She's crazy about you. That can lead a person to do all kinds of things they wouldn't normally do—"

I stopped cold for a moment and reflected on what I had just said. Apparently Brian was considering my words as well. "What exactly are you saying, Sally?"

"Nothing," I lied. "I only meant that she probably wouldn't have come to see me if she wasn't so crazy about you. You should talk to her and try to work things out."

"I'm not sure," he admitted. "I don't like the whole nontrust, jealousy thing. I understand that her ex was a real piece of work, but I'm not *him*. Trust is a fine line with me. I honestly don't know how I feel about her right now."

My phone buzzed, and I looked down at the screen. It was my parents' landline. "Mom? Is everything okay?"

"*Bella donna*," my father's deep voice greeted me.

Now I was really worried. My father *never* phoned me. "Is Mom okay? What's wrong?"

"She's fine," he assured me. "But you got another message on my blog today."

Icicles formed between my shoulder blades. "What did it say?"

He cleared his throat. "It said *Too bad she lived. What's really a shame is that it wasn't Sally*."

My hand went numb, and I dropped the cell on the linoleum floor. Brian stared at me in surprise then reached down to grab the phone and handed it back to me. I clutched at it with shaky fingers.

My father was still talking on the other end. "Sal, are you there?"

"Yes," I managed to say. "Thanks, but I'm sure it's nothing, Dad." I hoped my lie had convinced him.

"Do you want me to answer them?" my father asked.

At that moment a crazy idea popped into my head. Maybe I could use the blog to somehow trap this person. Of course if I told anyone about this—Brian, Mike, my grandmother—they would never approve. I would have to keep the details to myself.

"No, Dad," I said. "But don't erase it in case the police want to see it."

When I disconnected, I told Brian about the message. "Can you track it somehow?"

Brian's expression was grim. "We've already looked into it. The user has a VPN, a virtual private network. It masks your IP so that your location can't be found."

My shoulders sagged. "So we struck out again."

A woman's voice sounded through Brian's radio asking for a certain badge number, which happened to be Brian's, and he rose to his feet. "I have to go. Remember what I said before, about calling Adam?"

I nodded. "Of course. I promise I won't bother you again."

His eyes darkened. "Sally, I was wrong to say that. If you need anything at all, I want you to contact me. We're going to find this maniac and put them behind bars where they belong. I don't want anything to happen to you."

My voice trembled. "Thank you."

The door opened, and Mike, Grandma Rosa, and Rob came back into the room together. Mike handed me a cup of coffee and pulled me close to him.

"You look exhausted, sweetheart," he said. "We should go home."

I shook my head. "Not until they let me see Josie."

"She's sleeping, Sal." Rob looked from me to Mike, his eyes tired and bloodshot. "I was wondering if I could ask you guys a favor."

"Name it," Mike said.

Rob shoved his hands into the front pockets of his jeans and shifted from foot to foot in front of us. "This is a *really* big favor."

"Whatever you need," I said. "Anything at all."

"My mother's sick with the flu," Rob explained, "and Josie's mom is out of town. She's due back tomorrow morning, but Josie hates to ask her for anything. You know they've never been close. I can't reach our regular sitter, and the one who is with the boys right now can't stay the night at our house. She's a neighborhood kid, and her parents don't feel she's old enough or up to the responsibility. I'd like to stay here with Josie but don't have anyone to watch them, so I was wondering if—"

I jumped to my feet eagerly. "Say no more. Of course we'll watch them."

There was an unmistakable look of sheer panic in Mike's eyes. "We will?" he asked. "How?"

"It'll be fun." I had newfound energy suddenly and was excited for this opportunity. Plus, it would be a wonderful distraction from everything else going on in my life. I adored kids. Sure, I'd never taken Josie's boys overnight before but loved going to her house to play with them on occasion. How difficult could this be?

"Where will we put them?" Mike wanted to know. "We only have one extra bedroom."

"We'll put two boys in there, another on the couch, and the baby has a portable crib that can go in our room," I said. "It will work out fine."

"I can grab them first thing in the morning," Rob volunteered. "Are you sure this isn't too much to ask? They—um, can be a bit of a handful at times."

Mike swallowed hard. "How much of a handful?"

Grandma Rosa looked at the both of us and chuckled. "Caring for babies when you two are very much like ones yourselves."

"What does that mean?" I asked, puzzled.

Grandma Rosa smiled in that all-knowing way of hers. "You will find out soon enough."

CHAPTER THIRTEEN

"Okay," I rubbed my hands together eagerly. "Who wants to take a bath?"

"He does," three grimy-looking little boys shouted and pointed to each other.

So far we were off to a roaring start. The baby, Jeremy, had spit up in the car all over Mike when he'd lifted him out of his car seat. Mike was upstairs showering while I was distributing McDonald's Happy Meals for a very late dinner.

A french fry zoomed past my head.

"Stop it!" Dylan whined at Robbie.

Danny was the eldest. He was almost eleven and had red hair like Josie's, with a face full of freckles to match. Dylan was seven, Robbie Jr. five, and the baby, Jeremy, was just over a year old. It was times like this when I thought Josie and Rob should have been nominated for sainthood.

Spike had entered the room and was having a field day mopping up the food on the floor with his tongue as fast as the kids managed to drop it.

Jeremy was in the high chair we'd brought from Josie's, wriggling around and banging his little fists on the tray. When food sailed past him in the air, he had an absolute fit and opened his mouth wide like a guppy. I put some Cheerios on his tray and tried to spoon some applesauce into his mouth, but he shook his head at me. Greedily, he shoved the Cheerios into his mouth at a rapid pace with tiny fingers.

"You have to watch the baby," Danny said to me, a tone of disapproval in his voice. "He eats too fast. That's why he always pukes."

Even though his name was Jeremy, everyone referred to

him as "the baby," so I found myself doing it too. I removed a few Cheerios from the tray, and as soon as I did, the baby started to howl.

Danny wrinkled his nose at me. "Don't you know how to cook?"

I filled the baby's sippy cup with apple juice which he grabbed from me and downed greedily like a drunken sailor. "Sure, I can cook. But it's awfully late, so it was easier to get you food already prepared."

"I was really hungry," Dylan whined. "Nancy can't cook. I hate it when she takes care of us. She always tries to starve me." He glanced at me pitifully with Josie's large blue eyes.

"She didn't starve you," Danny yelled back. "She let you eat a whole bag of potato chips. She's like Aunt Sally because she can't cook either."

"I can too cook," I said defensively.

Mike was standing in the doorway, watching the scene play out in front of him. His hair was damp from the shower and curling at the ends. He was barefoot, in jeans and a gray T-shirt, and smelled of that spicy aftershave I adored. He kissed me and wrapped his arms around my waist as desire flooded through my body. Okay, best to get rid of those notions now. Romance probably wasn't on the calendar for tonight.

He whispered in my ear. "Do you think they'll fall asleep soon? I have plans for us later." He was using that sexy bedroom voice of his that I knew all too well and had the power to send my heart racing.

Dylan watched us with a frown. "Ew, gross."

Mike suppressed a smile as he reached into the fridge for a beer.

Danny watched him with curiosity. "Do you drink lots of beer? My dad likes it sometimes, but he won't let me have any."

Mike narrowed his eyes at the child. "No, I don't. But I need a stiff drink to help me get through this night."

"How come?" Robbie asked.

I shot Mike a murderous glance. "Okay, guys, if you're done, you each need to take a quick bath. I promised your father you'd go to bed clean."

"You only have one bathroom," Danny protested. "It's

gonna take forever."

"Well, Robbie and Dylan can have their baths together, so that will save time," I said pragmatically. "And then I'll bathe the baby in the sink while you take yours." I was feeling good, great in fact. I was in charge, a regular Mother of the Year candidate in training. Hey, this wasn't so bad. Parenthood was going to be a piece of cake after this.

"I don't wanna take a bath with Robbie," Dylan whined. "He poops in the tub."

"No! Do not!" Robbie yelled. His feet connected with our small wooden kitchen table, and before I even knew what had happened, it was lying on its side. The floor was suddenly awash with soda, apple juice, milk, and remnants of hamburger and fries. Poor Spike howled and rushed into the other room to escape the chaos.

"God da—" Mike finished the curse under his breath when he caught my look. He sighed in frustration. "I'll go get the mop."

Danny yelled at Robbie who was stomping his feet in frustration while Dylan cried to anyone who'd listen. Josie had warned me before that the kid was a drama queen, but I had no idea it was this bad.

Dylan held out his hand to me. "There's soda all over my fingers."

I grabbed a dishtowel from a drawer. "That's okay. It won't hurt you. And you're going to take a bath anyway." I started throwing the empty cups into the garbage pail. Mike came back with a mop from the hall closet and started to fill the bucket in the sink.

I glanced up to see the baby in his high chair, staring at us and giggling. At least someone was happy. Then the stench hit me like a wall of bricks. I covered my nose with the dishcloth while the kids all gagged and plugged their noses.

"What the—" Mike glanced in the garbage pail. "Is there something rotten in there?"

"It's the baby," Danny cried. "He pooped his diaper again. That's all he knows how to do."

I started mopping the floor. "You guys go in the living room." I glanced at Mike. "Can you change his diaper?"

Mike looked at Jeremy still giddy from his recent accomplishment. His midnight blue eyes went wide with alarm as he stared at me. "Sal, I've never changed a diaper before in my entire life."

I winked. "You'll need to start sometime. It will be good practice for you. The diaper bag is on our bed. There's a changing pad in there too, along with wipes and diaper rash cream. Call me if you need help."

He began to say something else then watched as the two older boys ran into the living room to turn on the television and started fighting over the remote. He sighed, moved the tray, and lifted the baby out of his seat. Jeremy waved bye-bye to me over Mike's shoulder as they left the kitchen.

I finished cleaning up and shooed Robbie and Dylan away from the television and into the bathroom. I started the tub, made sure it was the right temperature, and then turned the other way to give them privacy while they undressed. Once they were situated in the tub, I left the door open and went out into the living room to find pajamas for them then took a minute to arrange a blanket and pillow on the couch for Danny, who I thought was in there watching television. No such luck.

I could hear the baby giggling from the bedroom, so I assumed all was well in there. After stealing another peek into the bathroom, I was about to go check in the kitchen for Danny when I heard Dylan crying.

"Aunt Sally!" Dylan called. "Robbie's splashing water at me."

I went into the bathroom again. Robbie stood up in the tub in full naked glory and pointed a toy pistol at me. The stream of water hit me straight in the face. I gasped and reached for a towel to wipe my eyes.

"Sal," Mike yelled. "These tabs won't stick."

Robbie and Dylan were both giggling and pointing at me. I reminded myself of the fact that they were children and to count to ten first. Okay, they might be part demon as well. I had to give Josie credit—I would have pulled my hair out long ago.

"Did you happen to get diaper cream on your hands?" I yelled back at Mike.

There was silence for a moment. "Damn it," I heard him

growl.

Dylan started jumping up and down in the tub. "Uncle Mike said a naughty word!"

I grabbed two towels off the railing and held them out to the boys. When they were bundled up inside them, I reached in and drained the water from the tub. "Tell Danny it's his turn. I don't know if he'd rather have a shower or a bath."

"Danny's not out here," Dylan called from the living room.

"He must be in the kitchen then." I hoped he wasn't feeding Spike on the sly.

Mike came into the bathroom with the baby in his arms. Jeremy was wearing the diaper and nothing else. There was a piece of black masking tape wrapped around the top of it.

My jaw dropped. "What the heck did you do?"

Mike gave me a satisfied smile. "The diaper wouldn't stick, so I figured, hey, why waste another one? This one will never fall off."

I placed my hands on my hips. "What happens when he wets himself again? You're going to need scissors to cut it off him."

Mike's satisfied smile disappeared. "Oh. I forgot about that."

We heard a noise from nearby and cocked our heads to listen. It was the automatic garage door opening. Then the rumble of an engine hit our ears.

Mike and I stared at each other for a second, and then he instantly paled. "The key to the snowmobile—it was in the ignition!" He thrust the baby into my arms, sprinted down the hall and out the front door, still barefoot.

The baby started to howl, possibly indignant about Mike deserting him when they had just started to bond. Dylan and Robbie were smacking each other with cushions from the couch. I rushed to the front door in time to see Danny zooming over the grass in the snowmobile.

My heart leaped into my throat. "Stop him!" I screamed at Mike.

Fortunately the machine wasn't going very fast, but I was terrified that Danny might topple off of it at any moment.

Apparently so was Mike because he ran to the side of it and wrapped his arms around Danny's waist. As he was about to lift him off the machine, Danny turned the handlebar, and it collided with Mike's nose. I shuddered and closed my eyes at the impact.

When I opened them a few seconds later, Danny was skipping toward me with a smug smile on his face that I longed to wipe off. Mike was lying on his back in the grass, struggling to move onto his side.

"Are you all right?" I examined the child quickly but secretly wanted to banish him to the corner until he left tomorrow. Fortunately there wasn't a scratch on him.

He nodded. "That was fun!" He pointed at the figure in the grass. "I think Uncle Mike might be dead though."

I hurried out onto the lawn and over to Mike's side, the baby still in my arms. "Are you okay?"

Mike grunted unintelligibly as he slowly rose to his feet. A swear word popped out of his mouth, and I covered the baby's ears. Mike's dark hair was standing up on one end, and his face had been drained of color, except for the blood that dripped from his nose as he staggered over to me. "I have no idea what just happened."

"Don't worry. He's fine," I assured him.

Mike looked at me, a dazed expression on his face. "Who?"

"Danny." I wondered if he was having some type of temporary memory lapse. "We're watching Josie's kids, remember?"

Mike moved unsteadily toward the front door beside me. He looked like he had aged twenty years in those few minutes. "Those aren't kids, Sal," he said in a hoarse voice. "They're tiny devils without pitchforks who've been airmailed straight from hell."

I didn't say anything to Danny about the incident since I was just relieved that he hadn't been hurt. Also, I wasn't comfortable disciplining someone else's children, even if they were Josie's.

Danny went into the bathroom to take a shower while his brothers continued battling each other with the cushions in the living room. I brought the baby into the kitchen and undressed him, carefully cutting the masking tape off his diaper, then gave him a quick bath in the sink. He looked like he was growing tired, so afterward I dressed him in pajamas and hummed to him before I laid him down in the portable crib. He was so soft and cuddly, and I loved inhaling the smell of him. For a moment I might have even pretended that he was mine.

I gave the baby his pacifier and pulled the blanket over his tiny arms. As he stared up at me, all sweet and utterly adorable, the sight tugged at my heartstrings. I couldn't wait to do this with my own child someday. I glanced over at Mike, who was stretched out on our bed, wanting him to share in the moment with me. He had an ice pack propped against his nose, and his eyes were shut. For some reason, I didn't think he would be as enchanted as I was.

There was loud giggling coming from the living room. Mike opened his eyes for a brief moment then shook his head at me.

"They're not that bad," I protested.

"Please tell me that our kids won't be like this, or I might have to arrange for a vasectomy tomorrow," he said.

Dylan and Robbie were sitting on the floor in front of the television with Spike situated between the two of them. They had taken one of my lipsticks and colored in the white patches on his fur. They'd even written *Hi Aunt Sally* on his back.

"Oh no!" I gasped. "That was very naughty!" I picked up Spike, who licked my face in what appeared to be relief. Children were a new thing for Spike. He was quite a docile little dog because of his advanced age, and I felt confident he'd be fine when Mike and I had our own children. Like Mike, though, he hadn't quite been prepared for the antics of Josie's little darlings.

"I like Spike," Dylan giggled. "Mommy won't let us have a dog."

Gee, it was difficult to imagine why. I struggled to keep the irritation out of my voice. "You two need to go brush your teeth as soon as Danny comes out of the bathroom. Then I want you to go into the spare bedroom and lie down on the bed."

"You mean with Uncle Mike?" Robbie said hopefully.

"No!" I was afraid Mike might jump out of the window if they went near him again. "I mean the bedroom across the hall from ours. You're both going to sleep in there. It's a big bed, and you'll be nice and comfy."

Dylan started crying again. "I don't want to sleep with him. He wets the bed."

"No! Do not!" Robbie argued.

"You do too!"

My patience was wearing thin, and I pointed in the direction of the bathroom again. "Let's go this minute, or I'll tell your father how naughty you've been for me and Uncle Mike."

Danny came out of the bathroom at that moment. "It won't matter," he said casually. "Dad tells us to stop all the time, and then he forgets about it."

I sucked in some air. It was annoying that a ten-year-old child knew exactly what he could get away with. He was testing me—they all were—except for the baby. I placed my hands on my hips, squared my shoulders, and leaned down so my face was level with theirs. Three sets of eyes stared back at me—four blue like Josie's and two brown like Rob's—and waited expectantly for me to say something.

"Well then, I'm going to tell your *mother*."

That did the trick. Robbie and Dylan went meekly into the bathroom to brush their teeth without saying another word. Danny laid down on the couch and immediately fell asleep. Sure, Josie had mentioned before that Rob was a wonderful father but not much of a disciplinarian. That part was left up to their mother, who was tough as nails. She'd grown up in a large family of siblings and had learned to take care of herself from an early age on.

I set Spike in the kitchen sink and filled it with a few of inches of lukewarm water while I took a soft cloth and dog shampoo to clean up his fur. Tears fell off my face into his bathwater as I thought about my best friend. I sent a small prayer of thanks up to God that she was going to be all right. I couldn't imagine my life without her. So many people needed her, especially her children.

I rinsed Spike off with the spray hose and then toweled him dry. He seemed happy to be rid of my offensive lipstick and trotted outside to the backyard through the doggie door to do his private business.

I was so tired that I couldn't see straight. I finished cleaning up the kitchen and then checked on all the kids one last time. It was almost midnight, but they were finally asleep. As I stood watching them peacefully slumbering, I promised myself that this maniac—who was obsessed with ending my life—would not get away with it.

Panic seized me again. Even when Mike and I were on our honeymoon, what if this nut continued to terrorize my family and friends? It was entirely possible. What if they hurt someone else and used it as a method to get me to return to town? No. I could run away, but I'd never be rid of this person. They had to be stopped, and I was prepared to do it—no matter what it took.

I switched off the lights and went into our bedroom, shutting and locking the door behind me. The baby was sleeping peacefully in the crib. He looked like a tiny angel in his blue pajamas. I went into the bathroom to wash my face and brush my teeth then threw on a yellow satin nightgown that Mike had always liked. It wasn't revealing, in case the kids woke up in the middle of the night. Feeling suddenly amorous, I ran a finger down the side of his face and kissed him lightly on the lips.

Mike was lying on his back, wearing a pair of plaid, blue boxer shorts and nothing else, his arm thrown across his eyes. The ice pack was sitting on the nightstand. His nose was bruised and noticeably swollen. Despite the wound, he was still so breathtakingly handsome. I kissed him passionately and then ran my hands seductively down his smooth, muscular chest. He made a moaning sound low in his throat.

I smiled to myself. Yes, I could always count on him to be receptive when it came to romance.

"Guess what?" I said softly. "Everyone's asleep. You know what that means."

He opened one eye and turned his head slowly to look at me. "Sal, I never thought I'd say this, but not tonight, baby. I've got a major headache."

CHAPTER FOURTEEN

The ringing of my cell phone woke me at seven o'clock. As my hand fumbled across the nightstand in an effort to grab it, I heard children's voices coming from the kitchen and smelled bacon frying. Mike must be feeding the kids breakfast.

A longing swept over me then, so sharp and pressing against my heart that it was almost painful. I wanted children so much that it hurt at times. Everyone had different goals in life. My greatest one had always been to be a mother. It hadn't happened during my first marriage. To Colin's credit, he had warned me from the beginning that he never wanted children, but I had been certain that he would change his mind over time. That was my way of not being able to face reality. Fortunately Mike was eager to be a father too. At first I had been worried he might be put off by the idea because of his own horrible childhood, but he claimed he wanted them as much as I did.

Just not Josie's kids though.

I sighed into the phone as the wailing started from the kitchen. "Hello?"

"Hey, Sal, it's Rob. Sorry to call so early."

I sat upright in bed. "No problem. How's Josie?"

"She's fine," he said. "Actually, she's sitting next to me and wants to talk to you."

I'd only seen Josie for a fleeting minute last night at the hospital, right before Mike and I had left. She'd been sleeping, and I hadn't wanted to disturb her, so I'd only kissed her on the forehead and squeezed her hand. Raw emotion swept over me when I heard her voice.

"Hey, partner." She sounded tired. "Are you coming to see me today?"

I wiped at my eyes. "Jos, I'm so sorry about—"

"Stop it," she said quietly. "I won't let you do this, Sal. You are *not* to blame."

Tears were running down my cheeks as I struggled to compose myself.

She sighed on the other end. "I know you're crying. Knock it off or I'm really going to be pissed."

I choked back a sob and tried to turn it into a laugh. "Okay, you win."

She sniffed. "I always do. Rob's coming by your house in a little while to get the kids. I was hoping you might stop and see me this morning, but I know you have to get to the shop."

I blew my nose with a tissue. "Forget about the shop. You're more important."

She was silent for a moment. "The doctor said I can't go back to work for a few days. Sal, maybe I could come in for a few hours each day to at least—"

This time I cut her off. "No, I won't hear of it. You need to rest. I'll close the shop down until I get back from my honeymoon."

"How did the kids behave for you?" Josie asked suddenly.

It was fortunate that she couldn't see my face at that moment. "They were as good as gold."

She snickered on the other end. "Man, you are such a liar."

At that moment a loud crash came from the vicinity of the kitchen. I put my hand over the receiver, jumped out of bed, and opened the door. Spike ran past me, jumped onto the bed, and buried his head underneath the comforter. His small body was shaking.

Dylan was crying. "Robbie made me spill it!"

"Did not!"

Mike stuck his head out of the kitchen, saw me standing in the hallway, and waved me off. "All under control. Go grab a shower while I hold down disaster central in here, baby."

I decided not to argue with him, but it was probably a good idea to hurry up and get dressed before they managed to knock Mike out cold this time.

"Sal?" Josie called. "Are you still there?"

After our experience with the kids last night, Josie was my new superhero. "Like I said, they were little angels."

Josie sniffed. "I can't wait to see them, but they'll be scared if they know I'm in the hospital, so I asked Rob not to bring them here. When I go home tomorrow, I'll tell them I had a little accident. You didn't say anything to them about the shooting, did you?"

I grabbed a towel out of the linen closet in the bathroom. "Of course not. I wouldn't do that without asking you first."

"Thanks, Sal," she said, her voice shaky. "For everything."

For everything? For what in particular—getting her shot and almost killed? I was afraid the waterworks were going to start again, and then she'd be sore at me. "Okay, let me jump in the shower, and then I'll be over. Do you need anything?"

"Don't rush. Visiting hours aren't for another hour. And yeah, I want breakfast. A real honest-to-goodness breakfast, not this junk they're feeding me here. Something fattening, greasy, and unhealthy."

I wrinkled my nose at the phone. "Is that allowed?"

"I say it's allowed because I'm starving!"

It was so good to hear her sarcastic mouth again. "Say no more. I know just what you need."

* * *

About an hour and a half later, I was placing a bacon, egg, and cheese biscuit, hash browns, and an apple pie on my best friend's bed tray.

Josie quickly unwrapped the biscuit and took a large bite, closed her eyes, and moaned. "You're an absolute angel."

I sat in the chair next to the bed. "How are you feeling?"

She shrugged. "I won't lie. It hurts like hell. And I'm going to need physical therapy too. But it could have been a lot worse." She took another bite of the biscuit.

Fortunately Josie was in a private room. There was an IV pole located next to me and what I guessed might be a heart monitor on the opposite side. She shifted in the bed as if trying to get more comfortable, and I could see the bandage covering her shoulder through the thin hospital gown.

I said nothing, but my face must have betrayed me when my lower lip started to tremble violently.

Josie rolled her eyes at me. "I told you to knock it off, Sal."

In desperation, I blinked back tears as my voice hit a high octave. "No, I won't knock it off. I'm upset and angry that this happened to you. Someone mistook you for me and tried to kill you because of it. This is personal for me."

She looked at me like I had two heads. "Of course it's personal. Someone wants you dead."

I shivered visibly as she leaned her head back against the pillows, frustrated with herself. "I'm sorry. That sounds so cold."

"But you're right." I took a sip from my McDonald's coffee cup. "And I refuse to live like this anymore."

She cocked an eyebrow at me. "What are you talking about?"

I wrapped my hands around the cup for warmth. "I have a plan. I'm going to set a trap for the killer."

Josie's face went pale underneath her freckles. "What sort of plan?"

"I'm not sure yet," I confessed. "But this person visits my father's blog. I think I'm going to stop over at my parents' and leave a message for them, courtesy of Father Death himself. Maybe I'll see if I can lure them to the bakery tonight."

I thought Josie would be excited by the news. She was always up for a new adventure and had constantly been my sidekick in investigations before. She compressed her lips tightly together, and the expression in her eyes was not one of anticipation but of cold, dark dread. "Don't do it, Sal. Please."

"You can't say anything to Mike," I told her. "He'd freak."

"Of course he would," she snapped. "He loves you. You're getting married in two days for crying out loud." She bit into her lower lip. "What the hell are you thinking?"

I was beginning to wonder if I should have even told her. "This isn't just about me anymore. I don't know when this psychopath will strike again or who could be the next victim."

She grabbed my arm. "Don't go by yourself. Promise me."

"Ralph will be with me all day." I didn't tell her but had already decided that I'd have to lose him somehow. The killer knew Ralph had been hired to protect me, so I felt confident they wouldn't make a move while he was around. This would be risky, but I didn't think I had a choice.

"Sal," Josie whispered. "Please be careful."

"You worry too much," I teased, quoting the line she always used on me. "I have to get to the bakery to finish the order for the Owens' birthday party tonight. I'll put a sign up saying that we'll be closed tomorrow and through next week, until I return from my honeymoon."

If we returned from our honeymoon, that is. I didn't want to mention Mike's insistence that we would relocate if my stalker had not been caught by then. Sure, Mike could run his business from anywhere, but what would I do? Plus I didn't want to leave my family and friends.

Josie cleared her throat. "It's awful nice of you to want to give me the time off, Sal, but I'll come in for at least part of the day. I—we really need the money. And I won't be out long enough to be able to get disability."

I hadn't even thought about that aspect and was suddenly ashamed of myself. "I don't want you to worry about money. Consider this a paid vacation—well, sort of a vacation anyway."

Now it was Josie's turn to cry. "You can't do that. It's too much money for you to shell out, plus being closed down for a week. I won't let you."

"Look," I said. "You've worked for me for a year and never taken any time off, with the exception of the three days when we went to Florida last January which I wouldn't call a vacation since we were there for a contest. I received the insurance payment on the old building the other day, and there's a little money to spare. I want to do this for you, so please don't argue with me, okay?"

She looked away from me and wiped at her eyes. "Okay, fine, but I don't know how to thank you."

I squeezed her hand. "You don't have to thank me."

Josie observed me thoughtfully. "What's going on with

the wedding? I still want to be a part of it."

I sighed. "To be honest I don't have any idea. Mike will be finished with his last job today. We have an appointment for city hall on Saturday, but he doesn't want us to wait. Mike thinks we should be married tomorrow so we can throw the killer off. He switched the plane tickets out already, and I believe my mother canceled the country club reception." At least I hoped so. My parents' house was the next stop on my list.

I tried to laugh it off. "We'll be married. I just don't know where or when."

"But I want to be there," Josie whined, her voice reminding me of Dylan's.

My heart was heavy. "I want you there more than anything, but I'm not sure if it's going to be possible. With the new flight, there are a few hours layover in Vegas. We might do it there."

She twisted her napkin in her hands. "This sucks, Sal. To have the most special day of your life ruined by some whack job. No one deserves to be happier more than you and Mike."

"We will be." Of course I wanted Josie and my family at the ceremony, but Mike was adamant about us getting out of town as soon as possible.

"I'm getting discharged tomorrow," Josie announced. "I wanted to leave today, but the doctor gave me a hard time about it."

"You're not ready to go home yet," I protested. *With those four kids?* I was exhausted just thinking about her trying to cope with a gunshot wound and her four highly energetic children.

"You don't have to worry about the kids tonight," she added, and I worried for a moment that she'd read my mind. "My mother's going to watch them. If there's any way at all possible, I *have* to be there when you guys say your vows. Stick with city hall if you need to. All I ask is that I be there."

I didn't say the words out loud, but my greatest concern right now was if *I* would be there too.

CHAPTER FIFTEEN

"Hello?" I called from the foyer. "Anyone home?"

"In the kitchen, *bella donna*," my father answered.

I walked through the living room and entered the large, sunny yellow kitchen with Ralph two paces behind me. My father was seated at the table, chowing down on a piece—or maybe it was three—of Grandma Rosa's sumptuous zucchini bread. My mouth watered. Grandma added chocolate chips to her version, and the effect was delicious. The bread had a rich soft texture and tasted even better than cake. I snitched a small piece off the plate on the counter.

My father looked up at me and then nodded to Ralph. "Is this the guy Mike hired to watch your back because he's too busy to do it himself?"

I wanted to pound my head against a wall. "Dad, please. Mike's been working around the clock to finish the jobs he's contracted for."

My father liked Mike well enough, or at least I assumed he did most of the time. Still, he was an old-school Italian who didn't think there would ever be a man good enough for me or Gianna. I think Johnny might have been winning the potential son-in-law contest, though. After all, he was Italian, while Mike was of Irish descent. That alone earned my sister's beau several stars in my father's book.

"Sir," Ralph extended his hand to my father. "Ralph Chang, R.C. Investigations. A pleasure to meet you. Mr. Donovan is not trained in security like I am. He wanted your daughter to have the best, and that would be *me*."

My father scraped his plate with his fork and snorted. "You're modest, too. Want some zucchini bread?"

Ralph shook his head. "No thank you." He turned to me. "I'll have a quick look around the house, and then I'll be out in the driveway, whenever you're ready to go."

"There's no one here," my father protested, but Ralph ignored him and opened the screen door that led into my parents' backyard. Dad turned back to me. "Your grandmother is next door at Nicoletta's, and your mother is upstairs taking a nap. Where does he think this person is hiding—on the roof? Some security. Yeah, I'll bet you feel safe, huh?"

"Come on, Dad. Ralph's only trying to do what he was hired for." I took a step in the direction of the living room. "How's the blog going?"

He puffed out his chest with pride. "I made a new post this morning, and it's already got over a thousand hits. I've called it 'Weddings and Funerals—They're All the Same.'"

"Gee, thanks for that, Dad."

He lowered his eyes to the floor. "Oops. I forgot about that, *bella donna*."

Okay, time to lie again. "Well, I'd still love to read your latest post, Dad. Is your computer opened up to your blog page?"

My father's face brightened. "Sure is. Take all the time you want. I'm going upstairs to take a shower." He rose from his seat and rubbed his chin thoughtfully. "Your mother canceled the reception for the country club this morning. She was real upset about it too."

"Mike and I will pay you back," I insisted.

He waved his hand in the air. "No worries. Besides, they had a last minute request for a graduation party. Guess the people waited too long to plan the darn thing and asked to be put on a waiting list if anything came up. So it looks like we won't lose much money after all."

I breathed a sigh of relief. "Oh, I'm so glad."

We walked out into the living room together. "You take your time and enjoy the post, baby girl. Maybe I could come to the bakery sometime and give a talk to your customers. I am famous now, after all."

"Um, I'll mention it to Josie." Yeah, like that was going to happen.

He started up the stairs, whistling, while I sat down in

his office chair and stared at his blog. According to the information on the side of the page, he had 989 followers. There were tiny pictures of these people in the corner, and they looked like respectable, normal individuals. *What gives?* A few morticians had posted entries asking my father if he was accepting paid advertisements for the blog. Yes, it appeared that my father and his infamous death blog were a hit. *Has the entire world gone mad?*

I clicked the button to publish a new post and stared at the screen, my fingers poised on the keyboard. What the heck could I say to attract the attention of a possible killer?

I glanced at my father's previous post from this morning and winced. *Weddings and funerals are the two most popular events you will ever see your loved ones at. There's a wedding in my future this weekend. At least I hope there still is.*

Ugh. Seriously, what was the matter with both of my parents? Why could they not keep anything a freaking secret? Yes, they meant well. They truly did. Perhaps they didn't understand how serious the circumstance was. My father had suggested that maybe someone had shot at Josie because she'd been rude to them in the bakery. He also thought that the messages on his blog might have been from someone playing a bad joke. My mother was probably upstairs crying because I wouldn't be able to show my wedding gown off to 200 people on Saturday. They just didn't get it.

I sighed in frustration and tried to get into my father's unique mind-set, which was not an easy task. Then all of a sudden, my fingers began to fly.

Hey, readers. Father Death here. Some special news to share. As I said earlier, there's a wedding in my near future. My daughter is getting married on Saturday. I'm all excited about the good food I'm going to eat, especially that delicious wedding cake. Well, I hope there will be wedding cake. My daughter owns a bakery, and her coworker was supposed to make the cake, but now she's ill, so my poor girl has to stay late tonight to make it herself. Can you believe it? What do you think? Is it bad luck for her to make her own cake? Yes or no?

My fingers were shaking so badly that I had to stop and correct a few misspelled words before I plodded on.

My family is expected at a viewing tonight for an old friend. Like I said, those weddings and funerals go hand in hand! My daughter has to miss it. I offered to pick her up at 8:00, but she said she'll only be getting started about then. The poor thing will be working all night, and alone too! Her fiancé won't even be around because he'll be finishing a job across town. What do you think? Wouldn't you rather go to a viewing than make a cake?

Okay, it was risky, and to me it sounded like a really idiotic post. My stalker might not fall for this scheme, but it was all that I had.

I held my breath and hit send. A tiny message popped up that said *Your post has been published.*

"What the heck are you doing?"

I must have jumped about three feet in the air. Startled, I turned around to see Gianna standing there watching me, hands on hips.

"Hey." My hands were shaking violently, and I noticed her looking down at them. "Ah, I was reading Dad's posts. When did you come in? What are you doing here? No work today?"

"I took today and tomorrow off because of the wedding and to move my stuff into the apartment," she said. "I pulled into the driveway, and your bodyguard was all over me. He wouldn't let me walk into the house until I had identified myself."

It was impossible for me to look her in the eyes. Gianna always knew when I was lying, so I was done for. Call it a sister's intuition, or perhaps it was one of those things that made her an excellent attorney. Unlike my parents, she could not be fooled easily. I started to close the laptop, but she placed her hand over mine. "Not so fast, Sal."

"Let's go out into the kitchen and have some zucchini bread." Hey, it was worth a shot.

Gianna refused to loosen her grip. "I came in through the kitchen. You were so wrapped up in whatever you were typing that you didn't even hear me." She narrowed her eyes. "Level with me. What's going on?"

"I told you. I was reading Dad's blog. That's all."

She snickered. "Give it up, girl. I know you too well."

Defeated, I let go of the laptop. "Okay, but you can't tell

anyone. I'm trying to set a trap for the killer."

Gianna leaned over my shoulder and read the post, which already had a few comments, much to my surprise.

Her jaw dropped. "Are you nuts? This is not a game. Someone is trying to kill you."

"Don't you think I know that?" I snapped. "They shot Josie, and I won't let them continue to hurt people I care about. No more living my life in fear. This maniac will be stopped and by me, if necessary."

Gianna's lovely face was pale. "No. Let the police catch them. This is far too dangerous."

"It may not even work," I said. "Do you honestly think they'd fall for it? I may need to come up with something else."

She glanced through the responses that were popping up on the screen. "No way. People are actually replying to this dumb thing."

"Apparently our father is good at what he does," I said.

Gianna kept staring at the screen in disbelief. "I don't get it. These people need a hobby, like checkers or needlepoint."

We started reading the responses that were pouring in. Most were well wishes for me. One suggested we have death by chocolate cake. Another recommended that we get married in a funeral home.

"Cripes," Gianna muttered. "These people are twisted. They're like—Dad!"

At that moment a new message popped up on the page under the title *Miscellaneous*. My heart stuttered in my chest as I read the one-line post.

I hope her wedding dress is black so she can be buried in it.

A chill spread from the top of my spine to my toes in a matter of seconds. "Well, it looks like they've seen the post. The question is—did they fall for it?"

"There's no way I'm going to let you do this by yourself," Gianna announced.

"What you do?" a voice called out.

We both let out a small squeak and turned around. Grandma Rosa and Mrs. Gavelli were standing in the doorway of the living room, watching us.

"N-nothing," Gianna stammered. "I'm going to help Sal finish making the wedding cake."

Grandma Rosa looked sharply from me to Gianna but said nothing.

"Hmmph," Mrs. Gavelli snorted and shook her fist at me. "It bad luck to make your own cake. And I hear you have enough of that lately, missy."

"Come," Grandma Rosa said. "We will go into the kitchen for zucchini bread."

"None for me," Mrs. Gavelli announced as Gianna and I followed them into the kitchen. "I see your car, so I come over special." She placed a fortune cookie in my hand. "You need this more. No one want to kill me."

Grandma Rosa wiggled her hand back and forth. "I do not know about that. Some days, maybe yes."

Mrs. Gavelli shot my grandmother a dirty look then turned to me. "You open. *Now*."

Cripes. "Where did this come from?" I asked.

"Johnny get them from your shop the other day," Mrs. Gavelli announced. "When I hear a person want you dead, I save one for you. It tell you what to do."

This was all I needed. "Thanks, but you keep it, Mrs. G."

"You no argue with me," she grunted.

With a sigh I snapped the cookie in two and nearly fell over when I read the message.

Things might not always go as you planned, but they'll always end up as they should.

Gianna read the message over my shoulder and spoke low in my ear. "You are *so* not going alone."

Great. What the heck did this mean—that I'd wind up dead instead? "These fortunes are silly." I flung the message into the garbage and hoped no one could hear my heart thundering inside my chest.

Mrs. Gavelli nodded. "See? Now maybe you make sure I always get good fortunes." She came closer and grabbed my face between her hands. "You be good girl, and be careful. And make sure you no wear white on Saturday."

"Nicoletta," Grandma Rosa growled. "I think it is time for your nap."

Mrs. Gavelli scowled. "What, I a child now?"

"Yes" Grandma Rosa said. "The doctor said you need to rest."

"I rest when I dead."

"Okay," Grandma Rosa agreed. "That can be arranged."

Mrs. Gavelli slammed the screen door behind her in fury. "I get you for that, Rosa!"

"And your little dog too," Gianna mumbled.

Grandma Rosa watched Mrs. Gavelli stomping toward her house and then turned to face us. "You two are planning something, and I am afraid that it is dangerous."

Gianna and I exchanged a look. How did she always know these things?

"Everything's fine, Grandma," I said. "I am worried about Mom, though. How's she doing?"

Grandma Rosa gave me a suspicious look that let me know I wasn't fooling her. "Your mama," she sighed. "Even when she was a little girl, I knew that there was something not right about her. She liked to play dress up all the time and carry on with the baby dolls. It was all she thought about then."

"What does that have to do with her acting like a psychotic mother-of-the-bride?" Gianna asked.

Grandma Rosa went to the doorway, peered into the living room and toward the staircase. When she was assured that my parents were nowhere in sight, she settled herself at the kitchen table and gestured for us to sit as well. "She canceled the country club after what happened to Josie last night. Your mama was crying when she talked to the manager."

The color rose in Gianna's cheeks. "She should be ashamed of herself. It's Sal's day, not hers."

Grandma Rosa wagged a finger in Gianna's face. "I know your mama is a nutsy cookie, but she has her reasons for what she does. Once upon a time, she wanted a big wedding."

"But they eloped," Gianna said calmly. "She told us that before."

Grandma Rosa folded her hands on the table in front of her. "Yes, but she did not tell you *why* they eloped. I had a talk with your mama last night. I told her the time had come and that you both needed to know the truth."

Gianna and I exchanged confused glances.

I wasn't sure how much more I could handle at this moment. "Grandma, please tell us what's going on."

She gave me a somber look. "Your mama was pregnant when your parents got married."

Gianna stared from Grandma Rosa to me with unabashed curiosity. My face immediately heated, and I pointed a trembling finger at my chest. "*Me?* I was the reason?"

I'd seen my parents' marriage certificate before, and of course I remembered the date and year. For a moment it felt like someone had punched me in the stomach.

"Oh my God!" I shrieked. "They lied about my age. How old am I really? That would make me, what, thirty-one?" Mike would get a kick out of it when I told him he was marrying an older woman, but I didn't find this amusing. I had aged two years in a matter of minutes!

Grandma Rosa smiled sadly. "No, *cara mia*. The baby I mentioned was not you. Your mama was pregnant with your brother."

We both stared at her in frozen fascination.

"What brother?" Gianna asked, and then she sucked in some air.

The realization hit me at the same moment, like a sledgehammer between the eyes.

"You had a brother," Grandma Rosa said again, her large brown eyes somber. "We believe that he died during labor. He was stillborn."

CHAPTER SIXTEEN

The expression in Gianna's eyes was pure horror and must have mirrored my own. I let out a sharp cry while she covered her mouth with both hands. Tears started to fall from my eyes and blurred my vision. Grandma Rosa calmly handed us each a paper napkin.

Gianna sobbed into hers. "I can't believe Mom never told us."

Grandma Rosa kissed her on the top of her head. "It was a big mess back then. Your grandfather—rest his soul—never did like your papa, and this only made things much worse."

"Go on," I urged.

"Anyhow, your mama was twenty-one when she met your papa who was thirty-four, a big age difference back then. When your grandfather learned that she was pregnant, he wanted to kill your papa. He refused to have anything to do with either of them for many years." Grandma Rosa snorted. "The old fool was so stubborn that he made my blood toil."

"It's *boil*, Grandma," Gianna sighed.

"Whatever. There was no time for a big wedding, and your grandfather would never have paid for one, even if we had had any extra money. Your mama always dreamed of an elegant affair, but she did not have a choice in the matter. So they were married at city hall."

Which explained why she was against me doing the same thing.

"I was the only one in attendance. Although your papa and I do not always get along, he loves your mama and has been very good to her." Grandma Rosa patted my hand gently. "You remind me of your mama, *cara mia*. She could not wait to have children. She was so excited about the baby coming. He was born two months early. I got to see him at birth—a beautiful boy—perfect, in fact. The doctor could not explain what went wrong. Your mama blamed herself and could not deal with his death, so we never talked about it after that. She would not allow it. She was very depressed for a long time, until you were born, my dear."

I blew my nose into the napkin. My heart ached for my mother. I couldn't even comprehend how horrible this must have been for her. This was why I tried to never judge people. Someone might act rude or mean, but my philosophy was to take it with a grain of salt because you never knew what trauma that person might be dealing with in life. Take Mrs. Gavelli, who'd never gotten over the death of her daughter, Sophia. My grandmother had once told me that I looked like Sophia, and that was the reason why Mrs. Gavelli acted nasty to me sometimes—in some odd way she thought she was protecting me and really did care about my welfare.

Gianna's face was full of misery. I knew my sister well enough to realize that guilt was threatening to consume her.

"I need to talk to Mom." Her face was streaked with tears. "I want to tell her how sorry I am. I've been so mean to her lately."

"No," Grandma Rosa said sharply. "You will *not* speak of it. When you see her later, give her a nice hug. That is all. I told her I would tell you both what had happened but promised that you would not talk about it to her."

"That isn't healthy though," Gianna remarked. "Mom's been carrying this around inside for so many years and is most likely still blaming herself. She needs to rid herself of those feelings."

Grandma Rosa shook her head. "Ah, my dear girl, you do not understand. Everyone has a different manner in which they cope with sorrow. This is what works for your mama—and always has. Do not try to take that away from her." She paused as if groping for the right words. "Your mama has never been able to deal with bad things in her life. She is fragile—like those stilts she likes to wear all the time."

Gianna smiled. "They're called stilettos, Grandma."

Grandma Rosa nodded as she rose to her feet. "I like that too. Is Johnny not helping you move today?"

Gianna shook her head. "He's in Syracuse at a conference for history professors. I'll probably see him later tonight."

"Maybe Johnny should stay at the apartment with you while we're away," I said. "I don't like the idea of you being in the building by yourself." I wondered if we could hire Ralph to watch over my family while we were gone. When I got home that night I'd talk to Mike about it.

Gianna grinned. "We'd have to say Johnny's staying with a friend. If Mrs. Gavelli found out her grandson was crashing with me, she'd go nutsy cookie, like Grandma says."

We all laughed as I dangled my car keys. "Do you want to come with me to drop off some of your things? I'm on my way over now."

"Do you need help running the bakery today?" Gianna asked.

I shook my head. "My plan is to stay open for a few hours, get things in order, and then close down until after my honeymoon. Josie can't work, so there's no other way."

Grandma Rosa eyed me suspiciously. "Perhaps you plan on it staying closed permanently."

Cripes. How did she always know these things? "Did Mike tell you something?"

She shook her head. "He did not have to. I know how much he loves you. Mike would never let you come back here if he thought you were still in danger after the honeymoon. I would miss you terribly, but your safety must come first." She clapped her hands. "Okay, you two should leave now."

After we had both hugged her, she stared at me with those eyes that always seemed to have the ability to peer into the depths of my soul. I was fairly certain she knew what I was planning to do.

"More than anything, be careful, *cara mia*."

* * *

The day flew by, and I was mobbed at the bakery. I had

a new appreciation for Josie and her talent as I tried to handle everything alone. Gianna moved her belongings in then insisted on helping me for a while, for which I was grateful. I managed to tell several of my regulars that the bakery would be closed starting tomorrow. Everyone wished me a happy wedding and a wonderful honeymoon and said they looked forward to seeing me in about a week.

If only things were that simple. After I had finished cleaning up, tallied sales, and checked on inventory, I glanced at the wall clock and was shocked to see that it was already after seven. Ralph knew the shop closed down at six every night, so he must be wondering what I was up to. He had sat inside the bakery at one of my little tables for most of the afternoon and had then been relieved by one of his employees for a while. He was back and sitting in his car across the street at this particular moment while talking on his cell phone. He didn't appear to miss much, his eyes roaming back and forth, settling on my figure by the front window for a moment before a quick nod to me.

Gianna finished washing the dishes in the sink. "So what are you going to tell Columbo out there?"

"I have to get rid of him somehow. If my stalker sees him, they might not make an appearance."

Gianna bit into her lower lip. "This is crazy, Sal. I'm scared for you. What about calling Brian for help?"

"Well, I called his partner, Adam, earlier and asked him to have Brian call me," I said, "but haven't heard anything back yet. Maybe he's angry at me for messing things up with Ally."

Gianna frowned. "That's not your fault. Besides, there's something about Ally I don't trust. She has stalker tendencies too."

I shook my head. "Nah, she's just a bit insecure about her relationship. I've been there myself."

The bells on the front door jingled, and I jumped. Gianna and I both peered out the doorway to see Mickey standing there awkwardly. Something about the way his eyes watched me creeped me out.

"He's our new helper," I managed to say.

She placed her hands on her hips and frowned. "You forgot to lock the front door?"

Defeated, I lowered my head. God, I was a mess these days.

Gianna squeezed my arm. "Everything's okay, Sal."

We both walked out into the front room. Mickey looked from me to Gianna, and his face reddened.

"Hi, Mickey," I greeted him. "Did you want something?" Secretly I was hoping to get rid of him soon.

He shook his head. "I wondered if everything was okay. Um, like, I came by first thing this morning, but the door was locked." His eyes darkened. "I thought something bad might have happened."

Gianna narrowed her eyes at the kid, and I could guess what she was thinking. Like Josie, she thought there was something off about Mickey. I hated to admit it, but I was starting to think the same thing myself.

I managed a smile for him. "Thanks, Mickey, but everything is okay. Actually I apologize for not calling you sooner, but I've decided to close down the shop until after my honeymoon."

He stared at me, shock registering on his face. "I thought you canceled that."

Now I was confused. "Canceled what?"

"The wedding. I thought you weren't getting married because Josie got hurt."

Invisible ice skaters danced across my skin as I stared into those opaque brown eyes that were cold and could have served as a skating rink themselves. "My wedding was never canceled, Mickey."

"Oh." He acted contrite. "I, uh, didn't mean that the way it sounded."

Okay, this was getting just a tad bit uncomfortable. "How about some cookies to take home with you?" *Like right now.* "What kind would you like?"

He glanced absently into the case. "Chocolate chip. And the jelly filled."

I motioned at Gianna. "Give him a dozen of each while I get his pay, please." I went into the back room and hastily wrote Mickey a check. *Breathe, Sal.* Maybe the problem wasn't with Mickey but me instead. I was too suspicious of everyone lately. I tried to remember if Mike had been like that at Mickey's age. Perhaps in some ways. He'd been insecure and as a result of it, insanely jealous every time I'd talked to another man. Then again, we had actually been dating. Mickey seemed strangely possessive of me, and I was his employer. I walked out of the back room and handed Mickey his check.

"Thanks," he said and withdrew his wallet from his jeans pocket at the same moment I chose to hand him the box of cookies. He seemed momentarily flustered and dropped the wallet. Pictures and papers spilled out of it onto the floor.

"Sorry," he mumbled and fell to his knees to pick up the mess.

"Don't worry about it," I said. My sister and I both stooped down to help him retrieve his goodies. I gathered up some receipts and a picture. As I handed the items back to him, I stared at the photo absently. Then my mouth went dry.

It was a picture of me.

My blood ran cold as I continued to stare at the photo. I wasn't sure when it had been taken, but I was behind the bakery counter laughing with one of the customers.

Gianna peered at the picture as Mickey snatched it back, and I saw her eyes widen in surprise. "What the—"

I elbowed her in the side.

Mickey rose to his feet and shoved the wallet into his pocket. "I like taking pictures," he stammered. "It's my hobby."

The heat rose through my cheeks, and my mouth was dry as flour. "Sure, Mickey. That's cool."

His face was crimson. "Uh, I gotta go." Without another word he turned and practically ran out of the bakery.

Gianna shivered visibly. "I can't believe you hired that kid. He makes my skin crawl."

Mickey's actions had finally gotten to me as well. "He's just got a bit of a crush on me. That's all."

"That's not a crush," Gianna muttered. "That kid has potential to become a full-fledged stalker. Why did you hire him?"

"Rob knows his family. He said he was a nice kid."

She reached over to shut the door on the display case. "No offense, but you realize that you have the worst luck when it comes to hiring employees."

Defeated, I slumped against the wall. "Yeah, so I've noticed."

As I went to the front window to draw the blinds, I noticed a Chevy Cruze pull up behind Ralph's car and bump the rear end of his vehicle. Ralph, who had been talking on his cell phone, jerked forward slightly from the impact. The offending driver got out of the car immediately and trotted over to Ralph's door. I blinked twice, unable to believe my eyes. It was Marla.

Gianna was watching the scene over my shoulder. "What, is she blind? How do some people ever manage to get a license?"

"That's the woman Mike used to date. You know, Mrs. Channing's daughter."

Gianna's eyes bugged out of her head. "What the heck is she wearing?"

"As little as possible, it seems." We watched Marla as she talked to Ralph. He emerged from the vehicle looking like a very intimidating and annoyed figure next to Marla who was dressed in an extra skimpy outfit tonight. She was showing way too much cleavage in a pink tube top that left hardly anything to the imagination, along with a pair of white, knit lace shorts that exposed a good chunk of her rear and had been paired with pink, high-heeled sandals. Every time I thought about Marla putting her hands on Mike, my blood started to boil.

Gianna's face was the color of powdered sugar, and she pulled me away from the window.

"What are you doing?" I asked.

"Maybe she's setting some kind of trap for you. Don't take any chances. Get in the back room," she ordered.

The thought seemed absurd at first, but I didn't know who to trust or what to think anymore. We backed away from the window and moved behind the display case. Ever prepared, Gianna took a small pair of binoculars out of her purse that had been under the counter. She peered out at the scene while I stood behind her.

"You should see Ralph's face," Gianna remarked. "It's so obvious he's ticked off at her. They're exchanging insurance information."

I reached into my jeans pocket for my phone. "I'd better text Mike and tell him I'll be late getting home." It was strange that I hadn't heard from him all afternoon. With the sad disarray my life was in, he was usually texting every hour.

I glanced down at my phone screen. There was a weird succession of colors, and no matter what buttons I pushed, they wouldn't go away. I couldn't access anything. "There's something wrong with my phone. I can't get it to work."

Gianna put down the binoculars and examined the screen. "Oh my God. Do you think it could have been hacked?"

Swallowing hard, I wound a strand of hair around my fingers in agitation. The fear was blinding and suffocating. I was starting to feel like a mouse in a maze, the only difference being that no cheese awaited me at the end of this journey. Someone was out there who wanted to end my life. This had to stop.

"We'll tell Ralph about it when he gets done with Miss Floozy out there. Let me go upstairs and grab my phone." Gianna's brow furrowed as she looked at me. "I think I left it in the kitchen when I was talking to Johnny earlier. I'll text Mike for you."

She ran upstairs, and I continued to watch the scene play out between Ralph and Marla. She kept putting her hand on his arm while she pointed at the fender of her car. Did she really think her so-called charm or that skimpy outfit would gain her any points with this man? Ralph's face was full of annoyance as Marla's arms continued to flail around him wildly.

I grabbed the bag of garbage and reached for the back door, unlocked it, and stepped onto the top step, glancing to the right and left before I exited. There was no one in sight. At that moment I heard a cracking sound from beneath me. I glanced down in time to watch the step collapse beneath me. I pitched forward onto the cement, letting go of the bag and extending my arms out in front to protect my face from the fall. It was only a few feet drop but still managed to momentarily knock the wind out of me. I'd meant to ask Mike to look at the stairs before but had forgotten all about it.

As I lay there, a vision of Josie's body from last night entered my head. I pictured her facedown, lying in the rain, motionless. The blood on her shoulder, a whispered plea. How defenseless she must have felt. Tears pricked my eyes, and a chill surged through me as I slowly rose to my feet.

A shadow moved into view from behind the dumpster. I glimpsed sneakered feet, jeans, and a white T-shirt topped off with a creepy clown mask. My body failed me, and I stood there motionless as the person stopped a few feet away and raised a gun between their hands.

I couldn't move or speak. My feet were frozen to the cement, and my hand was resting on the useless phone in my pocket. The blood started to roar in my ears, and my heart thumped wildly against my chest.

Run. Run away. Still, I couldn't move.

"Any last words, Sally?" a menacing male voice, unrecognizable, asked as he pointed the revolver straight in my direction.

The sound of his voice dragged me out of my mental stupor. Anger set in and flashed across my body, triggering a switch on in my brain. Was this really the way my life was going to end?

No. Oh, hell no.

My hand was still wrapped around the dysfunctional phone. Without thinking clearly and in a last-ditch effort of hope and frustration, I threw the phone at my assailant. At the same time a roar of an engine and sirens sounded behind me. Clown Man nervously fired the gun, but the shot went wide. In a panic, he turned on his heel and raced down the alley in the opposite direction.

Brian screeched the police car to a stop by me. Adam was riding shotgun and immediately jumped out of the vehicle to chase after the culprit. He pointed his gun at Clown Man's retreating figure.

"Drop the weapon, or I'll shoot!" Adam shouted.

The man kept running, and Adam fired the gun. The noise thudded and kept reverberating inside my head until I thought my brain might explode. Clown Man faltered for a second in mid stride then his body hit the cement with a loud thud. He lay there motionless as Adam ran toward him, gun still in hand. Brian was at my side, helping me to my feet. His face was pinched tight with worry as he looked me over. "Are you all right?"

I stumbled against him and nodded mutely, still too shocked to say anything. He placed an arm around my waist for support. The back door burst open, and Ralph appeared, gun in hand. Gianna was right behind him. Before Brian or I could attempt to say anything, Gianna moved forward past Ralph. He noticed the missing step and tried to grab her but was too late. She fell and landed on the cement. Without missing a beat she rose back up and threw herself at my body. Her arms wrapped around me.

"Oh my God!" she sobbed. "I heard the shot and thought the worst. Are you okay?"

My legs trembled like Jell-O as I sank back down onto the cement. Gianna dropped to her knees at my side and held me in her arms.

I spoke into her shoulder. "If Brian and Adam hadn't shown up, I wouldn't have been."

Brian frowned. "I sent you three separate texts after Adam gave me your message. You never responded, and I thought that was kind of odd. We were investigating a domestic dispute a couple of blocks away, so we decided to swing by and see what was going on." He stared at me soberly. "I'm glad we did."

Adam jogged back toward us. He and Brian exchanged a wordless message between them then Adam's brown eyes met mine. "Your assailant's dead. He won't be bothering you anymore, Sally."

Still shaking, I blew out a long ragged sigh of relief and continued to cling to Gianna as she helped me slowly to my feet. I'd given new meaning to the phrase trembling like a leaf. Adam went to the patrol car to call in the incident while Brian placed a hand on each of our shoulders and guided us down the alley.

"Let's go see who this sick bastard is." He instructed us both to move behind him and kept one hand on his gun as he led the way. Gianna and I held hands as we cautiously followed his lead.

Clown Man was lying motionless on his stomach. I spotted the bullet hole in his back and instinctively brought a hand to my mouth. Brian leaned down to roll the man over onto his back. Brown, curly hair framed the demented clown mask. Brian lifted it off his face, and we all stared down.

"Oh God," Gianna said as realization set in.

Brown curly hair, a babylike face, and large brown eyes that were open but unseeing, staring upward at a sky on fire, the sun sinking rapidly behind the clouds. On Clown Man's right wrist there was the vexing rose tattoo with a letter *M* beside it.

May you always have good fortune.

It was the waiter from my bridal shower.

CHAPTER SEVENTEEN

"The guy's name was Pat Milton," Brian said. "He'd been in a mental hospital in Upstate New York for several years and was released about a week ago. The guy was staying at a hotel outside of Colwestern up until last Saturday. After that we're not sure where he wound up. Maybe he was hanging around on the streets trying to get a shot at Sally."

We were seated in the living room of our house. Mike and I were on the couch, and Brian sat across from us in an armchair. Spike was lying at our feet, sound asleep. My parents and Grandma Rosa were at home, Gianna had gone to meet Johnny, and Josie would be discharged from the hospital first thing tomorrow morning. Everything was slowly getting back to normal.

Mike had come to the bakery looking for me right after the incident. He'd tried to text me a couple of times, but with my phone being hacked, I'd never received it, and he'd become worried. When he hadn't been able to reach Ralph because of the incident with Marla, he'd grown alarmed and headed over himself. Mike said that when he'd spotted the police cars with their lights flashing, he'd thought the worst for a moment.

I didn't think I would ever forget that expression on Mike's face when I looked up from talking with Ralph and Brian and saw him standing there watching me. His arm was now wrapped tightly around my shoulders as if he never intended to let go. He was tired and dirty and like me, exhausted from the entire ordeal. At least we could breathe more easily now.

"This doesn't make any sense," Mike said. "Why did this guy have it in for Sal? She didn't even know him."

Brian shrugged. "He's been in the facility on and off

since the age of eighteen. I don't want to upset you with all the details of how he got there, so let's just say he has killed before. I haven't been able to find any information on his family yet. We're checking on former visitors at the facility, so if I come up with any names of significance, I'll let you know."

Mike blew out a sigh. "Jenkins, I may not have always been your biggest fan, but if it wasn't for you and Adam looking out for Sal tonight—" He stopped midsentence and closed his eyes for a second then brushed a hand across them wearily. His voice shook as he released me and extended a hand for Brian to shake. "Thank you. Thank you for saving her life."

"Yes." My voice trembled. "I'm so grateful to you and Adam."

Brian's face flushed red. "To be honest it wasn't all pure coincidence. Sure, I thought I'd stop over to see why you hadn't answered my texts, but I also wanted to tell you that I heard back from my friend and fellow officer, Carl Riley, in Vermont. He stopped over to see Mitzi Graber earlier today. She had an alibi for Saturday when the shooting occurred at DeAngelo's Bakery. Apparently Mitzi has been working at her parents' shop in Bennington for the last three months. Several people reported seeing her there on Saturday as well."

"Her parents were fellow contestants on *Cookie Crusades* with Josie and me last January," I put in. "Mitzi had mentioned that they wanted to start up a storefront at the time, so I'm happy that worked out for them. How did she seem to Officer Riley?"

Brian grinned. "Carl said she acted normal, even flirted with him a bit. She admitted to him that she had stolen a recipe from you and Josie in the past and wasn't proud of her actions. Mitzi told him she was going forward in her life and not looking back anymore. She said she was going to phone you one of these days to apologize for her behavior."

To be honest I wasn't in any great hurry to hear from Mitzi again, although I was glad to learn things seemed to be going better for her. "That's good to know." The whole incident had been so unpleasant and unfortunate. Sure, I wasn't responsible for Colin's role in Mitzi's fiancé's death, but I'd be lying if I said the entire incident didn't weigh heavily on my conscience.

"So Pat was the one who shot at Josie and killed Alexandra?"

Brian's phone beeped, and he stopped to read a text before answering me. "We found car keys on him for a Chevy that was parked a street over from the bakery. It was reported as stolen last week. We checked with the DMV, and the guy didn't even have a valid driver's license."

He paused to look at the text again and then stared up at me, his green eyes without their usual vivacity. "A rifle was found in the trunk as well. Adam just sent me a message, and they've verified it's the same one that killed Alexandra. Of course we don't know for sure that this wacko is the one who fired it, but since it was inside the car he was driving, it seems to be a safe presumption."

Even with Mike's arm around me, I was cold, chilled to the very core of my being. Had Brian and Adam arrived even one minute later tonight, there was no doubt in my mind that I would have been a goner.

Mike shook his head. "So did this guy see Sal somewhere and decide to terrorize her? I don't get it."

He wasn't alone.

"We're still checking things out," Brian said. "Maybe you went to school together years ago, and he had a crush on you. Maybe he spotted you in the bakery one day and wanted to ask you out for a date. He could have seen your engagement picture in the paper and snapped. Who knows what his motive was. Have you seen the news lately? A woman was killed for unfriending another person on Facebook recently. We're living in a disturbed society." He sighed. "Some days I feel like I'm fighting a losing battle."

"You should never feel like that," I said quietly. "I have such great respect and admiration for the work that you and your fellow officers do. You saved my life, and I'm sure there have been many others besides me. Compared to my job—well, there is no comparison. What do I do for society? Besides make people gain weight."

He laughed. "I wouldn't say that. Your bakery provides fuel for people like me. Hey, we all have to eat, so why not indulge in comfort foods once in a while? Say, any chance I can get some of those famous chocolate chips before you fly off on your honeymoon?"

I smiled. "I'll slip in the shop tomorrow and make up a batch special. On the house, of course. Find out what Adam's favorite is, and you can pick some up for him as well."

Brian dashed off a quick text on his phone. "I thought you guys were taking off tomorrow."

Mike ruffled my hair and smiled. "Since this guy is no longer a threat to Sal's safety, I'm going to switch the plane tickets back to Saturday. That way we can get married as originally planned—with her family around her."

"Our family," I reminded him.

He kissed the top of my head and tightened his arms around me.

Brian rose to his feet, looking slightly embarrassed at our display of affection. "Sounds good." He extended his hand for Mike to shake and then gave me a broad smile. "I hope you two will be very happy."

I walked him to the front door. "Wait a second. Is it okay for me to ask if you and Ally got everything straightened out?"

He leaned against the door and gave me a wan smile. "We're meeting for dinner tomorrow night to talk. I'm really sorry about what she put you through."

"No worries," I assured him. "I've had my share of insecurities too. It's awful when you don't know who you can trust. I hope you guys can work everything out."

"Thanks, Sally. I hope so too." His voice turned from serious to teasing. "So what time should I pick up that cookie order? By the way, Adam said he'll take chocolate chip as well and two dozen sounds great. But you shouldn't be spending time on this. It'll be the day before your wedding, and I'm sure you'll have a million other things to do."

"Not as much as you think," I said. "After I get my phone taken care of, I'll text you and let you know what time to stop by."

"Sounds good." He nodded to Mike then shut the door quietly behind him.

I locked the door behind him, and when I turned around,

Mike gathered me in his arms and kissed me tenderly. "The nightmare is over, princess. Come on. Let's go to bed and celebrate."

"That sounds great, but I may pass out on you. I haven't gotten much sleep all week."

"Believe me, neither have I," he admitted. "But we haven't had any time to ourselves either, so let's fix that right now. Come on. I'll make you one of my fabulous caffeine concoctions that's guaranteed to keep you up for a while."

I laughed. "How can I refuse an offer like that? Besides, I can sleep all I want to when Sunday arrives. We'll be on our honeymoon."

We walked over to the kitchen, our arms around each other. I removed this morning's used filter from the coffeemaker while Mike rummaged through the cupboard for coffee.

"It's such a relief not to have to worry about you every minute of the day," Mike said. "I have to stop over tomorrow to see Ralph and thank him. He's also got a small job for me to do at his house, and given everything he's done, I said I'd take care of it right away. So all we have to do is find another place to get married on Saturday. We still have the priest, right?"

I nodded. "I don't think my mother canceled Father Grenaldi, so three o'clock would still work. Let's go ahead with city hall. The place isn't important." I turned to kiss him and ran my hands down his chest. "I want to be your wife. That's all that matters to me. Not the location, the gifts, or what we eat. If this experience has taught me anything, it's that I'm lucky to be alive and to be with the man I love."

He leaned over to kiss me and then opened the coffee can. As I dumped the used filter into the garbage, I noticed a red rose lying on top, and my stomach convulsed. I was no longer as fond of them as I used to be. "Where did this come from?"

Mike stared into the garbage at the offending flower and looked embarrassed. "I meant to tell you about that."

A chill ran down my spine. "Did someone leave that for me?"

He shook his head. "No. It was a gift for *me*."

I cocked an eyebrow at him. "From whom, may I ask?"

Mike grinned. "You're cute when you're jealous." He

kissed me and started scooping coffee into the machine.

Not amused, I said nothing and continued to stand there with my hands on my hips, waiting for an answer. Somehow I knew the offender's name before he even said it.

Mike sighed, defeated. "This morning, when you went to visit Josie, I stopped by the bakery. I had a new faucet for Gianna's bathroom. It was a five-minute job, and I remembered that she planned to move in this weekend, so I wanted everything to be perfect for her."

"That was thoughtful of you," I said. "Go on."

"Well, I was on my way out of the bakery, locking the door, when someone touched my arm. I thought it was a customer. You know, maybe wanting to ask why the bakery wasn't opened yet. Instead it was Marla from across the street, dressed in a see-through minidress. It might have even been a negligee. Whatever it's called, she wasn't wearing anything else."

I bit into my lower lip. "You *noticed*?"

Mike looked pained. "Sweetheart, it was impossible not to."

Ew. I thought I might retch. "Let me guess. Marla had a faucet for you to fix too."

He plugged the machine in and turned around, placing both hands on my waist. "She said she wanted to talk to me. Something about how she was sorry for pursuing me the past few weeks."

What the heck? "You never told me this had been going on for a while."

He shrugged. "I didn't want to upset you. It was right before the fire, and you had enough to deal with. I didn't even realize it might be Marla until you mentioned her by name the other day. She had sent me a few texts from a number I didn't recognize and kept asking if we could get together again. I just figured she must have been someone I'd dated briefly before and she'd stop when I didn't answer back."

"And you only went out a couple of times?" I struggled to keep the irritation out of my voice. There was no reason for me to doubt Mike. I knew how much he loved me, but I still hated the fact that this woman was running after a man who she knew was going to be my husband in a couple of days.

Mike was staring at me in earnest. "Yes. I *never* lead her on, Sal. Please believe me. I spent many years looking for you in every woman I dated. But I was never able to find you." His voice shifted to a lower volume, barely above a whisper, as he pushed my hair back, his fingers lingering on the strands. "There's never been anyone else for me. When I heard you were back home after the divorce, I told myself nothing was going to stand in my way again. Remember the first time I saw you, when you threw up on me at the bar?"

I laughed. That seemed like such a long time ago when in fact it had only been a year. "Yeah. Kind of hard to forget an intimate moment like that."

Mike's sexy smile illuminated the dark blue of his eyes as he cupped my face between his hands. "That night, when I was home cleaning up, I vowed that some way, some day, I was going to win you back. It didn't matter how long it took. I would have waited forever for you."

There was a lump in my throat the size of a mountain. This past week had been such a roller coaster of emotions, and it had all finally caught up to me. Tears began to roll down my cheeks.

"Come here." He hugged me tightly to him while I snuggled comfortably against his chest. "The nightmares are over, Sal. It's time to make our dreams come true."

CHAPTER EIGHTEEN

As usual, I had planned too many things for the day. The first stop was to my phone provider. They confirmed that my phone had been hacked, and since it had also been damaged when I'd thrown it at Pat, I was set up with a new one. Thankfully I was able to keep the same number. I texted Mike to let him know it was up and running again.

Brian had mentioned last night that Pat was something of a technology whiz. He had even managed to hack the computer system during his stay at the mental hospital. Logging into my father's blog without his address being tracked must have been a piece of cake for him.

As I pulled into my parents' driveway, my cell buzzed. I glanced down at the screen and saw Josie's number pop up.

"Are you okay?" she asked worriedly. "Gianna told me what happened. What I'd like to know is why didn't you call me last night?"

I figured that she was going to be ticked at me. "Um, hello, you just got out of the hospital this morning. I was going to wait and tell you today. You've had enough to deal with lately."

She sighed into the phone. "I'm so glad this is all over with, Sal."

"You and me both. Where are you, at home?"

That was a silly question because I could already hear one of her little darlings screaming in the background. "Yep. I'm back on the funny farm. And I'll be at the rehearsal dinner tonight too. We've already booked a babysitter."

Now I was confused. "I thought my mother canceled that. Well, I'll find out soon enough. I'm in their driveway."

"Rob's stopping over at the bakery," Josie went on. "I gave him the alarm code. He's going to bring the cake home so that I can finish it here."

Her words shocked me. "Jos, this is too much. Please stop pushing yourself so hard. I can frost a cake for crying out loud."

"Not like I can," she insisted. "Plus I don't have anything else to do."

"How about rest for a while? Someone almost killed you!"

Josie spoke quietly on the other end. "I want to do this, Sal. Please don't try to talk me out of it."

I knew that stubborn streak in her voice well and realized there was no point in arguing with her. "Okay, I'm sorry. I didn't realize it meant that much to you."

She chuckled. "That's because you're not thinking straight these days. All you're thinking about is becoming a baby factory in the near future."

"Well," I teased. "After spending a night with your kids, I might reconsider."

Josie laughed. "Maybe Mike will, but not you. I'm already planning to throw a huge baby shower in about eight months or so. And wait until you see the cake I have planned for that."

"Now that is one party I'm really looking forward to. Please don't do too much, and I'll see you tonight."

I disconnected and went inside the house. My father was in his usual position as of late, in front of the laptop, typing away. He was using two fingers today. Practice does make perfect sometimes.

"Hi, Dad," I called.

"Not now, Sal. I'm in the middle of an important thought."

Well, at least things were back to normal. Then again, normal was kind of a stretch around here. I went into the kitchen where my mother and grandmother were huddled together in a deep discussion. They didn't see me at first as I stood in the doorway.

"That is what he told me," Grandma Rosa said to my

mother. She looked up and saw me standing there and for once seemed a bit flustered. "*Cara mia*. Why did you not tell us what happened last night?"

I sank into a chair next to my mother. "I didn't want to worry you both."

My mother leaned forward in her seat and placed her arms around me. "Sal, I want to tell you how sorry I am about everything."

"Mom, it's okay. I'm sorry for—" I looked up over her shoulder and caught my grandmother's warning expression. "Are you okay?"

She brushed the hair back from my face. "Of course I'm okay. My sweet daughter is getting married tomorrow. You've been through a lot this week, and I feel like it's all my fault. If only I hadn't run those announcements in the paper." She released me and wrung her hands together in agitation.

"Don't do this to yourself," I insisted. "Everything is fine now. So, do you still want to have the rehearsal dinner tonight?"

My mother looked at me with a small glimmer of hope in those big brown eyes of hers. "Only if you want to, sweetheart."

"Sure, but only the immediate family. Of course I want you to come to the ceremony at city hall tomorrow too."

She gave my grandmother a coy look and then smiled. "We'll be there with bells on, darling. On one condition."

Oh boy. "What's that?"

"I get to be in charge of the baby shower for my first grandchild. I'm guessing maybe in about eight months or so."

Good grief. Another person who was making premature plans. "Let's talk about it when the time actually arrives, okay?" I wasn't even pregnant yet, and already the pressure was mounting.

My mother beamed. "Of course, honey." She pushed back her chair and stood. "So, I need to go get ready for tonight! I think I'll wear that new strapless black dress of mine, the one with the crystal beads." She kissed me on the cheek and giggled as she trotted into the living room. "Domenic," I heard her call, "want to go upstairs?"

"The blog, hot stuff," he replied. "It has to get done first.

People are waiting for my next post with bated breath. I'll be up shortly."

Grandma Rosa shook her head as she brought me a cup of coffee. "Some things never change around here."

"I'm kind of glad about that today."

She wrapped her hands around mine. "Gianna told us what happened last night. Someone was watching out for you, *cara mia*."

No doubt. "Yes. Thank goodness for Brian and Adam."

To my surprise she shook her head. "Do not misunderstand me. It is good that they were there. But it was simply not your time to go. That is my belief, anyway." She frowned. "You still should be careful."

The expression of concern on her face bothered me. "Why? What's going on?"

She shrugged. "I am not sure. It seems very strange that someone who did not even know you would target you like this. Be mindful, and be careful." She lifted my chin with her finger until our gazes met. "Tomorrow is the first day of the rest of your life. You deserve much happiness, *cara mia*."

I stood and hugged her. "I love you so much. All right, I'll see you at the dinner tonight."

She looked startled. "But you just got here."

"Yes, but I promised Brian and Adam some cookies as a thank you gift. Then I have to pack and pick up my dress later. And Mike and I have to figure out who is dropping Spike off at the boarding facility. Probably me, I'm guessing." I felt guilty about that, but my parents couldn't take him. My mother had pet dander allergies, and Gianna worked long hours at the courthouse with no doggie door in the new apartment. I'd thought about asking her to stay at our house for the week but didn't want to inconvenience her.

Grandma Rosa nodded in understanding. "Yes, go then, my sweet girl. I will see you tonight."

I stopped in the living room to give my father a peck on the cheek. He looked pleased with himself. "I've dedicated today's blog entry to you."

"Oh really?" Amused, I glanced over his shoulder. "Does it have an itinerary for my honeymoon in Hawaii?"

He snorted. "No smut allowed on my blog. Nope, I simply stated that weddings were a beautiful thing, almost as beautiful as a funeral." He stopped and stared at the screen. "Hey, look. I've got a new message."

Nice post, Father Death. But remember, no relationship is without its thorns.

Below the message the writer had included a meme of a long-stemmed, red rose.

Ice-cold shards of terror formed between my shoulder blades as I examined the post. "Dad, wh-who's that from? I can't see the name."

The post was near the bottom of the page, so he scrolled down and examined the email address. "It only says *Anonymous*. I get a few of them like that. At least we know it's not *Miscellaneous,* right? That weirdo won't be bothering you anymore, baby girl."

I forced myself to breathe normally. Okay, it must be some type of weird coincidence. "Dad, do you have any other posts from this—"

"Domenic!" my mother called from upstairs, a giggle punctuating her speech. "I think I'm more important than some old blog."

My father rose to his feet. "That you are, baby. Father Death *and* Prince Charming at your service!"

Ew. Some days my parents were too much to handle. "See you later."

"Hey, Sal." He turned around on the staircase. "Bring your old man some fortune cookies tonight. Maybe they'll have some good predictions for the blog."

"Sure thing, Dad." When he'd disappeared from sight, I stared down at the weird message again. I hovered the mouse over the name, and a blank photo came up. Then I forced myself to laugh. How ridiculous—I was acting so silly. Silly Sally, as Grandma Rosa used to call me.

* * *

As I drove toward the shop, my mind kept growing more and more distracted. Was I making too much out of this coincidence with the blog? Of course it didn't mean anything. I thought back to the other brushes with death I'd had since returning to Colwestern. These had all been circumstances where I had intervened in the crime, either because my business or someone I loved was in jeopardy.

This was the first time someone had ever intentionally come after me without my knowing why. The thought that a random person like Pat had simply seen me somewhere and decided to kill me was both terrifying and surreal. Could there be more to it?

No. I didn't want to think about this anymore. My thoughts returned to Mike, and with a smile on my face, I recalled our time together last night. Even though we'd been exhausted, sleep had not come easily at first. Both of us had still been running on adrenaline and caffeine. I'd lain in his arms all night, and we'd spent hours talking about how much we were looking forward to our life together. We didn't want much. A family of course and to always be there for one another. We'd watched the sun starting to rise outside our bedroom window before I'd finally drifted off to sleep.

Despite the lack of shut-eye, I'd awoken with a renewed sense of being alive, fulfilled, and happy. Now that euphoria had been replaced with doubt, and I wondered if someone was still out there threatening our life together. This feeling needed to go away. Who was this man who had insisted on terrorizing me?

I pulled up in the alley behind the shop. Mike had stopped by earlier and placed some concrete blocks out for me to step on. He said he'd build me a new staircase after the honeymoon. It was only a minor inconvenience and not a big concern of mine. Mike was currently at Ralph's house working on a project, and I felt that job should take precedence. After all, the man had been instrumental in keeping me safe this past week, and we were both grateful to him.

I unlocked the door and entered the back room. I shut the alarm off and immediately went to the freezer and removed cookie dough. I turned the oven on and lined the trays with parchment paper. I also took the opportunity to clear the display case of any leftover cookies. I would drop them off at the homeless shelter when I left today. Then I remembered my father's request for fortune cookies. There were only three left in the case. Probably not enough to satisfy his demands, but I had no desire to make any more, plus there wasn't enough time. As I placed them in a ziplock bag, I noticed one of the cookies had already broken, and the message had unraveled.

When fear hurts you, conquer it, and defeat it.

Easier said than done. I stuffed the message into the pocket of my jeans and placed the ziplock bag in my canvas tote. I knew what the words meant—I had to fight this mess and these overwhelming feelings of terror, and I fully intended to do so. I thought about Grandma Rosa's words earlier today. *It wasn't your time.* I'd had so many close brushes with death lately that it made me wonder if I might actually be running out of time. Someday there might not be a person around to save me, and I'd be forced to rely on myself. The words of the message rang out loud and clear for me.

While the cookies were baking in the oven, I wandered upstairs to Gianna's apartment. She'd said she had some errands to do before the wedding tomorrow but had left the door unlocked, knowing that the place was closed today and no one would be in to disturb her things. Well, except for me, that is.

I went into Gianna's bedroom and spotted her laptop sitting on her desk. I'd used it before, and we both knew each other's passwords, so I went ahead and logged in. That was the beauty about having such a close relationship with my sister. Nothing was off-limits. We borrowed each other's clothes, shoes, and electronic devices without even asking.

Gianna was more ambitious than me. While I enjoyed my business, I longed for a family more. My sister wanted a career before even entertaining thoughts about a husband and kids, and that was her right. She had spent several years working toward her law degree, and I was proud of her for finally achieving that dream. Our taste in men ran different as well. Although Johnny and I had played doctor together at a young age, there had never been a romantic attraction for either one of us. I hoped he would be a member of our family someday, although Gianna had indicated on more than one occasion that she was in no hurry to get married, if ever.

As my fingers touched the keys, realization set in that I

didn't have a clue as to who or what I was searching for. Was it possible someone was still trying to kill me? *No.* Brian had told me that the rifle was the same one used to kill Alexandra. Sure, random crimes were committed all the time, but why did this instance feel so much more personal?

I brought up Google and sat there lost in thought, hands poised on the keyboard. I found myself typing in the words of the message from this morning. *No relationship is without thorns.* It sounded like a phrase from a poem, but I had no idea which one.

I glanced at the results on the screen in front of me. There were quotes about thorns, idioms from TheFreeDictionary.com, nothing useful. I scrolled down to the bottom of the page. There was a headline entitled *Local Florist Full of Flowery Tales.* For the heck of it, I clicked on the link. The article was three years old. I found myself staring at a picture of an attractive man with dark hair and eyes standing inside a floral shop with a bouquet of red roses in his outstretched hand.

Stanley Milton said that the secret to his success with flowers was similar to a dating experience. No relationship is without thorns, he said. If you realize that early on, you'll come out smelling like a rose.

My heart stuttered inside my chest. *Milton! Is this guy related to my killer*? Then I remembered the apartment building across from DeAngelo's Bakery. The woman who had checked on the apartment the day before the shooting had said her name was Rose Stanley. This couldn't be a coincidence. Was someone else involved besides Pat Milton? Could the woman who viewed the apartment have played a part too?

I read through the rest of the article, but it told me nothing else of consequence. Stanley was originally from Upstate New York. There was no other information that helped me. I googled his name and added "New York" after it since I assumed there must be many Stanley Miltons out there. Several links popped up, but it was the very first one that caught my attention:

Services for Stanley Milton, aged 28, will be held on Friday afternoon. Stanley was the owner of Daisy Delights

Florist. He was killed Monday evening in a car crash in Tampa, Florida. The driver of the other vehicle, Ryan Peterson, had an alcohol level of .08 in his bloodstream.

Oh God. The poor guy was dead. So this wasn't the man I was looking for after all. I was about to close out the article when my eyes traveled further down the remainder of the story.

Then I froze, my hand on the mouse.

Stanley is survived by his parents, brother Patrick, and his fiancée, Mitzi Graber, who was in the car with him. She suffered head trauma and a broken leg but is expected to make a full recovery.

Mitzi. My blood turned to ice water as I read the name.

A beeping from downstairs jerked me out of my thoughts, and then I realized with a start that it was the smoke alarm. *Crap!* I'd forgotten to take the cookies out of the oven.

I ran down the stairs, removed the trays from the smoking oven then grabbed a broom, and started furiously batting at the air in front of the detector on the ceiling. I stopped to turn on a fan, and after a couple of minutes, the beeping stopped but still resonated inside my head.

I should have guessed. Mitzi had been totally off her rocker last January, swearing she wanted to ruin me. She had blamed Colin for not cutting Ryan off the night of the accident. Had Colin not been killed by someone else, there was no doubt in my mind Mitzi would have tried to commit the deed herself. Somehow she had roped Stanley's brother into helping her with the scheme to do away with me.

The most frightening part of this was that Mitzi was still out there somewhere…waiting for me.

There was no way I could stay here and bake cookies. I had to call Brian and give him the news. Maybe Mike and I should leave tonight after all. If Mitzi knew about Pat's death, she'd be even more crazed than usual. I had no doubt that she was coming for me.

I went into the front room to double-check the lock on the door. When I glanced toward the tables, that's when I saw it…an ominous red rose lying on the table and contrasting so well with the white crocheted cloth beneath it.

A small whimper escaped from my mouth. No, the rose

hadn't been there earlier. I was certain of that. Was she here—inside the building? The room started to close in around me. I placed a hand over my chest and struggled to breathe normally. Mike had been wrong. The nightmare wasn't over after all. Now was officially time to panic.

I checked the oven to make sure it was off, set the alarm, and started out the back door, looking each way before I jumped into my car. I locked the doors and breathed a long sigh of relief as I started the engine. Then I pressed the contact information on my phone screen for Brian's number.

The call went directly to voicemail as I placed the vehicle in drive and slowly made my way down the alley. "Brian, it's Sally. You won't believe what I found out. There's someone else who has been trying to kill me—"

My head was suddenly jerked back against the seat as something cold and hard pressed into the side of my neck. With a gasp I dropped the phone and frantically attempted to control the swerving vehicle. I managed to bring the car to a screeching stop in the alley, narrowly missing the backside of a building.

"Move over slowly," a voice commanded from behind me.

I winced as recognition set in. My legs were numb, but my assailant didn't wait and pushed me onto the passenger seat then settled behind the driver's wheel. The gun never wavered from the side of my head.

The car started to move forward, and the needle on my speedometer rose rapidly. I managed to turn my head slightly and observe my attacker.

The face beside me was ghostly white and devoid of any emotion. Eyes that were dark and foreboding regarded me with uncontained malice. If death wore a mask, then I was staring into it.

"Hello, Sally," Mitzi greeted me politely with the same mannerisms she might use if waiting on a customer. A brittle-looking smile formed on her thin, cracked lips. "Did you miss me?"

CHAPTER NINETEEN

Terror is an overwhelming emotion that can send you into a state of perpetual shock. For several seconds I couldn't move or speak as I continued to stare at the face of my tormenter.

Mitzi controlled the vehicle with her left hand while her right one clicked the hammer on the gun. "Try anything funny and you're dead. Oh wait, you're going to wind up dead anyway, so it doesn't really matter, right?"

Stay calm. Mitzi was like a dog trying to sniff the fear out of me. Maybe I could try to talk some sense into her. It was doubtful, but what else could I do at this point? Anger suddenly took over. "Why are you doing this?" I demanded.

She laughed. "Because you and that loser ex-husband of yours ruined my life. I can never be complete without Stan. He was my soul mate. Can't you understand that? What would you do if your fiancé died all of a sudden?"

Her voice was taunting, and panic overwhelmed me. I hadn't spoken to Mike since the text I'd sent him earlier today. Had she found him? What if— "You-you haven't done anything to Mike, have you?"

She stared straight ahead, her mouth upturned in a slight smile, enjoying my fear. "You've got yourself one fine-looking man there. He'll make someone a great husband someday. Well, someone besides you, of course."

"Where are you taking me?" I tried hard to swallow the bile that was rapidly rising in the back of my throat.

When we hit a pothole in the road, the gun swerved slightly in her hand while I gulped back a sob of panic. Was there a chance the gun might discharge on its own?

"Maybe we'll take a trip to Niagara Falls," she said. "The water's warm this time of year, right? Oh wait. Correction, maybe the car will take a trip *into* the falls. Do you know how to swim?"

"You don't want to do this, Mitzi. You'd end up dying as well."

Her mouth set into a firm, hard line. "It doesn't matter. I have no life since Stan died. And I'm more than happy to take those who are responsible for his death along with me."

She sped through the local streets, weaving in and out of traffic while I clutched the door handle for meager support. I prayed a cop would see us speeding and attempt to pull her over. Mitzi took an abrupt turn up the ramp that led to the Thruway. The speed limit was sixty-five, but she was already pushing close to eighty. Sweat started to gather on my forehead.

"Why have you been terrorizing me?" I asked. "I didn't have anything to do with Stan's death."

She gnashed her teeth together. "Don't you dare say his name. You have no right."

"I didn't have anything to do with his death," I repeated in a voice that sounded strangely calm to my own ears.

Mitzi laughed. "We fooled you pretty good, right? Did you know it was me doing this?"

"Not at first," I admitted. "The quote in my father's blog tipped me off today. I googled it and found Stan's name in a related article."

Mitzi tossed her hair back in defiance. "That was stupid of me. But it doesn't matter anymore. I knew you'd come to the bakery at some point today. Little Miss Betty Crocker. We *must* have cookies!" she squealed in a suddenly high-pitched voice. "When I saw you leave your parents' house, I followed you there. Lucky for me you hadn't locked your car, so the rest was easy. And I slipped the rose on the table while you were upstairs. Pat gave me an awesome set of picks to use."

"Pat was Stan's brother?"

She gave a curt nod. "Correct. He was an expert shooter and a fabulous computer geek. He was in and out of the mental institution for years. He even lived with me and Stan for a while. I don't believe he hurt those kids years ago. He's always seemed pretty normal to me."

That wasn't saying much. Mitzi had lost the ability to identify normal a long time ago.

"You couldn't be happy with just Stan—you had to take Pat as well. Pat adored Stan," she sighed. "I had to bide my time until he was released from the facility. He was only too happy to oblige and help make those responsible for Stan's accident pay. We decided to avenge his death together."

This was a new kind of demented rage I hadn't seen before, and frankly, I thought I had witnessed them all by now. I tried not to watch as she switched lanes without signaling and barely missed clipping another vehicle's bumper. To know that you were about to die was a horrific indescribable feeling, especially when there was nothing you could do about it.

"So you feel that since someone else got to Colin first, you need to make a kill to get even. Is that right?" I asked, somewhat in disbelief. "It won't bring Stan back if you kill me, Mitzi."

She turned her head to glare at me and angrily pressed the gun harder into the side of my head. Her face, which had once been pretty with its delicate features, was gaunt and so pale that she seemed devoid of oxygen.

"Don't say that again," she snapped. "God, why do you have to make everything so difficult? We could have ended all of this last week if that bitch hadn't stepped in front of you at the last minute."

"And Josie?" I asked. "You thought she was me?"

"She was wearing your coat," Mitzi growled. "Of course Pat thought it was you. He was watching you guys at the apartment complex that day. He assured me he'd take care of everything. When you sent that message on your wacko father's blog, I knew it was a trap. But I couldn't reach Pat in time." A tear rolled down her cheek. "He walked right into his death."

"Stan and I were engaged," she went on. "Just like you and Mike. How tragic and sad that you'll die on the eve of your wedding. The bride who never got to see her wedding day."

Those were the same words that I had uttered inside my head when I'd stared down at Alexandra's lifeless body. I bit into my lower lip. No. I wouldn't give Mitzi the satisfaction of seeing me cry. Had she always been so unbalanced? Maybe it could be attributed to her car accident with Stan. There was no way to know for certain, although the article I'd read earlier had mentioned that she'd suffered severe head trauma as a result of the crash. Perhaps that was when it all started.

As she drove I noticed the rose tattoo on her left wrist. It was identical to the one Pat had worn. This one had a letter *M* next to it as well. "Were roses Stan's favorite flower?"

She blinked again, and a tear rolled down her cheek. "Pat and I got the tattoos as a tribute to my angel months ago. Everyone called him Milty."

The tears began to stream down her face, and she became more agitated. As a result the car picked up speed. Okay it probably wasn't a good idea to bring up Stan's name again.

"Everyone loved him," she sobbed. "He was so special. Then you and that husband of yours killed him."

"What about the drunk driver?" I asked.

"He's dead," she said matter-of-factly. "He was killed in a prison brawl a few months ago. Just my luck someone beat me to him. Of course another person took Colin out as well, so you're the only one who's left now. Somebody has to pay, and it might as well be you."

Mitzi glanced sideways at me and smiled as she swerved in and out of lanes while people laid on their horns and waved the middle finger at us in salute. "I would have done this months ago, but I needed Pat's help. When the mile-long article appeared in the paper with all your wedding details, it was like someone had given me a gift. I mean, I knew where you would be every single day of the week. It doesn't get much better. If that pesky bodyguard hadn't been around, we could have resolved this so much sooner."

"And you went to scope out the apartments the day before? How'd you know I'd be at DeAngelo's? The article didn't hit the paper until Saturday."

"The online version always prints that stuff the day before. I'd been scanning all the bridal notices for weeks, so when we finally saw the article, the rest was easy. DeAngelo's Bakery was in a perfect location with the apartment building directly across the street. It would have been too hard for Pat to try something while you were inside your own shop. There was no place for him to hide because there were only single units and duplexes across from your bakery. Too easy for him to be spotted."

"Pat had his picks ready in case he needed to break into the vacant apartment," she continued. "Turns out he didn't even have to use them. That bozo landlord forgot to lock the unit after he showed me the place the day before. It was as if someone was sending us a message of sorts. All Pat had to do was wait around until you and Mike came in." Her face became suffused with anger. "Then that Walston chick walked right into his path and ruined everything."

We were approaching the next exit when the wonderful sound of a police siren hit my ears. I glimpsed a cop car in my side mirror—no—two, three cars. They were gaining on us rapidly. Mitzi glanced into the rearview mirror, and I saw her suck in a sharp breath. Instead of slowing down, she pushed the pedal to the floor, veering the flying car toward the next exit on the Thruway.

"Guess we'll both die today," she said casually.

This woman might have a death wish, but I'd be damned if she was going to take me along with her. What had happened to her fiancé was a horrible, unfortunate accident, but I was not to blame. As she approached the traffic light in front of us that had already turned red, it was obvious she had no intention of stopping. In a sudden fit of anger, I lifted my left arm and knocked the gun from her hand. It discharged, sending a shot through my side window and shattering it.

Mitzi shrieked and let go of the wheel then turned her full-fledged rage on me. There was no time to think, and my first reaction was to punch her in the side of the head as hard as I could. Her body went limp against the back of the seat. I grabbed the steering wheel with one hand and pulled hard on the emergency brake which was within my grasp, having no way to reach the floor brake in time. The car made a loud screeching sound and skidded across the road from the exit ramp, where a small convenience store was located. I let out a piercing scream. The car had slowed some, but there was no way to stop it completely in time, and we sailed toward the glass storefront.

People who were walking in front of the building saw us coming and jumped out of the way screaming. The vehicle crashed through the plate glass window, forcing our airbags to inflate with a loud popping sound. The world went still and dark, and the sunlight disappeared from my range of vision.

The impact had bounced me against the doorjamb on the passenger side, and my head was now ringing with the sharp pain. I struggled to free myself from the crush of the airbags. Claustrophobia was starting to set in as I clawed at the bag. As I was fighting my way through, the car door opened, and Brian stared down at me in astonishment.

"What the hell happened?" He knelt beside the car.

I was shaking uncontrollably as my heart hammered against the wall of my chest. Then the floodgates opened, and I started to bawl like a baby. It had all been too much to absorb this week and had finally come to a head for me. Brian looked me over without comment and let out a small ragged sigh, the emotion showing on his usually expressionless cop face as he gently patted my arm.

"You're okay, Sally." Brian spoke softly. "You've got some bruises on your face and a cut lip, but they don't appear serious. We'll have an EMT check you out as soon as they can. Looks like someone else took the brunt of the crash."

Adam was at the other side of the vehicle freeing Mitzi from her seat and the airbag. Her face was a mess of blood and contusions, and she moaned in obvious pain. An EMT appeared from nowhere and started administering first aid to her.

I tried to stand on my own, but my legs were wobbly, and my right knee where I had banged into the doorjamb felt as if it was on fire.

Brian shook his head at me and gently pushed me back into the seat. "No, Sally. Stay here until the EMT examines you. You're dazed from the accident, and you need to stay still."

"H-how did you find us?" I asked weakly and noticed for the first time a crowd of people—perhaps customers—who had gathered near the car. They shouted and pointed at the vehicle. Shards of glass surrounded my car, and from what I could tell of the smashed front end, it appeared that the vehicle was totaled. On the bright side, I was still here to tell the tale and beyond grateful that my life had been spared.

"Your voicemail message," Brian said. "It didn't disconnect when you stopped talking. We were able to trace you from it. Plus, Mitzi was overheard on the phone saying that she was taking you to Niagara Falls. We assumed you'd take the Thruway and put out an APB for your vehicle hoping that was the one you guys were riding in. I phoned Mike on the way too."

I winced inwardly. He must be going out of his mind. "What did he say?"

Brian cocked an eyebrow at me. "It's not what he said, it's *how* he said it. He started shouting and said he was getting on the Thruway immediately."

Adam had joined us. "I called Mike a minute ago to let him know you were okay and what exit we are at," he said. "My guess is that he'll be here soon."

I looked around again at the people gawking and saw another ambulance with flashing lights arriving at the scene. "W-was anyone…" Suddenly I was having difficulty talking. The adrenaline had left my body and exhaustion was quickly taking over.

An EMT rushed over to me. "Are you having pain anywhere, ma'am?"

I brought a hand to my head. "I think there's a bump where I hit it against the door. My knee is hurting too."

Thankfully I had worn sweats that day, so he was easily able to roll the pant leg up and examine it. The entire kneecap was an angry red and bleeding. "Looks like you're going to have a bad bruise tomorrow, but it doesn't appear to be broken."

I looked at Brian again. "What I meant to say, is everyone—"

"No one else was hurt," Adam said.

The EMT examined the bump on my head. "You should let us take you to the hospital, ma'am, to be on the safe side."

My head was throbbing, and my body ached all over. "No, it's not necessary."

Brian raised an eyebrow at me. "It *is* necessary."

I pointed to the ambulance that Mitzi was being loaded into. "Is she all right?" Really, I didn't actually care.

"She's conscious, although I'm unsure about the severity

of her injuries. Regardless, she'll be treated and then carted off to a pleasant jail cell," Brian said. "She really had that officer in Vermont fooled. He was thinking about asking her out."

I shuddered visibly. "Brian, if there's one thing that I've learned, crazy people often appear saner than normal ones do."

He nodded. "Yeah, you've seen more than your share. That's for sure."

Something made me look up, and I saw Mike pushing his way through the crowd toward us. His eyes met mine, and the expression I read in them was at first terror and then relief. Brian also saw him coming and moved away as he sank down next to me and pulled me into his arms. For an entire minute he said nothing as he continued to hold me. I suspected he was trying to get his emotions in check.

Mike stroked my hair softly. "Thank God," he whispered.

"I'm okay," I managed to say against his chest.

He released me and examined my face and arms with an anxious frown. "You look like you've been through a war."

"She has," Adam said. "But her assailant looks much worse. Hey, Sally, you didn't answer my question. How'd you get the wheel away from Mitzi?"

"I knocked the gun out of Mitzi's hand and punched her in the head." I shrugged as if it wasn't a big deal.

Brian and Adam both looked thunderstruck, and then slow grins spread across their faces.

"Wait a second," Brian said. "*You* punched someone? Sorry, but I can't see it."

Mike rubbed my shoulders. "That's my girl."

"My life was at stake. I had no choice," I said. "When fear hurts you, conquer it, and defeat it."

A flicker of amusement crossed Mike's beautiful eyes. "That sounds like it would make a great fortune cookie message."

I smiled but said nothing.

CHAPTER TWENTY

After the EMT had checked me out, they again suggested that I go to the hospital for some routine tests on my head. Mike drove me himself, despite my initial protests. We went back to Colwestern and the local hospital there. Once inside, a doctor examined me in the emergency room. I winced when he touched the knee I'd bumped that was still bleeding some.

"You're a lucky girl," he commented. "Very fortunate. I'll have the nurse grab you a new bandage for that knee."

When the doctor had left the room, Mike winked at me. "Is it my imagination, or did that seem like another play on words with fortune cookie messages?"

I laughed. "Yeah, I put the doctor up to it. Maybe those messages are finally getting to you too."

He shook his head. "Not possible."

At that moment the door opened, and Ally poked her head in. She was dressed in pink scrubs and had a patient's chart in her hands.

"Hi, Sal." The color rose in her cheeks, and she smiled. "I'm glad to hear you're okay."

"Thanks," I said.

Ally waved the bandage in her hands. "I saw Dr. Thorn, and he asked me to bandage your knee. I—uh, well, I was hoping that we could talk." She glanced shyly at Mike.

Mike seemed to understand her request for privacy and released my hand. "I have a call to make, so I'll leave you two ladies alone for a minute. Be right back, princess."

Ally bandaged my knee, and I rolled the leg of my sweatpants back down. She picked up her chart again and then forced her gaze to meet mine. "Sal, I wanted to apologize for the way I acted the other day. I was such a jerk to you."

"No worries, Ally. I understand."

She shook her head in frustration. "But that's not me, honest. Gosh, I came off sounding so desperate. You did nothing wrong. It's obvious how much in love you and Mike are with each other. Plus, Brian told me what you've been through this week." Her lower lip trembled slightly. "The last thing you needed was a former high school friend acting like a jealous lunatic around you."

Yes, it felt like I'd been to hell and back the past few days. My head was pounding, and exhaustion from a sleepless week was starting to have a severe effect on me. But all I could think about was that in twenty-four hours I'd be on a plane with the man I loved, headed for paradise. No vengeful stalkers, bodyguards, or well-meaning parents had been invited to accompany us.

"There's no need for you to apologize," I assured her again. "Like I said, I've *been* there. In my situation though, I found out a little too late."

She looked puzzled. "What do you mean?"

I sighed. "I walked in on my husband in bed with another woman."

Ally gasped, and her eyes widened. "Oh, Sal, I had no idea. I mean, I'd heard that you and Colin were divorced but didn't know the exact details."

She had to be the only person in town who didn't know the whole story. The Colwestern grapevine had been kept busy ever since I came back to town.

Ally extended a hand and helped me down from the examining table. I was sore, and my muscles had started to ache. I assumed this was most likely from tensing up during the actual accident.

"It was awful, and I didn't know if I'd ever get over it," I said honestly. "Colin's dead now, so I can't hold any ill will against him. For the record, I don't believe Brian would ever do anything like that to you. The man has too much integrity. Basically I was fooling myself when I married Colin because I was still in love with Mike."

"Maybe it was some type of weird fate," Ally said. "Maybe you were supposed to find him in a compromising position so that you'd go back to Mike. It's obvious you two were meant to be together." Her face grew pensive. "Brian and I are having dinner tonight to talk things out."

I didn't mention that I already knew about this. Call me crazy, but I didn't think Ally would be happy to learn that Brian had been confiding in me. "I hope everything works out. He's a wonderful man and great at his job. He's helped me out of numerous scrapes."

She shook her head. "Cripes, Sal, it's like you have a death wish on your head or something. No offense."

I couldn't take offense because I was starting to wonder the same thing myself.

Mike poked his head in the door. "Okay to come back in?"

Ally smiled. "Yeah. We're all through here." She glanced from Mike to me and then reached out to give me a hug. "Congratulations. I hope you both will be very happy. Where are you getting married?"

I looked at my fiancé, who was grinning from ear to ear. "Ah, well, that's a very good question. We canceled our original venue, so it looks like city hall is the place."

"Hey, that's okay," Ally said. "The important thing is that you'll be happy."

Mike reached for my hand. "That's one thing I have never doubted."

Ally gave us both a little finger wave and then closed the door quietly behind her.

I sighed and leaned against Mike for support as he opened the door for me. "I'm so tired."

We were met in the waiting room by my grandmother, Gianna, and Johnny. When Gianna spotted me, she threw her arms around my neck and almost knocked me over in the process. "Oh my God! Are you all right?"

I hugged her back then leaned over to give my grandmother a kiss. "Everything's good."

Johnny gave me a playful nudge. "Aw, Sal, you'd do almost anything to get out of that wedding. It's plain to see that you're miserable with this guy."

Mike chuckled while I punched Johnny on the arm. "Hey, I found out today that I have a pretty good right hook. Watch out because your turn could be next."

Johnny backed away in fake horror with his hands outstretched. "Whoa. Guess I spoke too soon."

"I hate to bring this up," Gianna said, "but Mom and Dad are already over at the restaurant for the rehearsal dinner, which starts in an hour."

I groaned and was tempted to smack my palm against my forehead, but my head was throbbing enough already.

Grandma Rosa observed me closely. "You do not have to go, *cara mia*. I know you are concerned about your mama, but she will understand."

"Did you tell Mom and Dad about the accident?" I asked.

My grandmother shook her head. "They have been out all afternoon, going to lunch and shopping. I did try but could not reach them by phone. You know your mama forgets to turn it on half the time."

I suppressed a smile. "We'll tell them at the dinner then."

Mike looked at me in surprise. "You still want to go?"

Gianna and I exchanged a knowing glance. "Mom's really been looking forward to this dinner, especially since we had to cancel the reception at the country club," I said. "Since we're not having a big celebration tomorrow, I think I can manage to put up with it for an hour or two."

Mike didn't know about the big family secret yet, so he was understandably a bit bewildered by my response. "Sweetheart, you were in a car accident today, plus a psycho tried to kill you. I know how much your mother loves to throw a party, but even she wouldn't expect you to go through with this."

"It's okay, really. I'm fine now. I want to do this, Mike."

He reached out a finger and ran it gently over the scratch on my cheek. If he suspected there was something more to my persistence, he didn't ask. I'd find a time later on to explain my motive.

Mike cupped my face between his hands. "All right, princess. Whatever you say."

* * *

The next day, I awoke to the drumming of rain on the roof. Content, I closed my eyes again and pulled the blanket up over my shoulders. The sound of a rain shower first thing in the morning, especially on days when I could sleep in and snuggle against Mike, left me feeling happy and mellow. I sighed and prepared to drift off again. Maybe I'd lie here all day.

I reached out my hand, but Mike wasn't in bed with me. Maybe he was in the shower. Then I jerked awake with sudden realization. Holy cow. This wasn't just *any* Saturday.

It was my wedding day.

I sat up in bed slowly. Stiffness from the accident had set into my bones, and my knee still throbbed. Wincing, I stared down at Spike who was lying across my feet. "Mike?"

There was no answer. I glanced at his side of the bed. He'd left a note on his pillow and a red carnation beside it. I was overwhelmed by the sweet gesture and also grateful he hadn't left a red rose. I'd seen more than enough of those lately. I sniffed at the flower, inhaling its fragrant scent while I read the words Mike had printed in his fine slanted handwriting:

Good morning, beautiful bride of mine,

A client had an issue at his house. I just did his roof last week, and it's only a minor detail, so I shouldn't be gone too long.

I shook my head in disbelief. Up on a roof, in the rain nonetheless, hours before his wedding. This was what made him so good at his job. He was dedicated to a fault and never wanted anyone to be unhappy with his work. I read on.

I'll be home by noon, but I expect to find you gone by then. I'm not supposed to see you until we say I do, remember.

I love you. Thank you for making me the happiest man on earth, today and every day.

A tear rolled down my cheek. After all this time and everything we had been through, I couldn't believe this day had finally arrived. Mike might be the happiest man, but I was definitely the luckiest woman alive.

I sighed and stretched in bed for a moment. Spike

crawled up beside me, and I wrapped my arms around him. "Sorry we can't take you with us. But you understand about honeymoons, right?"

He gave me what I thought to be a dubious look, stopped wagging his tail, jumped on the floor, and tottered out of the bedroom without even a backward glance. Okay, someone was not feeling the love today.

I grabbed my cell and limped slowly into the kitchen. Mike had made coffee, so I poured myself a cup then stared down at the screen of my phone. I had a new text message from Becky at the bridal shop, and it was plain to see from the wording that she was not happy with me. *You were supposed to pick up your dress yesterday. Are you getting married naked? Come over. Now! I'll be here until two.*

Cripes. I sent her a text back. *Sorry! Will explain when I get there. Can I come in about noon?* I glanced at my watch. It was ten o'clock, and I hadn't even packed yet. Plus with my injury I was having trouble moving at a fast pace right now. I went into the bathroom with my coffee, showered, washed my hair, and let the hot water seep into my sore bones for a few minutes. Afterward I felt slightly better as I dressed in jeans and a T-shirt and started throwing things in my suitcase. Bathing suit, lingerie, sandals. Oh, wait a second. What was I forgetting? Actual clothing might be a good thing too.

I zipped the suitcase shut and grabbed my cosmetic bag. Spike had relented and let me give him a quick hug. Mike had said last night that he would drop him off at the boarding facility later today, and for that I was grateful because it would be difficult for me to say good-bye to him there. I took Mike's Camaro and arrived at Becky's Bridals at twelve fifteen. I burst through the front door, and Becky looked up from the gowns she was arranging on a rack. She shook a menacing finger at me.

"Your mother called a few minutes ago," she said. "When I told her you hadn't picked up the gown yet, she started to lose it."

Great. "There's been a lot going on the last couple of days. I've been a bit distracted."

"Honey," she said in a soothing voice. "I know you and your family, remember? Distraction is your middle name." She glanced sharply at my face. "What the heck did you do to yourself?"

Ugh. I wasn't getting into this with her right now. "Oh, I tripped and fell. I can't believe how clumsy I am some days."

Becky glanced at me sharply, and I knew she wasn't fooled, but mercifully she didn't comment further. Instead, she went behind the front counter and handed me a garment bag hanging on the rack next to it. "Go try this on, love."

There was no time for me to try the dress on. "Becky, you're fabulous at what you do, so I'm sure it's fine. And I'm so late now that I don't have—"

She shook her head furiously and pointed at the dressing room. "*Go!*"

Yikes. I went into the dressing room and shed my clothes as Becky followed me in without even asking and helped position the gown over my head. She glanced at it critically, and then her fingers did the pinching bit at my waist again. She let out a small sigh of satisfaction as she stepped back to observe me. "It's perfect. You look stunning, hon."

I did a turn in front of the full-length mirror, pleased at what I saw, then gave her a hug. "Thanks, Becky."

"Careful, you'll wrinkle it!" Becky helped me off with the gown. "It's a shame you had to cancel your reception at the country club. I was looking forward to dancing the night away."

I lowered my T-shirt over my head. "I know, I'm sorry. Things didn't work out quite the way we had planned."

She frowned. "But city hall is so unromantic."

"We'll make it romantic," I said stubbornly. "Thanks again for everything."

Becky handed me the garment bag. "Be happy, honey. That's what counts."

In a frantic rush I drove toward my parents' house. My mother wanted me to get ready there, and then they would drive me to city hall to meet Mike for our three o'clock appointment. She had insisted I arrive at the house by noon, and now it was almost one. I braced myself for the reprimand that was surely coming.

I did feel guilty about letting all of our guests down and had told my mother I wanted to return the wedding gifts that had already arrived. My mother said no, that friends and relatives had assured her they wanted us to have them. Maybe Mike and I could plan a small reception for everyone when we returned from our trip. I'd have to speak to my mother about it.

I walked into the house and expected bedlam, but my parents had managed to surprise me once again. My grandmother was in the kitchen unloading the dishwasher, like any other normal day. No one else was around.

"Where is everyone? Upstairs getting ready?" I reached out to hug her.

Grandma Rosa shook her head. "They had to go out."

"Go out?" I asked, puzzled. "Go out where?"

"Your mother had an errand to run," Grandma Rosa said simply, "and she asked your sister and father to go with her. I will help you get dressed."

Okay, so I could see my parents pulling something like this, but not Gianna. She would have never deserted me. "This sounds really weird. I thought Mom wanted to help me get ready." Cripes, maybe she was upset about something else. "Is she mad at me?"

Grandma Rosa shook her head. "It is all good. Come." She took the garment bag from my hands and led the way up the stairs as I followed her to my old bedroom. The stairs were rough on my knee, and she waited patiently at the top as I hobbled my way there.

"Did you bring the brooch?" Grandma Rosa asked.

I opened my cosmetic bag. "Of course. I'd never forget that." Grandma Rosa had given me a beautiful silver cameo brooch for my birthday recently. She'd explained that it had been a gift from her one true love, many years ago, before my grandfather had entered the picture. The man had gone to Vietnam and never been heard from again.

The brooch had a beautiful blue topaz stone in the center. I also had a pearl necklace to wear that I had borrowed from my mother, and my gown was new. Therefore I had all of the requirements to fulfill the "something old, something new" traditional saying.

After Grandma Rosa had fastened the necklace, I handed her a square, wrapped package and card. "Happy Birthday."

She snorted. "Bah. I told you that I did not want anything."

"It's nothing expensive," I assured her. My grandmother didn't like presents that were costly. However, this was a gift from the heart, and I knew she'd love it.

Grandma Rosa unwrapped the present and stared down at it for a long moment before her gaze met mine and she smiled. It was a picture of the two of us I felt sure she had never seen before. We were standing in front of the church where I had made my First Communion over twenty years ago. My mother had taken the photo, sent it for developing afterwards, and then promptly forgot about it. Gianna had found it in a pile of old photographs up in the attic recently. In the white lace dress that Grandma Rosa had made for me, I looked festive and pleased with myself. She stood smiling next to me in a gray suit from Italy that she had worn when she married my grandfather.

The frame was one that I had made during a ceramics class when I was living in Florida with Colin. Outside of the bakery, I was not creative in the least, and this might be the one time that something I had made by hand had actually turned out halfway decent.

Grandma Rosa kissed me. "It is beautiful, *cara mia*, and the frame as well. I am so proud of you and will treasure this always." She set the frame down on the desk and unzipped the garment bag for me while I undressed. After the gown was on, my grandmother picked up the curling iron that was sitting there, sectioning out a strand of my hair to curl.

I hadn't thought to do anything with my mane and sighed despondently as I stared at my reflection in the mirror hung over the small, white vanity table that I had also used as a desk while growing up. At least makeup hid most of the scratches from yesterday's ordeal. Fortunately the earlier rain outside had stopped, but it was humid, which meant frizz fest for me.

"I wish the weathermen would get things right for once," I groused. "They said it was going to be beautiful today."

Grandma Rosa worked on my hair as I continued to complain. She managed somehow to keep the frizz in check, gave it a generous douse of hairspray, and then kissed me on the cheek. "The weather, like the location, does not matter. You are marrying the man that you love. That is what will make the day beautiful."

I smiled at her. "You're right, as usual."

Grandma Rosa stood close to me and reached for my hand. "I would like to think that nothing bad will ever happen to you again. But you seem to have a way of attracting trouble, by no fault of your own. Perhaps it is your destiny to somehow make this world a safer and better place for others. Learn to accept things for what they are. You are marrying a wonderful man today. Embrace your new life together."

There was a lump in my throat. "I don't know what I'd do without you."

Her eyes clouded with emotion, a rarity for my grandmother. "I will always be with you, *cara mia.* Someday, even if you cannot see me anymore, remember that I am still with you."

My phone buzzed in my lap, and I stared down at it in annoyance. What lousy timing. Who would dare interrupt such a special moment with my grandmother, the other love of my life? I was tempted not to answer.

"Go ahead," Grandma Rosa urged. "It may be important."

The number did look familiar, so grudgingly I pressed *Accept*. "Hello?"

A man's high-pitched voice greeted me. "Hello, is this Sally?"

"Yes, speaking."

"Hi, Sally. It's Ray over at Purrfecting Your Pet. I was wondering if you were still planning on dropping Spike off today."

I stared at the phone, confused. "Mike was supposed to have dropped him off by now."

Ray cleared his throat. "Oh. Well, I called his cell, but he didn't answer. I thought he said he'd be here by one. We close at two, but I'm running a bit late today with cleanup."

I glanced down at my watch, and a chill went through me. It was two thirty. "I'll call him and see what happened."

"I can hang out a little while longer if you like." His tone was polite but not especially friendly, and somehow I sensed that he didn't prefer to wait.

"No, that's not necessary. I don't want to inconvenience you any further. Thanks anyway."

I disconnected and dialed Mike's number which went straight to voicemail. I texted him once then again a minute later, but he didn't respond.

Grandma Rosa watched me closely. Distress must have registered on my face. "*Cara mia,* whatever is the matter?"

I bit into my lower lip, determined not to panic. "Mike didn't drop off Spike. What are we going to do with him? And why hasn't Mike answered me? He was on a wet roof this morning. What if he fell off and got hurt?"

"My dear," she said soothingly. "You should not worry. I am sure that he is fine. And do not be upset about Spike. We can keep him until Monday and then take him over to the hoarding house."

I winced inwardly. "Grandma, it's *boarding*, not *hoarding*."

She nodded. "That works too. Come. We need to be going."

I wrung my hands in frustration. "How can we go? I don't even know where Mike is."

"My dear granddaughter," she murmured. "You are letting your imagination run away with you again. Everything is fine. We need to leave, for it is almost three o'clock."

I followed her down the stairs and out the front door, careful to close and lock it behind me. "I can't believe this is happening on my wedding day." *Could I have just one normal day of my life?* "Do you want me to drive?"

She gave me a disbelieving look. "We will take my car. I want to get to your wedding in one piece."

CHAPTER TWENTY-ONE

Ten minutes later, Grandma Rosa turned the car onto my street. I looked around, confused, as she pulled into my driveway. "What are we doing here?"

She smiled but didn't answer. Mike's truck was in the driveway, and my parents' car and Johnny's Ford Mustang were both parked at the curb. "Did Mom and Dad come here to meet me by mistake? What's going on?"

My grandmother calmly got out of the car and came around to my side to help me out. "How about you go see for yourself."

As we started toward the front door, my father, dressed in the black suit he wore primarily for wakes and funerals, came out to greet us.

His warm brown eyes regarded me with pride. "You look like a million bucks, baby girl."

"Thanks, Dad. Will you tell me what's going on?"

He extended his right arm to me. "I'm here to walk you down the aisle for your wedding."

"What are you talking about? We're going to city hall to get married."

"Nope," he said cheerfully. "That's been canceled. Come on." He opened the door, let Grandma Rosa go ahead of us, and then escorted me inside.

Nothing could have prepared me for the site that met my eyes. My small living room had been decorated with streamers and paper wedding bells that hung from the ceiling. Our fireplace mantel had been adorned with a lace coverlet, on top of which sat several lit candles in white porcelain holders. There were small vases of pink and white roses situated in between each one of them.

Josie and Gianna stood to the side of the couch looking lovely in their pastel gowns. Tears had already formed behind my sister's eyes as she handed me a bouquet of pink and white roses.

"Here, love." Gianna leaned over to whisper in my ear. "I called the florist yesterday and asked if they could substitute pink roses for the red."

"Great idea." I kissed her on the cheek.

Josie was pale and had dark circles under her eyes but managed to give me a broad smile. Father Grenaldi was standing in front of the fireplace, book in hand. Rob was positioned to his right. There was only one person missing—my groom.

My mother, who had been sitting on the couch, came over to hug me. "Oh, darling, you look fabulous." There were tears in her eyes, and she stopped to wipe them with a tissue.

"Thanks, Mom, so do you." She was wearing a beautiful pink, strapless satin dress and a matching jacket with high-heeled silver stiletto sandals. I'd never seen this outfit before. The dress was knee length, something unheard of in my mother's world. There was no cleavage or anything else showing, with the exception of her fabulously shaped legs. Could my mother be turning over a new leaf?

Not a chance.

Before I could even attempt to ask about Mike, Josie gripped my arm and led me toward the kitchen. Mrs. Gavelli and Johnny were standing on either side of the doorway, and he stuck out his foot, his eyes shimmering with laughter as he pretended he was going to trip me. Although Josie was walking slow and still in obvious pain, she managed to give him a hard shove so that he almost lost his footing.

Josie pointed at the kitchen table that had been covered with a white satin cloth. On top of it sat her masterpiece of a wedding cake. My breath caught in my throat as I stared at it in awe.

"What do you think?" she asked.

I'd seen Josie's cakes before, of course. It was a means for her to earn some extra money on the side. This time she had truly outdone herself. Her creation consisted of a three-tier, white fondant cake, and each layer in the shape of a heart, the smallest one complete with a bride and groom topper on it. Both the figurines had dark hair, like Mike and me. The cake was decorated with white and pink fondant roses, and each tier was surrounded with white satin ribbons and pearls.

Josie smiled as she watched me. "The inside has a cookies and cream filling. I thought it was appropriate, in honor of the shop."

"You spent all of yesterday on this, didn't you?" I asked in disbelief.

She wiggled her hand back and forth. "A good chunk of it. Don't worry. I sat down for the most part. It wasn't a big deal."

But it was a big deal—to me. To think that someone who had almost lost their life three days earlier would go to so much trouble for my sake completely overwhelmed me. My throat tightened with tears as I hugged her. "Jos, I don't know how to thank you. It's absolutely stunning. But this was too much trouble for you to go through."

"Nothing is too much trouble where your best friend is concerned," she said in a shaky voice. "Especially one like you."

I wiped at my eyes with the back of my hand and hugged her again, not knowing what else to say.

"Now look," Mrs. Gavelli grunted. "She gonna ruin her makeup because of your cake."

For once, Josie chose to ignore her nemesis, while I choked back a laugh. We made our way back to the living room, arms around each other's waists.

"I'll freeze the top layer for you," Josie volunteered. "Then you can eat it at your first anniversary—with the new baby sitting on your lap."

"What new baby?" My father looked alarmed.

I laughed. "It's nothing, Dad. Josie's priming me for motherhood."

Father Grenaldi spoke up. "Excuse me, Sally. I hate to interrupt, but I think this young man wants to get married."

Mike was standing at the end of the hallway, having just come out of the bedroom. His eyes met mine, and then he stepped back a bit, as if to take me all in. A broad smile spread across his face.

As for myself, all I could do was dumbly stare back at him. He looked so handsome in his black tuxedo, his blue eyes shining with such happiness and love that I thought my heart might leap out of my chest at any moment. He went to stand in front of the priest and continued to watch me as my father escorted me toward him.

There was no music, but it didn't matter. My father nodded at Mike then kissed me on each cheek. He settled himself on the couch next to my mother. Josie and Gianna both stood behind me, next to Rob who was Mike's best man. Grandma Rosa sat in the armchair, nodding and smiling at us.

The way Mike looked at me made me feel like I was the only person in the room, or perhaps the entire universe. With the exception of children one day, I knew I would never want for anything else. Since that day over ten years ago when we'd broken up, something had always been missing from my life. A dull ache in my chest that I couldn't identify, or perhaps didn't want to. This man completed me. There was no doubt in my mind that I could handle anything life threw at me now, as long as I had Mike by my side. Life was good, wonderful in fact.

He leaned close and took my left hand in his right one. "You're breathtaking, my princess."

"So are you," I whispered back.

He extended his arm around the living room. "What do you think? Were you surprised? I thought it was better than getting married at stuffy city hall."

Yes, he had surprised me once again. "*You* did all this?"

Mike flushed slightly. "To be honest, no. I had the idea yesterday after your—incident. I called your mother last night when you went to bed. She and Gianna scoured the stores this morning for decorations and flowers."

My mother giggled from the couch. "I'm so glad I never canceled the florist. They were able to make us up some quick pieces for the fireplace. All the other flowers that we couldn't use will be dropped off at the nursing home later on."

I stared at her, trying to keep my emotions in check while thinking about the resiliency she possessed that I had never known about before.

Mom laughed at my expression. "Come on, honey. It's

time to get married! Hurry up so that we can get this party started."

Mrs. Gavelli called from the doorway, "Yes, you hurry. I like to party."

"She just likes the alcohol involved," Johnny teased. "Gram's more fun when she's tipsy."

"Hush." She gave him a light slap and then grabbed his face between her hands. "Be a good boy."

"Yeah," my father growled. "It wouldn't be a party without you, Nicoletta. That's for sure."

Father Grenaldi's expression was pained. "Are we ready to continue?"

I had to bite down on my lower lip to keep from laughing.

"Dearly beloved," Father Grenaldi said in his rich deep voice, "we are gathered here together to join this man and woman in holy matrimony. If anyone has reason that these two should not be joined, let them speak now or forever hold his peace."

My father snorted. "Hey, Sal, where's those fortune cookies I asked for? Let's see what they say."

Grandma Rosa gave him a death stare. "Hush, you fool."

"My goodness." Father Grenaldi stared at me sympathetically. "I never knew the Muccios were so—unusual."

"That's one way to describe them, Father," Mike grinned.

"Sally, Michael, would you like to say your vows? Please join hands."

I handed Gianna the bouquet and placed both of my hands in Mike's. He smiled down at me tenderly. "I'm not very good at this," he confessed. "All I can say is that I've loved you since the first day I met you. We haven't always had smooth sailing, that's for sure. I guess we'll never know exactly what's in store for us, but all I want is to be there to love and comfort you for the rest of your life. I'll be the best husband I can—and hopefully father someday too."

My mother sighed from the couch. "I can't wait to be a granny."

"Sal." My father grunted. "What's all this talk about kids? Are you pregnant?"

I almost choked. "No, Dad."

The expression on his face was pure relief. "Okay then, go on."

Father Grenaldi stared at my father, confused. "Okay, Sally, your turn."

My heart overflowed with happiness as I stared into the eyes of the man I loved, and my voice grew shaky. "I've always loved you. I tried to fight it for years, but it was no use. I'm thankful for so many things in my life. But to be with you, forever—nothing can compare to that. I love you more than anything on this earth."

Someone was crying. I assumed it was my mother, so I was very surprised to turn and see Josie bawling with Rob's arm around her. Now I knew where Dylan got it from.

Grandma Rosa beamed at both of us. My father and mother were sitting together, arms around each other's waists, and Gianna and Johnny were holding hands behind Mrs. Gavelli's intimidating figure.

All was as it should be. Everything was right in my world.

"Do you have the rings?" Father Grenaldi asked Mike.

Mike looked at Rob who reddened. "Shoot. I forgot. The ring bearer has them." He let go of Josie and hurried down the hallway toward our bedroom.

"Ring bearer?" I stared at Josie who winked. "Is it one of the kids?"

"Oh, hell no," Mike whispered.

Josie laughed. "I heard that."

Rob reappeared with Spike in his arms. He was wearing a little black jacket, and there was a white ribbon adorning his back. Attached to it were two gold bands.

"Oh my gosh," I squealed. "He looks *so* cute."

Gianna was busy snapping pictures of all of us with her camera.

"By the way," Johnny said. "We're taking Spike while you guys are away. Gram likes dogs."

I didn't think Mrs. Gavelli liked anything, so this was a major surprise. She caught me staring and narrowed her eyes. "He a good little doggie. Pets be better than people. Okay, most times."

Father Grenaldi glanced at her almost as if he was in pain then cleared his throat. "Are we ready to continue?"

Mike smothered a laugh as he put the ring on my finger. "Father, it's just the way the Muccios are. Nothing will ever change that. Now, do you want to finish telling us our fortune so I can kiss the bride?"

Father Grenaldi looked at Mike like he had corn growing out of his ears. "What does that mean?"

"*Shh,*" I whispered, holding fast to his hand. "You're supposed to be serious here."

Mike turned those beautiful midnight blue eyes on me, and as usual, I melted on the spot. "I am serious," he whispered softly. "Seriously in love with you."

"You're going to make me cry," I said. "Stop it."

"She ruin her makeup!" Mrs. Gavelli yelled. "You stop now."

"Michael James Donovan," Father Grenaldi said in an authoritative tone. "Do you take this woman to be your lawfully wedded wife?"

"I'm willing to take a chance," he teased.

Everyone laughed, with the exception of Father Grenaldi who obviously didn't get the joke. I nudged Mike in the side. "Do you realize what you just said?"

His face grew somber as he stared into my eyes, his voice thick with emotion. "I do."

CHAPTER TWENTY-TWO

As we walked along the white sandy beach on the last day of our honeymoon, hand in hand, I reflected on my life. Although not yet thirty, I felt considerably older. I'd been through a lot within a short time—both Mike and I had. None of that seemed to matter anymore. Although I'd always tried to have an upbeat attitude where my life was concerned, I now looked forward to the rest of it with a renewed sort of anticipation.

The beach was private, and Mike had hinted that he had a surprise for me. I noticed an umbrella set up in the sand, along with a cooler beside it and blanket underneath. He walked purposefully toward it while I followed.

"What's this?" I asked.

"I ordered us a picnic lunch," he said. "I arranged it through the hotel yesterday."

I grinned. "You do think of everything, husband. This is perfect."

The entire honeymoon had been perfect, in fact. We'd slept in late, gone on a couple of excursions, been on the Pearl Harbor cruise, and attended a luau. I still smiled when I thought of the hula dancer who had picked Mike out of the audience to dance with her.

The ocean view from this particular spot was breathtaking, which is probably why Mike had chosen it. I could sit for hours watching the shimmering blue water with the foam skimming the top of it. The pleasant smell of hibiscus teased my nostrils as palm trees swayed softly in the warm breeze.

"I wish we could stay here forever," I sighed.

He reached for my hand and brought it to his lips. "Me too. It's beautiful here, isn't it? But that doesn't matter. We'll have paradise wherever we go, just you and me." He reached into the cooler and brought out a bottle of Pinot and some plastic stemware. There was also a platter of fruit, bread and cheeses, and what looked like seaweed. He poured a glass half full of wine and handed it to me. "You, me, and someday a houseful of kids."

I hoped I was already pregnant but wouldn't know for a while yet. "I want that so much. I even enjoyed taking care of Josie's."

Mike narrowed his eyes. "Our kids won't be like *that*."

Famous last words. "Yeah, right," I mocked. "Ours will be perfect, I'm sure."

"Of course they will. So, do we have a long layover on the flight this evening?" Mike asked. "I changed the reservations so many times last week that I can't remember."

I reached into my canvas bag for my phone. "Shoot. I must have left my cell in the rental car."

He gave me a wicked grin. "It's probably my fault. I've managed to distract you quite nicely on this trip. Not that you seemed to mind much."

I laughed. "You are so bad."

"Thank you, Mrs. Donovan. By the way, I do love saying that name."

My lower lip trembled. "And I love hearing it. For a while I never thought that would happen."

He gazed out at the ocean. "I don't know. Something deep down inside told me that someday I would get you back. Even after you married Colin, I never completely lost hope. It was what kept me going all those years."

I wrapped my arms around his neck, and Mike turned his head so he could kiss me. "I know something about that too."

We were silent as we sat there and continued to watch the sky streaked with sunlight and listen to the sounds of the waves hitting the shore. Reluctantly, I released him so that I could rummage through my bag again. I found our itinerary crumpled up inside one of the pockets and studied it for a minute. "Let's see. A two-hour layover in Seattle for the first change and then one hour in Detroit for the next. Not too bad. It's a good thing we checked out already because we won't have much time to get to the airport when we're done here."

"Damn." He grinned at me like a little boy with a secret. "And I had more plans for you."

"You never quit, do you?" I put the paper back inside my bag, and my fingers connected with something. I drew the object out and sucked in a breath. "Uh-oh."

"What's wrong?" Mike asked.

I held up the plastic bag for him to see. There were two smashed fortune cookies inside. "My father asked me to bring these to the house the night before the wedding. With everything going on, I forgot about them. They've been buried in my bag all week."

There was a trash receptacle nearby, and I rose to my feet. "Let me get rid of these."

"Hang on a second." Mike grabbed my arm. "Let's see what they have to say."

"Come on," I implored. "Let's not start this again."

He pinned me with his direct gaze. "Sal, the first thing you have to do is stop worrying about these cookies."

"So it's better that I throw them out."

"No, it isn't," Mike insisted.

I didn't want this to turn into an argument. Our trip had been so perfect. "Are you suggesting we read them?"

"Come here," he said and patted the spot on the blanket beside him.

I sighed but did as he said. Mike immediately placed an arm around my shoulders. "Even if there was something to these cookies—and I'm not saying there is—it won't do any good to keep avoiding them. Didn't we say we needed to tackle our fears head on?"

"Well, yes, but…"

"If you're going to keep serving these cookies at the bakery," Mike continued, "and I'm guessing you will because they're so popular—you need to deal with this. Don't be afraid of what they might say. Learn to embrace them instead."

I raised an eyebrow at my husband. "Embrace fortunes that tell me to stay in the house or that revenge can be sweet?"

He grinned. "Well, not exactly. What I'm trying to say is that you can't let them run—or ruin—your life. There's an old saying. 'Worrying doesn't stop the bad things from happening. It just keeps you from enjoying the good.'" He wove his fingers through my hair. "And I don't want to waste a minute of our life together worrying about something that might never occur. Anything that happens, we'll tackle together. Okay?"

I looked into his rugged handsome face and for about the millionth time this week, couldn't fathom how lucky I was. "Okay," I whispered. "I'll try. When did you get so wise, by the way? You sound like my grandmother."

"Don't I wish," Mike admitted. "If I had one tenth of the wisdom that woman has, I'd be satisfied forever."

I handed him the plastic bag. "Here you go."

He barked with laughter. "So I have to read one too?"

"Of course. We're a team," I reminded him.

Mike removed a cookie from the bag and pulled the fortune strip from it. A shadow passed across his face as he read the message, and he didn't smile. "Hmm. Interesting."

Despite the warm temperatures, a chill ran through me. "It doesn't say anything about the airplane crashing tonight, does it?"

Mike looked at me in disbelief. "No, darling. It simply says *Don't let people from your past haunt your future.*"

That was odd. Nevertheless, I squeezed his hand reassuringly. "I'm sorry. I know that you don't like talking about your childhood. It was hell for you."

He leaned his head on my shoulder. "Someday we'll talk about it. But not today. I won't let anything spoil the rest of my honeymoon with my beautiful bride. Plus, I've learned to live with it. So there's no way that could ever affect our life together." Mike waved the bag gaily at me. "Your turn."

Ugh. I sighed and removed the other cookie then glanced down at the strip. Mike leaned over my shoulder as we read the words silently together.

The sure way to predict the future is to invent it.

I raised an eyebrow at Mike. "So, according to this message, I am the one in charge of my future, so there's nothing to worry about, right?"

Mike laughed and removed both the strip of paper and cookie from my hand, rose to his feet, and tossed them into the nearby receptacle. "There's no reason for us to worry anymore. We're young, in love, and happy. No one can ever take that away from us. There's nothing else in this life that I want except to have a family and be a good husband to you. The rest will work itself out. Okay?"

I smiled up at him in adoration. To heck with the cookies. My fortune was standing right in front of me. "Whatever you say, my love."

He reached for my hand and helped me to my feet. "Come on. We've got a life to go live."

RECIPES

MAAMOUL COOKIES

Author's Note: Maamoul is a traditional Middle Eastern cookie made with a wooden mold that can be found in specialty stores. Different molds are required depending on whether you use dates or nuts. If you are making the cookies without the mold, you can use both dates and nuts.

The cookies are similar in style to Italian Wedding Cookies. This recipe was the creation of my beloved aunt who passed away over ten years ago, and I consider it a personal tribute to her memory.

5 cups all-purpose flour
2 lbs unsalted butter
1 jigger rye whiskey (approximately 1.5 ounces)
2 eggs, beaten
1 cup sugar
1 lb walnuts, finely chopped (or whole seedless dates can be used instead)
1 tsp rose water
Confectioner's sugar

Beat sugar and butter together. Add flour a little bit at a time. Knead until dough starts to fall off your hands.

In a separate bowl add nuts, ¼ cup of sugar, rose water, and rye whiskey.

Coat your mold with flour to prevent sticking. Add dough, flatten it out in the mold, add a teaspoon of nuts or a date, and close over with more dough.

To make the cookies by hand without a mold:

Coat your hand with flour to prevent sticking. Take a

dough ball about the size of a walnut, flatten it slightly, and lay in it the palm of one hand. Take a date, and flatten it slightly then lay it on top of the dough. Finally, take a smaller dough ball, about one inch in diameter, flatten it slightly, and place it on top of the date filling. (Basically the palm of your hand becomes the mold.) Gently press the dough on top into the dough on the bottom so the date filling is completely covered. Shape the cookie into a slightly flattened circle. Use a fork to make a decorative crosshatch pattern on the top.

Bake at 325° Fahrenheit for 20 to 25 minutes or until cookies are lightly browned around the edges and light on top. Cool for five minutes before dusting lightly with confectioner's sugar.

Makes about five or six dozen cookies.

BUTTERSCOTCH PARFAIT

1 cup flour
½ cup (one stick) butter, softened
1 tbsp sugar
8 ounces cream cheese, softened
1 cup powdered sugar
8 ounce tub whipped topping, divided
3 cups whole milk
Two 3.4 ounce packages of instant butterscotch pudding
One full-sized Butterfinger candy bar, crumbled

Layer number one: Combine flour, butter, and tablespoon of sugar, and mix well. Press to the bottom of an ungreased 9x13" pan, and bake at 350° Fahrenheit for 10 to 15 minutes or until the edges start to brown. Cool completely.

Layer number two: Mix softened cream cheese and powdered sugar. Then incorporate 1 cup of whipped topping. Spread over the first layer.

Layer number three: Combine milk and both packages of instant butterscotch pudding. Mix well, and spread over the second layer.

Layer number four: Spread the rest of the whipped topping over the first three layers, and sprinkle on the crumbled-up Butterfinger.

Refrigerate until ready to serve. Makes at least 15 servings.

COOKIES 'N CRÈME CAKE

12 crème-filled chocolate cookies
1 pkg of white cake mix
¾ cup water
½ cup sour cream
3 egg whites
2 tbsp vegetable oil

Icing:
6 crème-filled chocolate cookies
1½ cup powdered sugar
¼ cup sour cream
3 tbsp butter

Preheat oven to 325° Fahrenheit. Spray Bundt pan with nonstick cooking spray. Coarsely chop up cookies. Combine cake mix, water, sour cream, egg whites, and oil. Mix well. Pour one half of the batter into pan. Sprinkle chopped cookies evenly over the top of batter, making sure they don't touch the sides of the pan. Spoon remaining batter over the cookies. Bake 50 to 55 minutes or until a tester toothpick comes out clean. Cool completely.

Icing: Chop cookies. Combine sugar, sour cream, and butter. Beat until smooth. Spread on top of cake. Sprinkle on chopped cookies. Cake makes about 10-12 servings.

ZUCCHINI BREAD

3 eggs
2 cups sugar
1 cup vegetable oil
2 cups grated zucchini
2 tbsp cinnamon
2 tbsp vanilla
2 cups flour
1 tsp salt
¼ tsp baking powder
2 tsp baking soda
Chocolate chips or M&Ms (optional)

Preheat oven to 350° Fahrenheit. Mix eggs, sugar, and oil together. Add in zucchini. This will be a soupy consistency. Stir in cinnamon, flour, salt, baking powder, and baking soda. Mix in vanilla. Add chocolate chips or M&Ms.

Grease and flour two loaf pans. Pour batter into pans, and bake for 1 hour. Bread may also be frozen after cooling completely by wrapping in aluminum foil and then placing inside freezer bags. Use a straw to remove any excess air. Makes about eight slices per loaf.

ABOUT THE AUTHOR

USA Today bestselling author Catherine Bruns lives in Upstate New York with a male dominated household that consists of her very patient husband, three sons, and assorted cats and dogs. She has wanted to be a writer since the age of eight when she wrote her own version of Cinderella (fortunately Disney never sued). Catherine holds a B.A. in English and is a member of Mystery Writers of America and Sisters in Crime.

To learn more about Catherine Bruns, visit her online at www.catherinebruns.net

Enjoyed this book? Check out these other series starters available in print now from *USA Today* bestselling author Catherine Bruns!

And coming soon...

www.GemmaHallidayPublishing.com

Made in the USA
San Bernardino, CA
04 January 2018